Ziegfeld Girls

Center Point
Large Print

Books are
produced in the
United States
using U.S.-based
materials

Books are printed
using a revolutionary
new process called
THINKtech™ that
lowers energy usage
by 70% and increases
overall quality

Books are
durable and
flexible
because of
smythe-sewing

Paper is
sourced using
environmentally
responsible
foresting methods
and the
paper is acid-free

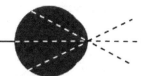

**This Large Print Book carries the
Seal of Approval of N.A.V.H.**

Ziegfeld Girls

Sarah Barthel

Center Point Large Print
Thorndike, Maine

This Center Point Large Print edition
is published in the year 2018 by arrangement with
Kensington Publishing Corp.

The text of this Large Print edition is unabridged.
In other aspects, this book may vary
from the original edition.
Printed in the United States of America
on permanent paper.
Set in 16-point Times New Roman type.

ISBN: 978-1-68324-684-8

Library of Congress Cataloging-in-Publication Data

Names: Barthel, Sarah, 1981- author.
Title: Ziegfeld girls / Sarah Barthel.
Description: Center Point large print edition. | Thorndike, Maine :
    Center Point Large Print, 2018.
Identifiers: LCCN 2017052054 | ISBN 9781683246848
    (hardcover : alk. paper)
Subjects: LCSH: Large type books.
Classification: LCC PS3602.A83894 Z54 2018 | DDC 813/.6—dc23
LC record available at https://lccn.loc.gov/2017052054

For L. and R.
You inspire me every day
with your passion and joy.

And
for anyone who has ever lost themselves
in a musical, this book is for you.

CHAPTER 1

New York City, March 1914

This was not how opening night should feel.

The Dancing Duchess had been in rehearsal for a few weeks, but the production was nowhere near ready. Jada had relearned so many moves she had to write down the latest changes just to be sure she was teaching Suzanne the right routine.

Just that morning the composer added a new song with complicated choreography. But, through it all, Jada was truly proud of Suzanne. Despite all the missteps and bruises, Suzanne hadn't complained once. Both of them knew the consequences of a flop. They couldn't return to Richmond, and vaudeville didn't pay them enough to continue there. They had to make Suzanne a star.

In the small dressing room, Jada clapped out a beat while Suzanne went through the new moves. *Tap. Tap. Spin. Lunge. Tap. Spin. Stop.*

"Damnit!" Suzanne cried. She rubbed her face in frustration and turned her back on Jada while trying to calm down.

Jada's stomach lurched. Two hours to curtain and Suzanne kept messing up these simple moves. She needed to tap twice after the lunge. If only there were more time to work with Suzanne, it might be easier, but they were out of time.

Jada forced a smile. "You are overthinking this. Take a break and drink some of Mr. Buxton's tonic." She gestured toward the glass on the vanity. Suzanne wrinkled her nose at the cloudy concoction. "It smells."

"He promised that it'll help with nerves." She held the glass out. "Seltzer water, ginger, and . . . other ingredients. All the stars drink it."

Suzanne grimaced, but Jada knew if all the stars drank it, she would too. Suzanne closed her eyes and downed the liquid in one gulp.

"Oh! It's fizzy!" Suzanne exclaimed with a nervous grimace. She leaned against the wall and looked up at the ceiling. "I'm not sure if it'll help."

"Close your eyes and count to one hundred," Jada suggested.

It was the same before every opening they'd ever had. At some point, Suzanne's nerves got the better of her and she couldn't perform accurately. The last time they opened a new routine, Jada stood on the side of the stage feeding her moves when she stumbled or forgot. The Chicago theater had threatened to terminate their contract, but changed its mind when Suzanne performed the routine flawlessly at the second show. And yet, despite all that, they'd made it to Broadway.

Suzanne mouthed the numbers as she counted.

Jada grabbed a pile of clothes and shoved them into the hamper. Then she shined the powder jars. Just those small actions made the room feel calmer and less chaotic.

"One hundred." Suzanne spoke the last number aloud. She rolled her shoulders and shook out her arms. Jada tried not to get her hopes up, but Suzanne looked like she might be ready.

A coy smile spread across Suzanne's face as she walked to the mirror. She tapped her foot to count the last beats before starting the move again.

Tap. Tap. Spin. Lunge. Tap. Tap. Spin. STOP.

When the sequence was done, Suzanne looked to Jada hopefully. It wasn't perfect, but Jada wasn't sure she should tell her that. Not so close to the opening performance. And yet she had an obligation to make Suzanne the best actress and dancer possible.

"Beautiful, but you are missing a step," she offered. "After the spin, you sidestep and meet Friedrich for the brief tango before you sing."

Moving through the steps slowly again, Suzanne said, "The side step. Of course. Leave it to me to forget the easiest move in the number." She pinched her own forearm in frustration.

"Want me to show you?" Jada asked.

Their eyes met and Suzanne nodded. Today was not the day to turn away help.

Tap left. Spin. Lunge. Tap right. Spin. Sidestep. Stop.

9

Jada moved through the dance effortlessly. She could feel the beat and could hear the music in her mind. It was all she could do to stop moving once she'd completed the steps. Suzanne watched as she always did with her legs crossed and head tilted as if Jada's ease threw her off-kilter. Neither could help what came naturally to them. Neither doubted that Suzanne's beauty booked most of their venues, but Jada's fluency with both choreography and music made the most of Suzanne's talent.

"When you come out of the spin, be sure you are on your right foot so that you and Friedrich will be in unison once you start dancing together," Jada explained. "Let me show you again."

Jada did the sequence again, but this time she grabbed Suzanne at the end. They stepped toward the vanity and burst into giggles when they caught their serious expressions in the mirror. Suzanne's blond ringlets bounced, and Jada's white smile contrasted against her dark caramel skin.

The door opened and a red-haired man popped inside. "Miss Haskins, this is your thirty-minute call," the stage manager announced.

Jada's smile dropped. "Thanks, Alex."

"I'll be onstage soon," Suzanne promised before shutting the door in his face. "Time to get dressed."

"Are you ready? We could go over the steps again." There was still so much to do.

Suzanne shook her head. "None of that will matter if I'm not dressed."

"What a headline that would make—'New Star Performs in Bloomers.'" Suzanne pretended to gasp in horror as Jada took the gown from the hanger. "Let's lace you up." She took the loose laces and began pulling them tight while Suzanne stood as still as possible.

"Another pull," Suzanne demanded. "I need the audience to admire my figure." She sucked in her stomach as the corset constricted her torso.

"There you are." Jada finished the laces and stepped back.

Slowly, Suzanne walked to the mirror. Turning from side to side, she smiled.

"You are a gem, Jada."

In a few moments her waist had gone from a slim, boyish washboard to a round and curvy woman's frame. The audience wouldn't know what hit them. Jada could see the reviews now: "Great beauty steals the show!"

Jada collected Suzanne's dressing gown and hung it up while Suzanne stepped into her costume. The bright blue flowered gown was monstrously large, but that was what Louis XIV's court wore. Jada turned back to lace up the dress.

"Jada?" Suzanne's voice was soft. "How bad is the show? Honestly?"

Jada looked up in surprise. Suzanne hadn't ever asked for her opinion about the show before.

11

"Accepting this role was the right move for us. It gives you experience to land a role in a bigger and better production."

"Oh." Suzanne nearly swallowed the word.

Jada knew where Suzanne's mind was racing, and an insult wasn't what Jada intended. She put a hand on Suzanne's shoulder.

"It *is* a good show," Jada insisted. "And you are wonderful in it. *That* is what matters."

"Yes, that's true." Suzanne's voice was full of hope. "Has any news come from London?"

"No," Jada said in as level a voice as she could find. Every few months Suzanne asked after her former fiancé, and the answer was always the same. "Elton hasn't replied to your last letter."

"Nor any of them," Suzanne muttered. She shook her curls and laid her hand on her stomach. "Just as well, really."

"Do you think he'll ever return home?" Jada shifted the lace cloth on top of the vanity so it lay perpendicular to the table's edges.

Suzanne met Jada's eyes in the mirror. "I really didn't think he was that ill. And he's been gone so long. I don't know." She sniffed and examined herself in the mirror. "If he could see me now, he'd be sorry he left."

The past eighteen months of living on her own had been good for Suzanne. Working in vaudeville was a necessity neither woman anticipated. While some women looked gaunt when they lost weight, Suzanne's cheeks became rosy and her eyes sparkled. When the times were rough, Suzanne would accept a dinner out with one suitor or another just to obtain a well-plated meal and let Jada eat her share of their food at the hotel. Jada never forgot the horrible men Suzanne forced herself to spend time with just to help them out. Many wouldn't worry about their servant's diet, but Suzanne was different. She treated Jada like family, and that made all the difference.

News of Elton's departure reached them quickly after they started performing in Philadelphia. When he started courting Suzanne, people made quite a fuss. The oldest banking family merging with one of the oldest plantation owners—it was exciting to think of the possibilities. But not too long after Suzanne accepted his hand, Elton became ill. It was never explained with what, but once Suzanne had left, he quickly retreated to London to spend time in a clinic. Jada couldn't help but think Suzanne's betrayal was the thing that pushed him over the edge to seek treatment. Perhaps if he had remained healthy, Suzanne wouldn't have been so keen to run away with Jada.

Suzanne appraised her figure again in the mirror. She fiddled with the top of her gown a bit, adjusting her breasts.

"You're better than this," Suzanne hissed to herself. "You have to look your best."

Something in her tone affected Jada and she motioned for Suzanne to raise her hands up in the air. Without saying a word, Jada grabbed the sides of the corset and, with one try, lifted it higher up her sides. When Suzanne turned around, she stared miraculously at the cleavage that appeared.

"How did you . . . ?" Suzanne trailed off as she examined herself.

"There are some tricks even Houdini doesn't know." Jada winked at her. "You should go upstairs if you want to get a stretch in before the curtain opens."

Suzanne opened the door and nearly walked over Alex, who was pacing in the hallway outside her room.

"Am I late?"

"No, early in fact. I just—I'm not sure if I should tell you this." Alex fidgeted with his clipboard and tried to make eye contact with Suzanne.

Alex's nerves were contagious. Jada's heart beat quicker just watching him fidget. Alex rarely looked out of sorts. What had happened? Not another song change! Jada stood behind Suzanne, her shaky breath shifting a loose strand of Suzanne's hair over her shoulder.

"Tell me," Suzanne demanded.

"I've been trying to get him to watch you for weeks and now, oh my." Alex swallowed. "Mr. Ziegfeld is in the audience. Why did he have to come opening night?"

"Florenz Ziegfeld? *The* Ziegfeld?" Jada's voice carried down the hall. She nudged her friend, but Suzanne didn't move. It was too much to think through. Ziegfeld, the star maker, was here.

Alex nodded. "Apparently some of the dancers left the company last year and he has been looking for new talent. I thought it would be a great boost for your career." He turned slightly red as he added, "I mean, you are prettier than any other girl on Broadway."

"Yes, thank you, Alex." Suzanne fidgeted with her skirt.

"Well, see you onstage." Alex gave her an odd look and rushed off to complete the rest of his preshow duties.

Jada's heart raced. Florenz Ziegfeld didn't visit just any woman. Alex must have begged for him to see Suzanne. She ignored the seed of jealousy that pinched her heart.

"This is good news. Just the break we wanted. I just knew this show would pay off."

Suzanne stepped away from Jada's excitement. She met Jada's gaze and frowned.

"I wish Alex hadn't said anything," she admitted. "Now it's even more important that I get every note and dance step right. Some of the numbers we ran through only a handful of times. How impressive can I be while I'm falling over the steps?"

"Calm down," Jada directed. She waited for

Suzanne to follow her suggestion before she explained. "Ziegfeld doesn't care about the production or the music or the lyrics. He is after beautiful women. And you, Suzanne, are breathtaking."

Suzanne looked up and down the hallway, where various actors were coming out of their dressing rooms and heading for the stage. "I just—I can't be a joke. Not to such a respected producer."

The fear was plain on Suzanne's face. "You are good in the show. That is all that matters. Shake this from your mind and have fun on that stage."

With a gentle squeeze of Jada's hand, Suzanne rushed to wait in the wings for the show to begin. Jada followed an appropriate distance behind.

Even from the wings the hum of the audience pulsated through the air. Jada adjusted one last ringlet of Suzanne's hair so that it lay against her back perfectly. Suzanne's whole body shook. Jada didn't blame her friend for being nervous. On the other side of that beautiful green curtain sat hundreds of people, all here to be entertained by Suzanne and the rest of the cast. And now they knew one very important person was also there, waiting to possibly change the course of Suzanne's career.

The audience erupted in applause and Jada's heart leapt. She couldn't help but bounce on her toes to keep from shrieking with excitement.

"This is it!" she exclaimed.

The overture began and the hair on Jada's arms rose.

"You are about to become a Broadway star!" Jada squeezed Suzanne's hand. "Your dream is about to come true."

"Our dream," Suzanne corrected her. "I wouldn't be here without your help."

The music stopped and the audience's applause roared in their ears.

From the opposite wing, Friedrich entered the stage and took his place among the silk-upholstered furniture. Suzanne rolled her head to stretch her neck. Friedrich started his first solo and Suzanne bounced on her toes. Jada stepped back. Suzanne's excitement was almost too much for her. Right on cue, Suzanne stepped onto the stage into seventeenth-century France and out of reality.

Jada's stomach lurched as she heard the audience's reaction. Of course they were impressed. The director chose that shade of blue to draw attention to Suzanne's pale skin and beautiful face. Her stardom had been well designed, and yet Jada had to remind herself to smile as she stood in the wing as promised until Suzanne finished her first song.

Jada stayed in the shadows but couldn't help mouthing along the dialogue. Suzanne broke into a short song and Jada glanced at the corner of the audience so she could see their reactions. It was a river of faces. Most likely Alex had exaggerated the chances of the "star maker" seeing the show. Suzanne's voice climbed to the height of her register and the clarity pulsated through the audience. The audience seemed to hold their breath as her voice rose to the back rows of the balcony. Perhaps the modern rhythm didn't match the seventeenth-century setting, but no one would forget hearing Suzanne's singing. The song ended and the audience applauded. Jada took her cue early and retreated to their dressing room.

The audience seemed to love Suzanne, even in this mediocre show. It was too much for Jada. Too many conflicting emotions. When her parents died, Jada knew she had to run away to avoid their fate, but never once imagined Suzanne would join her. But she did. The pair found a career in theater, fulfilling Suzanne's dream to be an actress. There never was room for any goal other than Suzanne's. And while Suzanne could sing well, her acting and dancing were more graceful movements than actual talent. Stardom was a pipedream, one she never really expected to find for them.

And yet, after eighteen months of eking out a living in vaudeville, Suzanne had managed an audition for a Broadway lead and then, amazingly, she got the part! Jada was happy for Suzanne's success. And as unrealistic as the dream was, Jada longed that it were she onstage instead of Suzanne. As a black woman, her options were limited to vaudeville, blackface, or the church. Not one of those options appeased Jada's dream. Either they paid too little or didn't offer the right sort of class for her taste. Jada wanted to dance across a large stage and belt out bold melodies written just for her. But that was virtually impossible. Instead, she would make that dream come true for Suzanne, which was the least she could do as thanks. Suzanne left her fiancé and family behind to help save Jada's life. She had sacrificed everything for Jada. There was no conversation in which Jada could confess her own hopes. And now, the chance to be a Ziegfeld girl . . . Jada would never be able to speak up.

Jada gripped the vanity table and glared at her reflection. Her dark brown eyes and tightly wound hair met her gaze. She looked tired. No producer in their right mind would audition such a dull, tired woman. It wouldn't matter what her voice sounded like or what her tired limbs could do.

"Pull it together. Grandma would laugh at this little problem. At least you are in a theater! Be happy." But even as she tried to convince herself, her mother's mocking tone filled her ears: *Filling that white girl's dream instead of your own. You deserve more, child.* Tears fell down Jada's cheeks.

Abruptly she stood up and shook the thoughts

from her head. She would not wallow in this jealousy or self-pity. Instead, she went to work. All the little jobs that kept the room looking spotless wouldn't do themselves: rubbing the spots off the mirror, folding all the clothing so they looked perfect inside the wardrobe, even refilling the powder container. By the time everything was done, it was intermission and the hallways were once again abuzz with performers.

Suzanne burst into the room and dropped onto the chaise, dramatically perching a hand to her forehead. Both girls quickly giggled at her forced pose.

"Oh, Jada," Suzanne swooned. "I've never had such fun."

"I'm glad for you," Jada replied. She hesitated, unsure if she should ask. "Did you see—"

"Ziegfeld?" Suzanne finished for her. A bit of the joy drained from her face. "I didn't see him. But I'm not sure I'd know him if I saw him. I mean, it isn't like I could walk out into the audience and gaze at each face." She laughed at the thought. "If it is meant to be, he will call." The yearning in her voice was palpable.

Jada handed her a glass of water and sat beside her. "That is true."

Suzanne leaned her head on Jada's shoulder for a moment. Jada closed her eyes, imagining they were back in Richmond with the warm summer breeze filtering in through the windows.

Abruptly, Suzanne stood up and started unfastening the laces to her costume. "Enough, I need to get dressed for act two."

The silk violet gown hung on the dress form across the room. Jada slipped it off the figure while Suzanne stepped out of her current gown. As Jada slid the new dress over her head, Suzanne bit her lip.

"Do we have to go to the party tonight?" Suzanne asked.

The dress nearly fell out of Jada's hands. "But it's opening night! Surely you want to celebrate with everyone."

Suzanne slid her arms through the sleeves of the dress. "Jada, the audience isn't laughing where they should laugh, and Friedrich has flubbed more lines than he has gotten right."

"But you just said you were having such a good time."

"Well, they are laughing at *my* lines. I just can't see everyone's faces if the reviews are bad."

It was Jada's turn to hesitate. "You should go for a little bit and celebrate the opening. Once you've made an appearance, you can claim a headache or nerves or something and come home. I'll corroborate whatever story you choose to use."

Suzanne nodded. "Thank you, Jada."

A knock came at the door.

The women looked at each other and Jada quickly finished tying the dress. She gave Suzanne a brush to start on her hair as she opened the door.

"May I help you?" she asked the stranger on the other side.

The man was tall and thin. His light brown hair was perfectly combed over and his suit tailored too well for him to be just anyone.

"Good evening. I am here to speak with Suzanne Haskins."

Suzanne turned from her vanity and pulled the brush through her perfectly curled hair. "I am Suzanne."

The man nodded. "Florenz Ziegfeld requests your presence at his office tomorrow morning. The meeting should last no longer than half an hour. You will make it?"

Suzanne's mouth dropped open and her hand froze, her brush halfway through her hair. Quickly she regained her composure and flashed the man a dazzling smile in the mirror.

"I believe I can accommodate him. What time?"

He handed a card to Jada.

New Amsterdam Theatre
214 W. 42nd Street
New York, NY
10:00 am, Mr. Ziegfeld's Office

Suzanne nodded again. "I will be there."

The gentleman nodded his head in a half bow before saying, "Mr. Ziegfeld will be pleased."

"And, if I may be so bold—who do we have the pleasure of meeting now?" Suzanne asked. Jada turned in surprise at the question and saw Suzanne's demure smile and coy expression. Was it possible she found this thin man attractive?

"Jonathon Franks, miss. I am Mr. Ziegfeld's personal assistant. It has been an honor watching you tonight. We both think you are a bright light in an otherwise bleak production."

Before Suzanne could defend her costars, Jada held the door farther open and insisted, "The second act will be starting soon. We really must get ready."

"Oh, yes, of course. Until tomorrow, Miss Haskins." He walked down the hall, his long legs making short work of the space.

The moment Jada shut the door, Suzanne's nerves rose to the surface.

"Can you believe it? During intermission? A meeting with Ziegfeld himself . . . I don't know what to make of that."

Jada pressed down on her friend's shoulders, grounding her and regaining control at the same time. "We will find out tomorrow. Right now, you need to get back onstage."

In a matter of moments, they had tucked all of Suzanne's beautiful hair under a wrap and placed the foot-high white wig on top of her head that was supposed to indicate the rise of her character's station from one act to the next.

"Never mind what that man said. You are talented and wonderful and this show is good. Go enjoy yourself." Jada kissed Suzanne's cheek and pushed her toward the door.

The intro started and Jada stood in the center of the small room. She danced along the steps she'd worked so hard to perfect in Suzanne. She knew them all by heart and no one would ever know. Jada grimaced and stopped before the applause trickled through the walls.

She knew the applause was not for her.

CHAPTER 2

New York provided a unique solitude. Here everything grew as if it longed to touch the sky. It was so different from Richmond's quiet calmness. Walking beneath these buildings, Suzanne felt small, yet empowered. Men in suits bustled to and fro, ignoring everyone but themselves as they hustled down the street. Their energy gave Suzanne focus. This was the city where dreams happened if you worked hard enough.

Suzanne had worked for her dream. No one could deny that. Perhaps this meeting with Mr. Ziegfeld would be the end of that kind of hard work. The Ziegfeld Follies were legendary for both the stars they attracted and for the beautiful women, the Ziegfeld girls, who paraded through the productions as anything from bees to battleships. Surely learning to walk as a flower or standing still in representation of a tree would be easier than the mountain of steps she had to learn for *The Dancing Duchess*.

On their last trip to New York, for Suzanne's sixteenth birthday five years ago, her father had surprised her with tickets to the rooftop Follies. In 1909, the Ziegfeld Follies were still an after-hours production, and attending such a late performance made Suzanne feel mature and just a little scandalous. The Jungle Scene was particularly moving. Men in suits hunted women operating puppets of lions and bears, while other women clad in glorious leaf-covered gowns stood in the back and held branches to create the illusion of a jungle. It was exotic and enthralling, and Suzanne couldn't get enough of the glamour. The evening was ruined, however, when Mother and Father got into a huge fight over his comments about the women's curves. After that, Suzanne hadn't thought much of the production. And now, she was on her way to possibly star as "one of the most beautiful women" her father had ever seen.

Her one regret that morning was leaving Jada behind. Her mother and she had read countless gossip rags while lazing out on the sun porch. If there was one thing she knew about Ziegfeld girls, it was that they were not only beautiful, but independent as well. Bringing a servant could be seen as an advantage, but also a weakness. Besides, that horrible hotel clerk had been bothering her again, and she didn't trust him not to riffle through their room if no one stayed behind. He had remarked too brazenly about the jewels she wore to the party. Once they had more money they would move to a nice boardinghouse.

Suzanne stopped next to the Saks on Fifth Avenue windows, examining the styles they were presenting that season. The ornate beading and layers of lace made her want to reach out and touch the gowns. She might be able to afford one of them if she impressed Mr. Ziegfeld. The thought sent a shiver of excitement down her back. She hadn't splurged on a new gown since they left Richmond. Jada had worked wonders on their wardrobe to keep it looking fresh and current, but Suzanne missed having new clothes.

But she didn't miss Richmond. Leaving was the best thing she ever did for herself, but she couldn't tell Jada that. It had been nearly two years of hard work and many sacrifices, but her dream was finally staring her in the face. She was the lead in a Broadway musical, and Mr. Ziegfeld, the star maker, wanted to meet with her.

Nearly two years ago, Suzanne had been pouting in her room after another fight with Elton. His health wasn't improving and he refused to set a date for their engagement party, let alone their wedding. She'd hoped Mother would understand his reasons, but Mother was not good at understanding such frivolities as illness.

When Jada came bursting into her room with the news she had found her parents' dead bodies on the grocer's land and that she was certain he was after her as well and had to run away, it was like a gift to Suzanne. The circumstances were horrible, of course, but the opportunity to leave home—to run away and make her own future— was too wonderful to pass up. She insisted she

27

accompany Jada. Mother's former beau ran a small theater in Philadelphia and she knew he'd give her a chance. It turned out to be much smaller and grimier than Mother had let on, but it didn't matter as Suzanne made her debut on that stage.

Although they didn't speak of it, Suzanne knew Jada wrote her mother every few months to let her know where they had performed and that they were well. That was her choice. Suzanne, however, could not forgive her mother for not coming after them and insisting on bringing them home. Cicely's death would have been a relief for Mother, or so Suzanne assumed. Was Jada's disappearance also a relief? Was it cause enough not to come after her only daughter? Not so much as a letter was exchanged between them until Jada sent the first newspaper clippings nearly three months after they left.

Suzanne raised her chin and smiled at her reflection. This was a life she had created for herself, and it was better than anything she'd ever imagined back home. Instead of drooling over the gown, she quickened her pace so she'd be sure to arrive at the New Amsterdam Theatre on time.

She turned a corner and walked down Forty-second Street. A trolley swooshed by her and the garbled voices of the passengers flitted in the breeze. The street was marked left and right with large signs hanging from the second and third floor of buildings. Advertisements for Turkish Trophies, C/B Corset, and Williams Talcum Powder hung over her as she walked down the street. At eye level a few buildings were plastered with sheets offering beautiful girls in revues and other theater spectaculars. Suzanne felt both gaudy and exhilarated to walk through an area with so much activity.

After walking for a block, she looked up and there it was: the New Amsterdam Theatre. A slight thrill washed over Suzanne. It was more than a mere playhouse, the building housed two complete and separate playhouses and had an eleven-story office tower rising up above all the other theaters on the street. On the top few floors of the building, a sign was painted on the side to identify the opening attraction. A man sat on scaffolding painting the lettering THE ZIEGFELD FOLLIES OF 1914. Above, the names of the star performers had already been painted: ANN PENNINGTON, BERT WILLIAMS, and ED WYNN. The names looked down at Suzanne as if they were waiting for her to do or say something to their grandeur. The front awning jutted out over the sidewalk into a point with ZIEGFELD FOLLIES in bright white letters shining in the morning sun. Ziegfeld's name almost covered the intricately carved lettering NEW AMSTERDAM THEATRE that hung upon the building. A man sat on a gurney touching up the paint on the Follies sign.

"Excuse me?" Suzanne called up.

The man looked down, his paint dripping slightly on the sidewalk. Suzanne jumped out of the way.

"Yes?"

"I have an appointment with Mr. Ziegfeld. Do you know how I can get into the office building?"

The man wiped his brow and nodded. "Go inside these doors and up to the fifth floor. His office is at the end of the hall. Good luck." He winked.

Suzanne flashed him her brightest smile. "Thanks!"

She tiptoed around the small droplets of paint and pulled the front door open. The entryway shone with art nouveau opulence. The elevator doors carried a flower and vine motif that was reflected in the vines on the columns inside the entryway and on the sconces hanging on the wall. The lobby was dark, but the bronze friezes that hung above the mirrored walls depicted scenes from various Shakespeare plays and Greek dramas. Even the box-office windows were adorned with metal flowers and vines. The box office was closed that early in the day, and the doors to the theater were locked.

Suzanne pushed the button to call for the elevator, but when a minute had passed she decided to walk up the stairs instead. The marble stairs were wide and smooth and she found herself marveling at the details. Even the stair rail had roses carved into it to make it melt into the scene. No other theater that Suzanne had played in had such a cohesive design.

After her climb she hoped her cheeks would be appropriately bright with the exercise, but she pinched them just the same. The man downstairs had directed her to the room at the end of the hall, but he needn't have bothered. There was only one door on the fifth floor and that was Ziegfeld's. She swallowed her nerves and walked down the red carpet to her meeting.

The clock in the hall rang nine forty-five with a loud chime. Suzanne stood in the hallway until it had completed its chords; then she knocked and entered the vast office. A crystal chandelier glittered high above her head. Sunlight glared through the ten-foot window, reflecting off the crystals and sending tiny rainbows bouncing off the walls. The dark oak desks complemented the red walls and golden frames. A huge marble mantel took up one entire wall and had a large portrait of Mr. Ziegfeld hung above it. His dark mustache and gray hair complemented his round cheeks and amused eyes. He stood in such a way that you knew he was a force to be reckoned with. She took a step toward the portrait, but halted when she heard a man clear his throat. Collecting herself, she changed directions and walked toward the desk in the center of the room where Ziegfeld's assistant sat.

Suzanne held her handbag in both hands and waited for Mr. Franks to acknowledge her. In her mind she quickly went over her outfit, hoping she hadn't forgotten some small accessory at the hotel. Her sage suit made her golden hair shine and was snug in all the right places. Jada had spent nearly an hour making sure Suzanne had perfect Mary Pickford curls. The long, thick curls were pinned up on one side and set to flow over the other shoulder, ensuring she looked both in fashion and endearing. She raised her hand slowly to her hair to make sure they had remembered to place her diamond comb just above her left ear. They had. At least she looked the part of a Ziegfeld girl.

"Hello, Miss Haskins." Jonathon rose to his feet. "I'm glad to see you."

"I am pleased to be here, Mr. Franks."

He smiled. "Please call me Jonathon. Most of the girls here do."

"Thank you." She didn't know what else to say.

His hand extended and his warm fingers took her hand. His fingers were long, like Elton's, and Suzanne was reminded of how safe he had always made her feel while they courted. Her hand looked small in Jonathon's grasp, but instead of safe, Suzanne felt a flutter of excitement. Instinctively, she pulled her hand back and clasped her handbag.

"You did say ten, correct?" She looked at the cherrywood clock hanging on the wall.

Jonathon flipped through a stack of papers. "Yes, ten. I'm very sorry. He was needed onstage but shouldn't be too much longer." Gesturing for Suzanne to follow, Jonathon opened the high double doors to the office behind him. "You may wait in Mr. Ziegfeld's office."

"Thank you." His formal tone felt awkward after his friendliness the day before.

He led her into the rectangular room. Jonathon walked directly to the fireplace, opened the grate, and stoked the fire back to life.

"How many girls is he looking to hire?" Suzanne blurted out. She meant it to sound conversational, but instead it hung in the air like an accusation.

Jonathon stoked the fire so that its glow brought warmth to the room. "The Follies are always open to beautiful, talented women. However, this year, we have been left to fill the stage after a few . . . unexpected departures."

She put her handbag down on the side table. "Yes, I heard some of the girls left abruptly."

"Yes, well, I wouldn't listen to all the street gossip." Jonathon cleared his throat. Placing the poker back in its holder, he turned to Suzanne. "Mr. Ziegfeld can make you a star, but he can't make you loyal."

"Oh, of course." Suzanne fell over the words. Somehow she'd stumbled into the middle of an argument she didn't quite understand. A silence fell between them.

"Can I get you anything else while you wait?" he asked.

"I don't think so," Suzanne replied.

Jonathon abruptly tipped his head at Suzanne and said, "I have much work to do. Please let me know if you change your mind."

Once the door clicked shut, Suzanne stood in the center of the room with the fire crackling behind her. The tall ceiling towered over her, with carvings of vines and flowers continuing the theater's motif. The walls were draped with dark pink velvet curtains that made the room look taller. Without another person in the office, Suzanne was left feeling insignificant. She wished she hadn't asked Jonathon about the rumor. She had hit a nerve, she felt. She'd find a way to regain his good graces. Being in with Ziegfeld's assistant could have its perks.

The high ceilings made the crackling embers of the fire echo loudly throughout the room. Two tall chairs faced the fireplace. On the other side of the room sat Ziegfeld's desk with another pair of short leather chairs. Two tall windows bridged the gap between the two areas. Velvet curtains flowed from the ceiling, framing the wall.

Between the fire's soothing cracks and sputtering, Suzanne could hear the typewriter keys from the outer office. *Busy little bee,* Suzanne thought.

Ignoring decorum, she moved behind the desk

and examined the wall of photographs: groups of women standing in rows with their legs extended straight out and portraits of girls in costumes that sparkled in the camera's flash covered the wall. Suzanne could soon be one of them. The idea made her both apprehensive and exhilarated.

If Jada didn't send word, the papers would report on one of Richmond's own joining the Follies. Mother wouldn't be pleased knowing her baby girl would soon be photographed with exposed elbows and ankles. Somehow that made the idea even more desirable.

She walked to the two chairs on the other side of the desk and carefully lowered herself into one. The leather cracked as it adjusted to her figure. The noise was loud and she suddenly found herself sitting as straight as possible in an attempt to stop the adjustments.

Shaking her head clear, she focused on Ziegfeld's desk. The large oak desktop was covered in photographs. She leaned forward and picked one up. Ziegfeld stood next to a man so wide with muscles Suzanne wondered how he found clothing that fit him. She placed it back on the table and shuddered a bit. That many muscles was unnatural. She picked another frame and turned it toward her. A gawky young woman stood, looking amused at the camera. She wasn't beautiful, but she had a charm that made Suzanne instantly smile. The girl was in her early twenties, about Suzanne's age, and perched on a stool, turned slightly away from the camera. A string of pearls and a fur were draped loosely about her shoulders and arms to hide the girl's bosom. It took Suzanne a moment to realize that the girl was naked. The tilted pose hid the most delicate parts of her body, while also highlighting the girl's curves. Nothing improper showed, but everything scandalous was implied.

Suzanne could hardly take her eyes off the captivating image. The woman possessed something none of the other girls photographed had: an inner glow that made her presence wink at the camera. In scrawly handwriting the girl had written, *With much love and gratitude, Ann.*

Ann? Suzanne looked at the girl's face again. Dark curls, pale skin, and those big eyes. That was Ann Pennington! She'd become a star last year in the 1913 Follies and was rumored to be chased by Ziegfeld himself. Is this what the girls rebuffing his advances gave him? Suzanne's stomach lurched uneasily. What would Jada say if she saw this photograph? What would her mother think? She pushed that thought away from her. What anyone else thought did not matter. It only mattered what she was comfortable with and she'd know that once she met Mr. Ziegfeld.

As in answer to her question the door opened and Ziegfeld himself entered with Jonathon at his side. He was shorter than Suzanne imagined, but an air of power and confidence gave him an attraction to which Suzanne couldn't help but feel drawn. His gray suit was impeccably tailored and his shoes freshly shined. Few men could make a lavender shirt look stylish, but Mr. Ziegfeld could. He was a bit rounder in the face than his portrait illustrated, but his slender build made up for it.

"This is Suzanne Haskins, sir," Jonathon said as they walked to her.

"Ah, yes. The Dancing Duchess." Mr. Ziegfeld's smile made his mustache twitch. "Pleased to make your acquaintance." He reached for her hand and bowed his head in greeting.

"Will you bring us some drinks, Mr. Franks?" He smiled at Suzanne. "Miss Haskins appears pale."

"Right away, sir." Jonathon tipped his head and departed.

Mr. Ziegfeld walked to his desk and set his briefcase down before he adjusted the photograph of Ann and smiled at the image.

"She is the epitome of my empire." He gestured toward the frame.

Suzanne nodded. "She is a beautiful woman."

"All girls are beautiful, but mine possess something other women can't quite obtain. They have an inner glow. That is what makes a Ziegfeld girl."

Jonathon reappeared with a glass of water with

several ice chips floating in it and a cup of coffee for Mr. Ziegfeld. Suzanne sipped the water slowly. It had been too long since she'd had ice in her water. Most of the places she and Jada stayed in had ice only for keeping the meat and milk from spoiling.

Suzanne caught Mr. Ziegfeld's eyes as he appraised her. Instead of feeling sexual, his gaze was that of a businessman appraising a new building development. Suzanne pushed her shoulders back and twisted slightly toward him to show off her slim waist and good posture. A silence sat between them, but Suzanne refused to speak first. He had requested the meeting; she'd not ruin this chance by assuming the wrong thing. Instead, she appraised him with the same intensity.

Having worked in theaters for nearly two years, she was used to dancer-turned-directors and somehow imagined Ziegfeld to be the same. Not only was he short, but he probably weighed little more than she did. What he lacked in size, he made up for in charisma. Ann's photo was in Suzanne's side line, but she resolutely put it from her mind. Anyone who wore a pink shirt and spats was hardly someone to fear.

He pulled the chair out and lowered himself slowly onto the fine leather. He moved so gracefully that the leather didn't make one creak as he settled onto it.

He was waiting for her to speak, as if only she could command the room into action. His eyes focused on her face as if he was memorizing every line to immortalize her immediately. She noticed his eyes never lowered to other, more improper regions. She took one last sip from the glass before placing it on the table and looking him straight in the eye.

"You requested this meeting. How can I help you?" She smiled to soften the frankness of her words.

Mr. Ziegfeld chuckled and nodded. He took a sip from his own glass. "Very good. Stand up, Miss Haskins," he demanded, standing up himself.

Suzanne did as she was told, walked to the center of the room, and stood before him.

"Turn around, please," he said, spinning his finger in circles as an example.

Forcing a natural smile, she again did as she was told. However, instead of feeling special, she felt like the prized pig at a slaughterhouse. He didn't leer at her, nor did he make her feel in any way uncomfortable, but that was what made her uneasy. Shouldn't such appraisal feel awkward? If he wanted the most beautiful women in the world, shouldn't she feel attractive from his gaze? Her confidence faltered slightly. Perhaps she was not destined to be a Ziegfeld girl after all.

"That is enough, Miss Haskins," he said. He motioned to one of the chairs in front of the fireplace before continuing. "Please have a seat."

"Thank you," Suzanne said as she sank into the chair. The cushion was softer than she expected and as she sank lower, her corset cut into her rib cage. Tightening her smile, she regained her composure and perched on the edge of the chair's seat instead. It was more ladylike.

"You are an impressive woman, Miss Haskins," he began. "Not only does your beauty command attention, but your dancing is unique and your voice, although limited, has a clear tone."

"Thank you, Mr. Ziegfeld," Suzanne said, ignoring the slight rebuke.

"Given your limited vocal range, I am impressed that you've been able to have the career you've had. You must be a wonderful musician to accommodate your talent."

Suzanne pushed her lips into a smile. Instead of admitting to Jada's assistance, she simply smiled and said, "Thank you for noticing, but it is my dancing that has made my career."

"I would have said it was your beauty." Mr. Ziegfeld smiled. "You know that my primary concern for my girls is that they possess unique beauty. I also need girls who have an extra-special quality. Girls who have star potential. I would not have chosen you had I not believed you were truly gifted."

"Thank you." True praise indeed!

"With a bit of training you could be a star. Does that interest you?"

Suzanne met his gaze and shifted so her whole body leaned toward him. What a question to ask. Yet, she knew that she had to answer.

"Yes, I want to be a star."

The words felt light in Suzanne's mouth. They flowed out so easily that she knew she was in the right space at the right time.

Ziegfeld became serious as he leaned forward in his chair, coming very close to Suzanne. "I expect you to do every dance perfectly. Each head turn or toe twitch is timed down to the second and must happen in unison. I will not stand for laziness or tardiness. Rehearsals are at nine AM promptly and do not finish until we are satisfied. Work hard and you will be rewarded. If you shine, you could become the toast of New York."

A part of her was ready to commit body and soul to Ziegfeld, but something held her back. She glanced again at that photograph of Ann Pennington. It was art, yes, but it represented so much more. Was she capable of being all Ziegfeld wanted her to be? She stared into Ziegfeld's dancing blue eyes and could almost see his vision of her.

She saw herself holding crystal leaves, acting the part of the tree in a Grecian temple. She saw red rubies bending back, forming a line of sparkling rainbows. She saw herself tap dancing alongside Leon Errol while the audience hooted with joy. For the mere price of sweat, time, and perhaps a little art, all that could be hers.

As she was about to reply the door burst open and a raven-haired woman stormed in.

"I am sorry, Flo," she said. "I know I promised to give it the night, but I am done. No more."

Mr. Ziegfeld slowly turned toward the woman. "Kitty, I wasn't expecting you."

"I'm sorry, Flo," she said again. "But I refuse to work under these conditions. I've never been treated in such an abysmal fashion."

Suzanne thought she saw a look of sadness cross Mr. Ziegfeld's face, but when he spoke it was with a calm tone. "We have been nothing but generous with you. You had time off when your mother took ill, despite needing to work on the opening solo. Fanny says the two of you have become friends, and you are well-liked by many of the girls. You are welcome in our little family."

Kitty's mouth opened and closed a few times as she took in his words. After a moment her face flushed and tears came to her eyes. "I can't, Flo. I can't stay in this company. I am sorry." She spun around and rushed from the room.

Jonathon appeared in the empty doorway. "Mr. Ziegfeld?" he said.

Mr. Ziegfeld exhaled a deep breath and waved

a hand dismissively. "Please send Kitty's money to her room."

"Yes, sir." Jonathon let the door close behind him. It remained slightly open. Suzanne wondered if he was listening to their conversation.

"I am sorry you had to witness that display," Mr. Ziegfeld said.

Suzanne shifted in her chair. "Yes, well, I suppose this life isn't for everyone." She winced at how lackluster her words sounded. "Of course, I couldn't imagine doing anything else. When can I join rehearsals?"

A look of excitement spread over Mr. Ziegfeld's face. "I knew I saw a star in you. I will have Jonathon send over the contract for you to sign. You will need to complete your contract for *The Dancing Duchess* before we write in your start date."

The Dancing Duchess. Suzanne's heart plummeted. She had a contract to uphold for that horrible show. She forced a smile. "I look forward to starting here."

Mr. Ziegfeld glanced at his desk calendar. "Our official rehearsals don't start for a few weeks, so you won't miss much."

"Well, that is good at least."

"The reviews were not good. You may be with us sooner than we expect. The contract will be the standard starting wording for my girls. You must maintain your appearance and weight to our specifications and attend all required events. The starting salary is seventy-five dollars a week." He smiled knowingly.

It took every ounce of concentration to keep the shock off of Suzanne's face. Seventy-five dollars a week was more than triple what she'd ever made before.

"I look forward to the challenge."

CHAPTER 3

Jada brushed glue onto the back of the *New York Times* review cutout of *The Dancing Duchess*. She almost didn't put it in Suzanne's scrapbook as the review was brutal. The one thing all of the critics had praised was Suzanne's poise and beauty. But she was not enough to save the show. Carefully, Jada pressed the paper into her scrapbook, which was about half-full. Photos of Suzanne's inspirations and clippings from the venues they played filled the album. Jada hoped that someday Suzanne would be glad to have it all recorded.

From the trunk, she pulled the newspaper from two months ago. A photographer had published a snapshot of Suzanne taking a bow onstage in Philadelphia. The article was about the theater's renovation to a motion picture house, but the photos showed Suzanne's tango costume to full effect. Enough time had passed since they played there. It was safe to send it on to Richmond now. Jada carefully cut out the article, folded it, and slid it into an envelope. She wrote Mrs. Haskins's name and address on it.

Suzanne may not care to keep her mother informed of their success, but Jada couldn't bear the thought of her not knowing if they were surviving or not. Like it or not, Mrs. Haskins was the only mother figure Jada had left.

She pushed the thought away. Ma and Pa had been dead for a long time. Twenty months and three days, to be exact. Jada refused to think about that day. She still saw their bodies swaying from that tree and their still eyes glossed over with death. They haunted her, but luckily it had been some time since the nightmares had bothered her. She couldn't help but wonder what would have happened if they'd never gone to town that day . . . never been accused of stealing by that horrible grocer. Perhaps she and Suzanne would still be in Richmond. Jada sealed the envelope with more force than necessary.

"Back to work," she muttered, and stood up.

The new boardinghouse was perfect, but the unpacking process was more work than Jada anticipated. With all the traveling in vaudeville it had been some time since the entire contents of their trunks had been emptied. Jada rubbed her neck. All the day-to-day clothes were hung, and a pile of clothes sat in a basket waiting for her to mend rips and holes that had developed from disuse.

With the offer from Ziegfeld signed, Jada had moved them from the run-down hotel to the upscale boardinghouse within walking distance to the theater. Money would be a little tight until she officially started at the New Amsterdam

Theatre, but it was worth it. Miss Mitzi's was highly recommended both for her discretion and her food.

Their room was periwinkle and pink with small roses on the wallpaper. Jada smoothed the comforter and nodded to herself. This was good. Just nice enough without being gaudy. She closed the trunk that contained Suzanne's vaudeville costumes. It would be bad luck to keep those out.

She tucked the pieces that needed mending into the smaller trunk along with the scrapbook and pushed it into the corner of the room. With it out of the way the room looked neat. One of the serving men would come pick up the rest of their trunks and put them in storage. She glanced around the room, making sure there wasn't anything else that needed to be packed away.

She caught her reflection in the mirror. Her long braids, which she'd earlier pinned up about her head, now were dangerously close to falling out. Worse than that, straggles of hair had escaped from her braids, giving her a rough resemblance to the boardinghouse maid, Sally.

A lady is always put together properly, Suzanne's mother always said. Perhaps she only told Jada such things so Suzanne would always follow her guidance, but Jada kept those words close to her heart and lived by them.

Immediately dropping all other thoughts, Jada walked over to her corner of the room and pulled

47

out the thick ivory comb Suzanne had given her for Christmas and began the arduous task of unbraiding and untangling her hair. She sat down at the vanity table and moved the newspaper and teacup out of her way. Starting at her temple, she put the comb in her hair and pulled it smoothly down to the tips. Relaxing into the rhythmic motion, she closed her eyes and withdrew back to her childhood, when her mother would comb her hair and sing at night.

Absentmindedly she opened her mouth and began singing one of the old tunes her mother always hummed as she worked:

> Go down, Moses.
> Way down in Egypt land.
> Tell old, Pharaoh,
> Let my people go.

The slow, cool notes soothed her and soon she felt like she was back on the plantation, letting Ma brush her hair while Pa fiddled on the banjo. She could almost smell the grass and feel Ma's cool breath on her shoulder. As if they'd never met Mr. Sims . . . as if they'd never died.

"Your hair is sure straight." Sally's words shot through Jada's memories. Jada dropped the comb and spun around to face the boardinghouse servant who stood in the doorway with her hip jutted out to one side.

"Don't you knock?" she exclaimed. She felt as if she'd been exposed somehow.

"I did knock, you just didn't hear me with all your singing. You've got a great voice." Sally shrugged as she sat on the bed and crossed her arms. "How'd you get your hair so straight? You use one of those fancy creams?"

Jada picked the comb up off the floor with a shaky hand. "It's always been this way," she replied, shrugging her shoulders. She should have kept her hair pulled back. Something told her Sally wouldn't leave the topic there.

"My hair don't do that—no matter what I do." Sally gestured to her hair. Despite being covered with a bonnet, there were frizzy sections that had escaped and gave her a slightly crazed look.

Jada turned back to the mirror and pulled her hair back into a braid. Sally moved from the bed and leaned over Jada's shoulder, her face appearing in the mirror. Sally's eyes were moving all over her face as if inspecting a dog.

"Where I come from it's rude to pry into other people's affairs," Jada said, sitting up as straight as possible. She prayed the strange girl would just go away.

"Oh, please. Get off your high horse. Think you're the only mixed girl in New York? There are so many inbred families, I'm surprised we aren't all colored." Sally took a few steps toward Jada, as if daring her to tell the truth.

"What?" Jada asked, quickly pinning her hair up against her scalp. Out of sight, out of Sally's mind, she hoped. Mixed girl? She opened her mouth to correct her when Sally continued.

"There's this woman I used to run errands for, a Miz Walker. She's made makeup and hair stuff for us colored women." Sally came over to Jada and pulled her braid off her back, fingering it slowly. "Supposed to make us look lighter or something. 'Course I don't see how that's for us, I look great. Anyways, I hear she's looking for a new face for ads and whatnot. Hair and skin as white as yours . . . you should look her up."

Jada wasn't sure if Sally had just paid her a compliment or an insult. "I don't think that is for me," she said, hoping to put an end to the conversation.

"Just as well, now that I think about it, I think she moved to Indiana. You'd make great money doing it, though. If I had your looks, I'd do it, but my hair'll never look like yours." Sally shrugged her shoulders. "We'd better get going if I'm going to show you around 'for dark."

"Show me around?" Jada asked. She turned around and stared at Sally.

"Miss Mitzi wanted me to make sure you knew where everything was, seeing as you and Miss Suzanne gonna be staying here awhile."

Jada pressed the last pin into her head. "All right." She hoped the trepidation didn't show in her tone.

Taking one step out of the room, Sally confronted her with a stack of sheets. "Might as well get some work done while we're walking around the place," she said.

Jada rearranged the stack in her arms until she was sure she could see over them and followed quickly behind Sally. They walked briskly through the hallway and down the servant's stairway. Instead of going toward the linen closet, Sally swung open the back doorway and motioned for Jada to follow her. Without so much as a warning, Sally skipped down the steep cement steps from the door to the alley's ground. Jada, on the other hand, lost her footing on the top step and nearly tumbled down them. Luckily for the laundry, she managed to catch her balance.

"I'd like to see Suzanne pull that move off," she laughed.

"What was that?" Sally asked, turning around to look at her.

"Just wondering where we were going," Jada called out. They were standing in the center of an alleyway. Jada's boots grinded awkwardly with the gravel underneath them.

"To the washbasins, of course." Sally grinned and set off down the alleyway.

Jada felt suddenly skeptical. "The washbasins are in the alley? I thought you were showing me around."

"We share our tubs with the ladies around the

block," Sally explained before she turned the corner.

The ladies from the block? Jada hugged the brick walls of the building until they came upon an opening. Who would have thought that in the middle of all these towers was a gathering spot? There, in a makeshift circle were at least seven basins with various amounts of steam rising from them and groups of women hovering all around, cackling like only women could do. Their faces were dripping with sweat from the steaming-hot water.

"Come on," Sally said, practically running to the one empty basin.

Jada tried to plaster a smile across her face, but found she could only jog a little to keep up with her. By the time Jada got to Sally's side, the girl had already dropped one pillowcase into the water and was scrubbing hard against the washboard.

"Everyone," Sally called out, "this here is Jada." She sat her armload next to an empty basin. A few pitchers of steaming water sat beside it.

" 'Ello, Jada," the women called out.

Jada blinked as she glanced around the circle, realizing that she and Sally were the only Negroes among them. Listening closer to their conversations, she was amazed to hear that most of the women were Irish.

"Hello." Jada knelt beside Sally and poured the last pitcher of steaming water into their basin.

"What brings you to our meeting spot?" One woman asked as she scrubbed a set of white sheets against the washboard.

Sally took a set of sheets and dunked them into the steaming water. Jada watched her for a moment before replying.

"I was just being shown around." The steam wafted up from the tubs so that Jada could feel the sweat beads trickling down her face. She hated the feeling of sweat. Hopefully she and Suzanne could afford to have their laundry cleaned for them.

"Being shown 'round?" Sally reached for the soap. "Why don't you toss me another sheet to soak and be useful?" She winked.

Jada was about to respond when Miss Mitzi's voice rang out over the laughter, "Suzanne, what's wrong?"

Jada dropped her pillowcase into the tub. Wrong? What could be wrong? Had Mrs. Haskins written with bad news? Had Mr. Ziegfeld reneged on his offer?

"I'm sorry, I'll help you another day. I have to go to see Suzanne." Jada pulled the pillowcase out of the tub and handed the soppy mess to Sally.

Sally gave her an unreadable look. "Of course you do." She held out her hands for the rest of the bedding. Her friendly attitude shifted quickly to a rehearsed coldness. Jada didn't have time to worry about her, however.

"Suzanne?" Jada said as she came inside the back door and entered the kitchen.

Miss Mitzi was fussing about the small room. A tea kettle was brewing. Suzanne sat at the small wooden table in the center of the room, nervously picking at her nail.

She looked up and saw Jada. "It's so embarrassing."

Miss Mitzi handed her a cup of tea. "Oh, dear me now. These things happen."

Remaining by the door, Jada waited for Suzanne to explain further.

"The show is closing," Suzanne said. "Tonight is the last performance."

Miss Mitzi took Suzanne's hand. "There, there, child. It will be all right. I can extend some credit until you find another show."

Jada nearly interrupted as she asked, "Have you told Mr. Ziegfeld?"

"Not yet. I just found out myself." Suzanne took a sip of tea.

"Ziegfeld? Did you say Ziegfeld?" Miss Mitzi looked at Jada for the first time. "*The* Ziegfeld?"

"He's offered Suzanne a spot in this year's Follies," Jada explained. "Just as soon as her contract at *The Dancing Duchess* was up."

"A Ziegfeld girl? In my own home?! This is a cause for celebration!" She jumped to her feet. "I must make preparations. We shall have a feast for you tonight!"

"A feast?" Suzanne held her stomach warily.

"Perhaps we could postpone until another time?" Jada's tone was soft, but firm. "Costume fittings and such, you know."

Miss Mitzi's face fell. "Well, of course. Perhaps we could have a tea to celebrate and you could invite the other girls here as well. Yes, that would be lovely." Without another word, she left the room muttering plans to herself.

"Are you all right?" Jada took a seat across from Suzanne.

Suzanne leaned back and stretched. She took a sip of tea before giving Jada a gleeful look. "Thank goodness *The Dancing Duchess* is over! I am now a Ziegfeld girl! It feels unreal still. We must go shopping!"

Before Jada could even think of protesting, Suzanne had collected her handbag and she and Jada were walking toward a shop.

"No arguing about cost, Jada," Suzanne insisted. "I must be the toast of the town and that requires fashion."

"But . . ." Jada said, trying to keep up with Suzanne.

"You've done a great job this last year, truly, but I need more now. That's all there is to it. And with Ziegfeld's salary, we can finally afford it."

Jada swallowed her pride. The gowns she

created and the suits she tailored were well made. She hoped to do more in the future, but as she practically jogged alongside Suzanne, she knew that was over. For a moment she felt the pang of . . . something. Disappointment? Resentment? But she quickly moved on. Suzanne was right, of course. She needed a perfectly tailored wardrobe. Ziegfeld paid well, and surely part of that was because he expected so much from his girls.

"Where are we going?" Jada asked again.

"It's on the end of the next block, I think," Suzanne replied, looking around them with a pinched expression.

"Don't you know?" Jada half laughed. How like Suzanne to speed ahead without direction.

"Well, I haven't been there personally," Suzanne confessed. "I heard one of the girls mention it."

Jada raised her eyebrow. Suzanne was resorting to her mother's tricks. But, as it never seemed to backfire on Mrs. Haskins, why shouldn't Suzanne try? People had to learn the tricks from somewhere. Even Jada had to admit to using some of Mrs. Haskins's expressions to move them along in either mood or money.

On the end of the block was a corner building with tall glass windows. The window displays showed beautifully ornate hats on stands of various sizes in front of an off-white gown covered in pearls. Suzanne and Jada stopped.

"Gosh," Suzanne gasped, and pointed to a straw hat with a satin flower perched on one side. "That is beautiful."

"Look at all the workmanship." Jada admired the pearl gown. Each pearl hand sewn. Surely it had taken someone days, if not weeks, to finish.

"These are fit for a Ziegfeld girl. Let's go in." Suzanne tugged on Jada's arm.

Jada grinned and let herself be pulled into the small shop. Bells above the door jingled as they entered. A wave of cinnamon greeted them, as did voices from the back room.

"I said you were being foolish!" a woman insisted. "Don't bite the hand that feeds you, girl!"

Suzanne's eyes widened and she mouthed to Jada, "Oh my."

"You don't understand! They aren't giving me my due!" another high-pitched voice whined.

Jada nodded back to Suzanne. It felt like they had intruded on some family dispute. She checked the door's sign again. It read, OPEN.

"It doesn't matter," the first speaker said. "They pay you to do a job, you do it."

"Jada," Suzanne whispered. "Jingle the door again."

"I deserve just as much as any of those other girls. I work twice as hard!"

Once Jada did as asked, Suzanne cleared her throat. "Oh, Jada, look at the bird on this hat. Don't you love it?"

The voices in the back stopped abruptly and the skirts rustled as they moved to come into the shop. Jada picked up the mauve fur hat with a blue bird perched precariously on top. She held it out for Suzanne. *Please don't like this,* she silently pleaded.

Suzanne took it and set it upon her head. Almost instantly she cracked a smile.

"Jada?" she asked. "How do I look?" She whipped her head around so quickly that the bird bobbed up and down.

"I am speechless." Jada tried to conceal her laughter.

Suzanne turned toward one of the mirrors and looked at herself. The bird bobbed each time she moved. Jada turned away and covered her mouth until Suzanne started laughing. She turned around to Suzanne forcibly nodding her head to make the hat move in various directions. A giggle escaped Jada's mouth, and soon the two were doubled over the counter laughing together.

Behind them the curtain flung to one side and a statuesque blond woman said, "It is the latest fashion from Paris."

Suzanne pulled herself together quickly. "Perhaps, but I do not believe it will be *my* latest fashion."

Jada couldn't help herself this time and her laughter continued.

"Some fashion is not for us, but for those we

are looking to impress." The tall woman looked down her nose at both of them. "I am Miss Steel. What can I help you with?" Her tone was so level all the amusement in the room evaporated.

"I need a new dress. Something fashionable," Suzanne said. She glanced up at the bird hat and quickly unpinned it. "Fashionable, but classic. Nothing too new."

"Is there a special occasion for which this gown is needed?" the woman asked.

Suzanne smiled. "No occasion in particular. I have recently accepted a position with the Ziegfeld Follies and need a few new gowns to spruce up my wardrobe."

"A Ziegfeld girl! Oh my." The woman walked around Suzanne and nodded to herself. "I have some designs in the back. If you wouldn't mind following me, we can get started right away."

The girls followed Miss Steel behind the velvet curtain. There was a small platform surrounded by mirrors and a plush sofa next to a table piled with catalogs. Being a Ziegfeld girl was a much different world than either of them was used to. Even in Richmond, Mother chose Suzanne's gowns. The local tailor had her measurements on hand and things arrived every few months. Jada often was given Suzanne's old gowns.

Once Suzanne was seated on the sofa, Miss Steel pulled the catalog off the top and opened it to a page in the middle. "With your hair and figure, this suit would look fantastic."

Suzanne handed her bag to Jada and looked at the illustration. "I'm not sure such wide shoulders would work."

"We will tailor it to fit your desires. The wide shoulders will make your waist appear small. It is a trick of the eye. Just as that bird will make you appear taller." She smiled.

Suzanne's eyes lit up. "The bird will make me appear taller?"

Jada glanced at Suzanne, expecting her friend to meet her gaze, but Suzanne was leaning over the book, examining the suit Miss Steel had suggested for her. It was something Jada would never create. It wasted too much fabric and was a bit too on the trend to make it worth Jada's time. Even knowing all of this, Jada felt slighted.

"Fashion is all about deception. Take your girl, for example." Miss Steel turned to Jada and gestured for her to come forward. "With her skin tone and thin frame she could be from anywhere. Is she a Negress? A Spaniard? Italian? No one knows until you style her."

Jada reached and adjusted the collar of her dress. The pale yellow gown was a favorite of hers, but she'd never once imagined that it said something about her. Did people look at her clothing to uncover her race? She never suspected they noticed her at all unless she forced them to by speaking. She now wondered what this dress said about her.

Suzanne stared at Jada, her eyes dancing. "Jada could pass for Spanish?"

Miss Steel nodded. "She does not have the Negro nose, nor the wide, ape-like face. With her high cheekbones and smooth hair, she could pass for Spanish."

Never in her entire life had Jada felt so disgusted. Suzanne was not defending her at all, but was staring at Jada's features along with Miss Steel and nodding in agreement. Jada's family had come over from Africa, were raised as slaves, and then maintained a life on the plantation in Richmond. Miss Steel was peeling her heritage away from her with this assessment.

"But I am not Spanish," Jada pointed out.

Miss Steel's gaze hardened. "It does not matter what you are. It only matters what will be best for your employer, and European servants are very hard to come by."

Suzanne nodded. "I'd be the envy of all the girls."

Suzanne cocked her head and looked at Jada. For the first time ever, Jada felt like an actual servant around her friend.

"It is something to think about," Miss Steel stated before pulling another catalog and pointing out another pattern.

Jada stepped back and sat in the chair against

the wall with Suzanne's purse in her lap. Miss Steel gushed over Suzanne's creamy skin and insisted on a baby blue to highlight her complexion. Suzanne nodded to everything the woman said without another glance at Jada.

CHAPTER 4

The following Monday, garbed in a new suit and a bird-topped hat, Suzanne strutted down Forty-second Street. Yes, the hat felt ridiculous at first, but they were all over Paris, and Anna Held, Ziegfeld's ex-wife, had been seen wearing one here in New York. Knowing such a woman wore them made the hat feel exotic to Suzanne. Jada wore one of Suzanne's old gowns, a periwinkle number that they had to take in a bit, but it did the trick. No one would guess Jada's race now, which gave Suzanne an air of mystery. She grinned with delight. Streetcars and buggies passed by as the street's pedestrians moved on either side of them.

"Stay by my side today, Jada," Suzanne said again. "I need you to watch the dances so we can practice at home. I need to impress Ziegfeld."

"You will," Jada assured her. "No one will expect you to be perfect right away. It takes time for everyone to learn new numbers, and you have to learn the Ziegfeld style on top of the dance steps."

Suzanne groaned. "I hadn't thought of that." Her pace slowed. "Jada, I can't fail at this. I can't give up like that other girl. We've come too far to go home. He can make me a star!"

"Look, you aren't some frail lady," Jada said.

She linked arms with Suzanne and pulled on Suzanne to walk faster. "You work hard. We will make sure you shine. Don't worry about those weaker than you."

Suzanne stopped and looked at Jada. "Don't you think those others had talent too? Mr. Ziegfeld chose them, the same as me. That girl in his office . . . you didn't see her. She looked scared."

"Of what?" Jada's forehead crinkled in confusion.

"I don't know."

Jada didn't reply. Instead, she started walking again. Suzanne maintained the silence, but inwardly she was concerned. When Elton first became ill, Jada offered dozens of solutions for how to bring him out of his depression. She was always full of ideas. This silence was new. Suzanne knew that the adjustment to theater life had been hard. Not only had her parents died, but Suzanne was the one onstage and not her. A cloud had come over Jada lately, but Suzanne could do little to help. Every choice they made was needed. Once Suzanne was a celebrated Ziegfeld girl, Jada would see that it was worth it. But Suzanne missed the glint in Jada's eyes. There must be something that would add to her excitement.

She grinned as she realized the one thing she'd forgotten to tell Jada.

"Bert Williams is performing in the Follies again."

Jada tripped over a bump in the curb. "Bert Williams, really?"

Suzanne nodded. "His name is on all the advertisements."

"Do you think you'll meet him?"

"I would think so!" Suanne laughed, delighted with Jada's excitement. "And if I do, I'm sure you will see him at the very least."

"I've seen others do his cakewalk, but never thought I'd see him do it. Is he performing with Leon Errol again? I wonder what he is like." Jada practically bounced. "He is so talented. He'd have to be to headline the Follies."

"Especially since he's a Negro," Suzanne added. Instantly she knew she should have kept race out of the conversation. A bit of the joy melted off of Jada's face. Suzanne tried to find a way to bring the conversation back to herself. "Perhaps I'll get to dance with him."

"You onstage with him?" Jada shook her head. "That will never happen. You read the papers when they hired him. People nearly revolted. Putting you beauties on the stage with him would be scandalous."

"Oh, of course." Suzanne turned down the back alley of the theater.

Jada grabbed for the stage door and held it open. "Sometimes I don't know where your head is." She shook her head and grinned at Suzanne as they walked into the building.

After some wrong turns they eventually found the dressing room. Each room was assigned to three or more girls. Suzanne and Jada walked down the hallway, looking at the various names written on chalkboards beside the doors. After passing two rooms, Jada motioned for Suzanne to stop. On a crooked slate it read: RUBY BOOTH, LILLIAN DARMIN, AND SUZANNE HASKINS. Suzanne reached up to straighten the slate. In *The Dancing Duchess* she had her own dressing room. She crossed her fingers and promised that by the time 1915 rolled around she would have star billing in the Follies.

The door opened and revealed two of the prettiest girls Suzanne had ever seen. One had a long pink silk dressing gown tied loosely at the waist and falling off one shoulder to reveal a lace undershirt. The other wore practical bloomers and a crisp white linen skirt with a shawl draped over her shoulders. Both had pale, smooth skin and bright brown eyes. Suzanne thought of her own overly bleached bloomers and plain jersey top and felt very plain next to Ruby and Lillian. Why waste clean garments on sweaty hours in a dirty rehearsal room?

"You must be Suzanne!" the girl at the door cried. Her perfectly curled hair bounced as she spoke. It was her pale skin that made her so luminous. It made Suzanne instantly regret the few freckles she had. The girl held out her hand. "I'm Ruby. This is Lillian."

Lillian pulled her robe on tighter and turned toward Suzanne, a raised eyebrow wrinkling her forehead. "You brought a servant?"

"Is she European? She looks Spanish." Ruby gushed and gestured for them to enter the room.

The room itself was not large, but it was designed with the girls in mind. Along the long wall was a row of vanities and large mirrors and bright lights. On one end was a wide wardrobe that Suzanne assumed they were all to share. Lillian's vanity already had various photographs of stars tucked into the mirror frame, while Ruby's table was covered with a purple shawl and had a vase of yellow roses. Suzanne's area was bleach white, waiting for her to put her own personality into it.

"Jada is a treasure," Suzanne replied vaguely.

Ruby took Suzanne's word as confirmation and nearly jumped up and down with excitement. "That's wonderful! I tried to find immigrant help, but all we have is a black girl at home. I couldn't bring her. We must keep up with the trends, you know. Where ever did you find her?"

"I am just one of the lucky ones. Isn't she lovely?" Behind her, Jada stuttered as if about to speak, but said nothing. Suzanne refused to feel guilty. They had discussed this. Any deception was worth it if it added to Suzanne's stature.

Ruby moved a pile of shirts so Jada could put the bag down and start unpacking. "I just love her skin. I wish mine tanned like that."

"You have perfect, porcelain skin. Don't let some fad make you question your beauty." Lillian's voice was filled with passion.

Suzanne cleared her throat as Jada adjusted her stance. Neither was prepared for the animosity in the girl's words. Jada hung Suzanne's rehearsal attire on a hanger and set to unpacking the few containers they brought for her to use at the theater. Powder, lavender water, and her good-luck brush didn't personalize her space like she hoped it would. She and Jada would have to find something to make her space special, but that was for another day.

Ruby nudged her friend. "Stop that, Lillian. Because of Suzanne's girl, we won't have to clean up now. It's perfect. We'll be first to rehearsal! Thanks, Suzanne!" She grabbed Lillian's arm and the two hurried down the hall to rehearsal. Lillian glanced at them briefly over her shoulder, but followed her friend.

"Clean the room?" Jada repeated once they were out of earshot.

Both girls looked around the small dressing room. There were garments and powders scattered across all the counter and tables.

"I'm sorry, Jada. You can come to rehearsal

after lunch. I'll be sure to come down and get you. I promise." Suzanne moved a pile of chemise so she could apply some rouge to her lips. "It will just be introduction instructions and such."

"Of course." Jada's face was unreadable. "Do you want me to use an accent?"

Suzanne flinched. "I don't know. No, of course not. We'll figure it out."

The two stood in silence for a moment. Both knew there was more to say, but since Jada didn't say anything else, Suzanne didn't know how to start the conversation. Instead, she cleared off the remaining chair and table by the mirror and started to hang Suzanne's clothes. Suzanne let her work in silence as she quickly stepped out of her day gown and stepped into the short petticoat she wore for rehearsals. A soft linen shirt completed her look. She leaned over to tuck any loose strands of hair back off her face.

"I think I'm ready, Jada," she declared.

Jada looked up from the line of glass jars she was pulling out of the bag and said, "Knock 'em dead."

"Thanks!" Suzanne hugged her friend before rushing out into the hallway and up to the stage, leaving Jada to clean up whatever mess was lurking in the dressing room.

The stage was positively abuzz with excitement. Dozens of young women were standing in groups of three and four, stretching and leaning in close for the best gossip. A few of them glanced at Suzanne, but none came to speak to her. Suzanne kept her head high, she knew what to expect as the new girl. Soon they would all be laughing together. And, if she made it to next year's Follies, she would be able to look down and laugh at whatever new talent was brought in as well.

She pretended to adjust her chemise as she looked for an empty spot to warm up. At the far left corner at the very front of the stage was a large, empty section. Suzanne made a beeline for it, quickly sat, and began her stretches. The walk to the theater was enough of a warm-up. If she was lucky, she would have time for a lengthy stretch before the day's activities began. She opened her legs as far as they would go and leaned forward. She was so close to doing splits that she could nearly roll forward and lay flat on the ground. One girl close to her gasped. Suzanne smiled to herself. Had she managed to truly impress someone?

"Hello there."

Suzanne looked up into the long dark curls of Ann Pennington herself. The woman was even more beautiful than her photos. Her hair sat in a low ponytail down her back, and her big brown eyes were rounder than any Suzanne had seen. From the corner of her eye, she could see other girls watching to see what would happen. Had she somehow made a faux pas on her first hour?

"Hello," Suzanne replied. She rolled into a sitting position and brought her legs together.

Ann sat down across from her and tilted so her back was to the other girls. "You are new?"

Suzanne nodded. "Mr. Ziegfeld saw me in *The Dancing Duchess*. It closed last week." Suzanne forced a bit of laughter. "But for two weeks, I was a headliner."

"Isn't that the worst?" Ann leaned over her legs and grabbed her toes. She was so short, it was like warming up next to a child. "At least the performance got you his attention."

Lillian and Ruby appeared beside Suzanne. "Can we warm up with you?" Lillian asked.

Suzanne was about to respond when Ann waved at them dismissively. "I would prefer to get to know Suzanne alone."

"Oh, of course," Ruby said, then pulled on Lillian's arm.

"You do like the pretty girls, don't you, Ann?" Lillian replied before letting Ruby pull her away.

"Ugh, those girls!" Ann whispered to herself.

"I share a dressing room with them." Suzanne held her elbow to her chest to stretch her arm.

Ann snickered. "They are such ninnies. They started last year same as me and have been trying to get in my good graces after they poured ink on my gown at the opening night party. Lillian

71

swears it was an accident, but I overheard her later telling Leon how clumsy I was and shouldn't she take over my number in case I embarrass myself."

"Oh my," Suzanne swallowed. "That is horrible."

"It is childish." Ann sighed. She leaned in as if to tell a secret. "Flo himself told me to look for the new girl with shiny golden hair. He thinks you are quite unique."

All strength fell from Suzanne's arms and they flopped down to her sides like lumps of lead. "What? He thinks I'm . . . what?"

"Special." Ann clarified. "Come now, Suzanne. You wouldn't be here if he didn't see something in you. In me he saw beauty and lust, in Fanny Brice he saw hysterical talent, in Lillian Lorraine he saw sex appeal, and in you . . . I'm not sure what he saw. But he saw it." Ann winked.

Suzanne glanced over at Lillian and Ruby, who were talking quietly a few steps away. Lillian met her eyes and the smile she plastered to her face was all too obviously fake. Suzanne steeled herself to a difficult discussion later.

"What is your talent?" Ann asked.

"Well, I was known for my tango performance when I was on the circuit; however, when Mr. Ziegfeld saw me, I was dancing and singing. I didn't ask what caught his eye." Suzanne laughed. "Though that might have been good information to have."

Ann laughed. She spread her legs wide and held out her hands for Suzanne to take them. They matched their legs and Suzanne pulled gently back on Ann's arms, giving her a deeper stretch.

"You have excellent turnout," Ann observed.

Suzanne shrugged. "I've always been flexible."

"That might be what Flo noticed," Ann muttered. "Why the tango? With that blond hair, you hardly look Spanish."

Ann leaned back, pulling Suzanne forward in a deep stretch. Her legs burned so much that Suzanne had to focus on her breathing. When Ann stopped pulling on her arms, Suzanne let her grip go and stood up, rolling her shoulders and shaking her legs. "We needed an act and it was a dance I performed well. It just happened." Suzanne prayed Ann didn't ask more questions. She didn't want to go into what lead her to vaudeville or the countless nights they went without food because of the decision. To this day, Suzanne prayed never to have to eat beans again.

Luckily, just then a thin, balding man walked into the auditorium, down the aisle, and up onto the stage.

"Good day, ladies!" he said. "For those who don't know me, I am Leon Errol, your director. For those who I've worked with before, welcome back."

There was a general muttering of greetings and comments about the previous year's schedule.

"I want to address the elephant in the room before more gossip spreads. As many of you already know, Bert Williams is back this year, and he has the good fortune to be onstage with some of you lovely ladies this year—"

"That is indecent!" a raven-haired girl in the back cried out. Soon the stage was abuzz with complaints and cheers regarding Bert Williams.

Ann leaned over to Suzanne. "Bert is the kindest man you'd know. Lord knows only a man's skin color can make a woman fear for her virtue so drastically."

Another girl stood up and stomped her foot. "You can't be serious, Leon. I won't risk my safety for this job. I won't do it."

Leon frowned. "Now, Mary, we went through this two years ago. As Flo said, Bert is irreplaceable, you are not."

That threw the room into a wave of whispers.

"That isn't fair!" Mary exclaimed.

Suzanne rolled her eyes at the commotion. "Mr. Ziegfeld can make any girl a graceful beauty. From what my girl tells me, talent like Bert Williams can't be taught."

The girls around her had grown silent and her words carried throughout the auditorium. She had meant her supportive words for Ann's ears only. Suzanne met the accusatory stares from some of the girls. Whether she wanted it or not, her stance had been chosen on the subject.

74

Mr. Errol looked approvingly at Suzanne. "That is exactly what Flo said to the few girls who already demanded Bert's removal. If you look around you'll see more than a few new faces. I suggest any of you who have a problem performing with talent like Bert's to think seriously before complaining again."

While others frittered about Leon's threat, Suzanne breathed a sigh of relief. This was why so many girls left: Bert Williams.

Next to her, Ann grinned. "Bert is really doing it," she whispered.

"What?" Suzanne asked.

"He is changing the game for colored folk. And he is doing it single-handedly." The pride on her face for her friend was contagious.

"Will you introduce me?" Suzanne asked before she could think about it.

"Of course!" Ann replied.

"And, could I . . ." Suzanne stopped herself. She barely knew Ann. She couldn't ask if she could bring Jada to meet him as well. It felt too forward.

Ann laughed knowingly. Suzanne gave her a quizzical look. Ann didn't know about Jada, what did she think Suzanne wanted from her?

"Let's see how you dance. If you have the right qualities, I'll get you in a number with him. These ninnies don't know it, but those girls onstage with him are going to be making history!"

Suzanne's stomach flopped. *Onstage with Bert Williams*. Fear and excitement battled for attention. If she got in that number she would be able to introduce Jada to Bert for sure. More than anything else, she wanted to make Jada's dream come true. In the end, all she could say was, "Thank you."

CHAPTER 5

Whatever Ruby and Lillian did before performing, it clearly did not involve cleaning. Jada jammed the last of the dressing gowns into the closet and slammed the door. It was as if they just opened their bags and dropped everything out without a thought as to what was what or where it should go. Everything might not be in the right place, but at least the clothes were all hung and the bottles were all cleaned and aligned in some order.

She perched on a chair and listened for some hint of what was happening upstairs. It was quiet.

Ruby's bottles were all made of pink glass. They sat in a line on the vanity. Jada stared at them. How could that silly girl think she was Spanish? She rubbed a smudge off one of the bottles. It moved and a small piece of paper stuck out underneath.

Slobs, Jada thought to herself. She pulled the paper out. It was a small card, perhaps a calling card or one that would accompany a flower delivery. Jada rolled her eyes. These girls must have dozens of suitors. Knowing who was courting these girls would help Suzanne steer clear of trouble. She unfolded it and read: *Don't think I've forgotten. Leave the Follies before it's too late.*

Jada's stomach lurched as she read the threat neatly scrawled on the pretty paper with a floral design. What had Ruby done? She threw the card in the trash and set the bottles to right. Suzanne didn't need to discover that and let it get into her head.

She refused to stay in this room and wait for them to return. Her curiosity about what was happening onstage was too much. She had to know what these girls were like. Suzanne had promised—no, begged for Jada to watch rehearsal, and that was what Jada was going to do.

She slipped out of the room and ran up the stairs to the theater level. Once she could hear the piano banging out a melody for rehearsal she stopped cold. It would be unseemly to just walk onstage, and it would surely embarrass Suzanne. Instead, she slipped back and went down the corridor that led to the theater lobby. From there she ran up to the balcony and slipped in through the door. The rows of red velvet seats sat empty in the darkness. Jada was thankful light from the stage did not reach them. Very carefully, she walked to the aisle and went down a few rows before selecting a seat. The hinge on the chair creaked as she sat, and her heart raced at the thought of being caught. But no one so much as glanced in her direction.

The theater was as beautiful as the lobby was.

Above the stage was a huge mosaic of Grecian mythology that was depicted throughout the theater in various paintings. The flower and vine motif continued inside the house as well as the mauve and maroon coloring. Jada took a moment to marvel at the beauty of the space before focusing on the women themselves.

Onstage, a group of girls walked in a circle, slowly waving their arms in and out of their formation as if creating a figure eight in the air. Another four girls sat at a table looking at a drawing of something Jada couldn't decipher.

Jada exhaled. The women were beautiful. Even from this distance, with all of them in rehearsal dress, they were stunning. A tall man walked to the center of the girls' circle and began barking directions.

"Shoulders back!" he barked at one girl. "Smoothly, Mary, we are not jumping puppies!"

Jada covered her mouth to suppress a laugh as she found Mary, who was indeed bouncing up and down as she moved, as if she might bounce away if tapped too hard. She scanned the girls for Suzanne's blond curls but was unable to find her. Alarmed, she leaned forward and counted as the girls continued their walk. Not a single one had Suzanne's particular shade of blond or her poise.

Something shuffled behind her, but Jada didn't move.

She scanned the rest of the stage, trying to

locate her friend. Finally, in the back corner, she found her. She was hunched over a few sheets of piano music, her head leaning toward a brunette woman. Jada squinted and drew back in surprise. It was Ann Pennington. Suzanne worried about a lot of things, but she always knew what connections to make.

Another creak sounded from behind her.

"Hello?" Jada whispered, suddenly aware someone else was with her.

"Ma'am."

Jada slowly turned around and found herself face-to-face with a light-skinned black man. "Can I help you?"

A crooked smile sprawled across the man's face. "Well, I was going to ask you the same thing. What are you doing here?"

Jada felt her face warm in embarrassment. She licked her lips and tilted her head in the way she'd observed Suzanne do in attempt to get the higher ground.

"I am observing rehearsal. What are you doing here?" The superior tone she adopted made her stomach churn. This was not the person she wanted to be, but she also didn't want to get in trouble.

"Same." The man stood up and hopped over the seats to sit beside her. "Leon and I think it's better if I observe from up here for a few days before I interact with the girls."

"Leon and you?" Jada leaned back and looked at the man. She'd only seen publicity shots, but from his smirk and ease of the name of Mr. Errol, she knew who he was. Bert Williams.

Her head fell to her hands. "Oh, Mr. Williams. I am so sorry. Please. I just wanted to watch the rehearsal. My friend—I mean, I work for one of the girls onstage and she wanted me to learn what was needed so I could help her with nightly rehearsals."

Bert chuckled. "No need, girl. You can sit with me and help me learn the names of all the new girls. Which one is your friend?" He settled back and propped his foot up against the chair in front of them.

"She is the blond one in the back corner with Ann Pennington."

"She's Ann's friend?" Bert jumped and leaned forward again. "Blond curls? Oh, yes, I see her. She's a pretty girl."

"They were looking at sheet music earlier." Jada hoped Bert might have some insight over what that might mean. For Suzanne to get a prominent number would be a huge coup.

"Sheet music, eh?" he nodded. "Ann was hoping to get another girl in our act, but most of the gals she knows are . . . reluctant."

"Your act?" Jada asked. "You're dancing with girls onstage?" Her heart beat against her chest.

"We are going to try," Bert said. "It opens so

many possibilities. But these women can be very impractical."

Both of them were quiet for a time. Onstage, Leon tapped his cane in a beat for the girls to move. Suzanne and Ann were in line with the others now and were, to Jada, the best of the bunch. Ann had something that made you just want to watch her, and Suzanne moved with effortless grace. Jada's eyes welled with pride.

Wait.

She was proud of Suzanne for walking nicely when she and Bert Williams, *the* Bert Williams, were sitting in the dark, spying on rehearsal. It was ludicrous.

"I am sorry for your troubles," Jada said. "It isn't fair that someone of your talent is kept in the balcony watching rehearsal while these women are worshipped for just being able to walk."

Bert put his fingers to his lips. "You hush now. Getting all worked up won't do nothing, and I'd rather not have the girls know that I'm watching them yet." He shifted in his chair until his long legs were facing Jada. "For now we are up here and they are down there. But this season that all changes. This season, Ann and I and, God willing, your friend will take the stage and make history on Broadway."

"Intermingling the sexes and races onstage." Jada nearly whispered the idea. If they would dance with a man, perhaps a Negro Ziegfeld girl wasn't too far off?

Careful, Jada, she thought to herself. Such dreams would get her nowhere.

"It is already done abroad. But much is done there that we lag behind on."

Suzanne dipped down and picked up a scarf that had fallen off one of the other girls. She didn't miss a beat in her movements as she swept it up and placed it on the shoulder of the girl in front of her. Jada leaned forward and observed the movements.

"Why does your girl want you to watch rehearsal again?" Bert asked.

Without looking at him, Jada replied, "I help her rehearse." Then she realized Suzanne might not want that spread around. A colored girl helping her rehearse might not be good for her future reputation. Jada quickly covered her steps. "She humors me as I fancy myself a dancer."

"A dancer, eh?" Bert glanced at the stage and back at Jada. "Shall we see if you have talent?"

"What?" Jada snapped to attention. Quieter she said, "I don't think that is necessary. Besides, you need to observe the girls."

Down on the stage, Leon stopped his tapping. "All right, girls, take five," he declared. "And drink water. We don't want anyone fainting like last year!"

A general twittering came from the stage as

the dancers broke down into smaller groups and whispered with one another. Ann grabbed Suzanne and the two got glasses of water to drink from a woman onstage. Ruby and Lillian sat on the front of the stage, their legs dangling with a slew of other women, their laughs carrying well in the theater.

"Looks like we have a few minutes. Do you want to show me what you got?" He motioned to the door behind them.

"Um . . ." Jada's heart raced. Dancing with Bert Williams? This felt like a dream, and yet, she was rooted in place. "I can't."

"Why not?"

"I don't think Suzanne would like it."

Once the words were spoken, Jada instantly regretted saying them. She hadn't intended to be so brutally honest. Bert looked her up and down and shook his head.

"That is too bad. Too bad indeed." He tipped his head in her direction. "Until we meet again."

He turned and walked out of the balcony, leaving Jada sitting in her seat, kicking herself for missing her chance.

CHAPTER 6

"The better your posture the more alluring your form," Ann explained. "One of the things Lillian doesn't understand is that attracting a man has less to do with the size of your bosom and more to do with confidence. Keep your head high and shoulders back and few men will resist your charms." She winked at Suzanne.

A pile of apple cores and half-empty cups of tea sat on a small, round table beside them as Ann tried to instruct Suzanne, Vera, and Mary on the art of seduction. Their small group was tucked into the far left corner of the stage, practically in the wings. As it was, Suzanne kept moving the large curtain that hung in the wings. The heavy fabric was surprisingly responsive to Ann's stride.

"It isn't about what is obvious, but what is underneath?" Suzanne asked as she tried to copy Ann's posture. The small woman was hard not to look at as she circled Suzanne.

"Exactly!" She picked up a book off the pile beside them. "Watch."

She placed the book on her head and continued to move around the stage. A few of the other groups stopped and watched her as well. Not for the first time did Suzanne hear whisperings of why Ann had chosen her to befriend, but

Suzanne refused to let their jealous gossip detract from her good fortune. This group of women especially should understand there was more to a person than good looks. Ann returned to their small group.

"When a man calls your name, do you whip your head around in excitement or curiosity?" She moved her head fast as if to look over her shoulder. The book naturally fell to the floor. Mary picked it up and gave it back to Ann. "Most of us do. But if we move slower, not quite glancing in his direction as we turn, it becomes a dance between you, and for once we women take the lead."

She turned slowly, keeping her gaze down as she turned, and then lifting her eyelashes up and meeting Suzanne's gaze. Only someone devoid of a pulse wouldn't have felt their pulse quicken when Ann set those eyes upon them. Suzanne herself felt goosebumps rise on her arms.

"But who here are you trying to impress, Ann?" Vera giggled.

Mary hushed her. "Perhaps had we known this move Mr. Vanderbilt would be taking us out tonight instead of Ann. No offense, Ann."

"None taken. Cornelius is a good friend, but far too young to be anything more than that." Ann took the book off her head and handed it to Suzanne.

"I'd take a young admirer if he brought me

jewels like the Vanderbilts are known for." Vera sighed.

Suzanne raised an eyebrow. "I've only been here for the morning, but even I have heard of the diamonds that you were gifted with from a certain someone."

Vera blushed as the other girls laughed. She pulled her robe tighter around her waist. It was embroidered with hundreds of little roses. Suzanne itched the collar of her chemise. Tomorrow she would make sure she looked as glamorous as the other girls.

Suzanne placed the book upon her head, hardly daring to admit to Ann how much the muscles in her back ached from keeping her posture in the Ziegfeld style. Working with Jada, Suzanne assumed she'd worked every muscle possible. She was wrong. In the span of one day she felt as if she'd unearthed a new level of muscles that had never been used before.

Leon walked over to their group and removed the book from Suzanne's head. "Very good, Suzanne. You've proven yourself a force to be reckoned with. I'll tell Flo of your hard work."

"Thank you," Suzanne said. Any thought of pain floated away with his compliment. A personal mention to Mr. Ziegfeld was quite an honor.

"We'll be stopping now. I want to be sure all you girls have time for dinner and a good night's rest. We will start working on thematic movement tomorrow."

Vera's hand shot up in the air. Leon looked at her and nodded. "Are we dressing up as roosters like last year? That was fun." She grinned.

Leon laughed. "You had the best crow, if memory serves. This year we are focusing on love and glamour and the crime that sometimes accompanies it. Ann will be dancing a lively number where she is chased by a policeman. She and Julian just started choreography on it, and I think it will make even the dullest man laugh. Our ending will feature a row of chorus girls in a dancing contest that will then turn into a musical number called 'At the Ball.' Bert and Leon will put their usual comedic twist on a gentleman golfer and his caddy while Mr. Wynn is perfecting a number about a joke king. With all the talent in the room, we expect this year's Follies to be the best yet."

An excited murmur filled the room and a couple of the girls applauded Leon's declaration. Suzanne felt her stomach tighten with nerves. Her signature dance was that tango, which didn't seem like a fit with Leon's cops and robbers ideas. She would have to find other ways of being noticed if she was going to stand out in this sea of beauties.

Leon cleared his throat. "I expect all of you to be on your best behavior as we begin our journey together. The temptation to go out every night is great and there are plenty of gentlemen waiting in line to have a Ziegfeld girl on his arm. Rehearsals start at nine sharp. As long as you are on time and ready to work, I won't ask questions. The moment our time here is jeopardized there will be consequences. Are we clear?"

A chorus of "Yes, Leon" vibrated through the room.

"Good. We will see you tomorrow then." Leon gathered some of his papers and watched the stage empty.

"Thanks, Leon," Vera said. She rubbed her shoulder as she linked arms with Mary and headed toward their dressing room.

"Bring an evening gown with you tomorrow," Ann demanded. "We'll go out to dinner after rehearsal. I'll introduce you around."

Suzanne tried not to sound overeager. "I'd love to! As long as it isn't too late."

Ann glanced at Leon and smiled. "Of course. Leon's word is law."

"Thank you, Ann." Suzanne smiled at Leon.

Leon put a hand on Ann's back and led her toward the piano. "I'd like to discuss some of the music for your entrance, if you have a moment."

Ann waved over her shoulder to Suzanne as she headed backstage.

Hobnobbing with Ann Pennington. Suzanne couldn't believe her luck. Ann was the biggest star in the show. Suzanne herself had tried to achieve Ann's classic curls, but without her dark locks they never looked right.

Before entering her dressing room, Suzanne hesitated. She'd never gone back to find Jada and bring her up to the stage. She bit her lip. Had there really been so much work that Jada couldn't be spared? Or did Suzanne just not want her near the excitement? Neither answer pleased Suzanne. Tomorrow, she promised herself. Tomorrow she'd rectify the situation.

With that enthusiasm she swung the dressing room door open, ready to announce her news to Jada, but the room was empty.

Suzanne shut the door behind her and stepped inside. On Ruby's table was a beautiful bouquet of lilies. They filled the room with a sweet scent.

"Jada?" she asked, despite there being no place for her friend to hide. She spun around again before giving up and dropping onto the white vanity chair. She lifted one foot onto her knee, slid her shoe off, and rubbed feeling back into them. The new blisters burned, but Suzanne refused to stop. Instead, she stared at the lilies and tried to guess which gentleman caller Ruby had infatuated. Ruby wasn't as vocal as Lillian about her conquests. A fact that made her a better friend, but much harder to read than the other girls.

Just then Lillian's laugh carried down the hall. As Ruby swung the door open, Lillian declared, "No better homecoming than a clean room."

Ruby's face fell as she saw her vanity. "Flowers? Who for?"

Suzanne switched and started rubbing the other foot. She shrugged. "As they are on your table, I assumed they are for you. Is there a card?"

Ruby's face paled further and she darted to the vase. She pawed through the flowers trying to find the card.

Lillian plopped down on the floor and leaned against the wall. "The first day is always brutal. It gets better."

Suzanne forced herself to regain Ann's Ziegfeld posture and smiled. "Are you sore? I just need a good stretch to set me right." Her back ached with her efforts, but the look on Lillian's face was worth it.

"Well, it helps that you have been in rehearsal for that flop. I'm sure it kept you in shape. Ruby and I, of course, had a few months off between shows to enjoy life."

Ruby yanked the card out of the flowers. "Oh," she sighed with a hint of relief. "They are for you, Suzanne."

"Me?" Suzanne tried not to wince as she stood up to retrieve the card from Ruby. Her feet burned, but Suzanne refused to show Lillian any weakness.

"Who are they from?" Lillian asked. She had gotten to her feet as well and was huddled together with Ruby and Suzanne.

That was the question: Who had sent Suzanne flowers? She and Jada didn't know anyone in New York, and those who might send her flowers from home didn't know that she had accepted this position yet. Suzanne wrinkled her nose.

"Sorry, girls. I think this might be a private affair."

"Oh my!" Ruby gushed. "A private affair. That sounds so mysterious." She giggled.

Lillian swatted her with the tie to her robe. "Don't be silly, Ruby. She just doesn't want us to know who sent them. I bet it was Flo himself. She looks about the type who would attract his eye."

Ruby's gasp covered Suzanne clucking her tongue. The very idea that a man such as Flo Ziegfeld would chase her was absurd. She was no Ann. And yet, the way Ruby reacted and the glint in Lillian's eye made her think that his interest may not be quite as farfetched as she believed. Well, any man can pursue, but she was the only one who decided when she was caught.

Either way she slid the card into her pocket. These girls didn't need to know everything about her. She'd decide herself who deserved her trust.

"Well, I am not interested in getting involved with any man." She went behind the partition and began to change.

"Isn't that what they all say—especially those who are dying for a ring." Lillian pointed to her ring finger and rolled her eyes. She lifted a leg onto her vanity stool and powdered herself from toes upward. The room quickly filled with a cloud of the white dust.

Suzanne coughed and turned her back to Lillian. That woman did not deserve an explanation as to why she was not interested in marriage.

"Don't be cruel, Lil," Ruby scolded. She rubbed lotion into her arms. "We all have a right to privacy."

Lillian looked like she was going to say something, but was silenced by Jada walking into the small room.

"Hello," she said softly. "I trust rehearsal went well today?"

"Of course," Lillian replied. "Do you know where my rose water is?"

Jada walked over to Lillian's table and moved a picture frame to reveal a row of bottles. Lillian took one and dabbed behind her ear without a word to Jada. Suzanne clenched her fist to prevent herself from saying something. She needed these girls to be her friends, or at least not hate her.

"Thank you for putting everything away," Ruby offered. Suzanne softened at Ruby's words.

"Even if you put things in the wrong place," Lillian growled as she sniffed a bottle, made a face, and passed it to Ruby.

"Oh, good, I need that." Ruby grinned. "There

is something about a splash of lemon that clears my throat right up."

"Take note, girl," Lillian instructed Jada.

Heat rose in Suzanne's cheeks. If she'd taken Jada to rehearsal as she promised, Lillian and Ruby wouldn't be critiquing her now. Jada deserved better than this. She buttoned her last button and stepped out from the partition. Grabbing her boots from the floor, she smiled at Jada. "I'm about ready to go home. Are you ready, Jada?"

Jada nodded, a look of relief spreading over her face.

"See you tomorrow!" Suzanne sang before shutting the door behind them.

"You aren't going to the Ritz tonight?" Lillian asked.

Suzanne reopened the door. "The Ritz?"

Lillian rolled her eyes as if it was an effort to explain. "It is only the best place to see and be seen. You joined us later than the other new girls. Don't you want to show everyone that you've arrived?"

"I think not," Suzanne said. Leon's suggestion of dinner and bed sounded good to her.

"Your loss," Lillian called out as Suzanne shut the door.

Suzanne led Jada through the hallways until they were in the lobby. She sat in a large, overstuffed chair and jammed her feet into her tall boots. "I am sorry about them."

"Those girls are a dime a dozen." Jada waved her hands as if to show how minuscule they were. Despite Jada's pretense otherwise, Suzanne still felt a coldness directed at her.

"Where were you, anyway?"

Jada's cheeks darkened. "Oh, I finished a while ago and took a quick tour of the theater. It's quite beautiful."

Suzanne nodded. "This is the most beautiful place I've ever been." She tied the top bootlace and leaned back. As she did so, the note from the flowers crinkled in her pocket. She reached in and pulled out the paper.

"Love notes already?" Jada raised an eyebrow. There was an edge to her tone that made Suzanne pause.

Suzanne forced a laugh. "No, I don't know. Someone sent me flowers."

Jada's face fell to an unreadable expression. "Who do we know who would send you flowers?"

The lilac paper unfolded easily and both girls looked down at the perfect penmanship: *May your introduction here be memorable.*

Suzanne blinked. She turned the paper over, looking for a signature.

"Looks like you've attracted a secret admirer." Jada continued to walk toward the exit. "That was quick work."

Ignoring Jada's taunting tone, Suzanne shook

her head. "The only men I've met are Mr. Ziegfeld, Julian Mitchell, and Leon Errol. And none of them would send this."

"Don't forget Mr. Franks," Jada said.

"I highly doubt Jonathon would send me flowers unless Mr. Ziegfeld instructed him to."

"I saw the way he looked at you."

"Jada, please," Suzanne exclaimed. "He is Mr. Ziegfeld's assistant."

Jada was silent. Suzanne frowned and continued. She didn't like to think that she had hurt Jada. Was she really that upset about Suzanne not coming to show her the theater? And being thought of as Spanish should be a huge compliment.

"I've been here all day, Jada. I haven't had time to make an impression yet." Suzanne tucked the note into her handbag. "No, it must have been delivered by mistake. That is the only thing that makes sense."

Jada opened her mouth as if to say something, but quickly closed it again. "With cleaning up the room, I still have a list of errands to run."

Suzanne stepped around a wrinkle in the carpet. "And I have more to add to that list, I'm sad to say. Ann invited me out to dinner tomorrow night. I have to look my best. Can you pick up a corsage to match my navy gown and purchase a new set of ivory gloves? My old ones are stained and since I'm making enough now, I should look the part of a Ziegfeld girl. Don't you think?"

"Of course. I am at your service. Do you think—"

Suzanne interrupted Jada without hearing her question. "The only thing I can think of is putting my feet up and taking a long nap. If he is going to parade us day and night, I need to get my rest when I can." Suzanne tittered a slight laugh, but stopped when Jada didn't join in. "Another time, I promise."

An uneasy silence settled between the two friends. Jada leaned backward as if afraid she'd burst with words, but Suzanne shook as if she couldn't wait to get away.

"I'll see you at Miss Mitzi's tonight. Wake me for dinner." Before Jada could say anything else, Suzanne slipped out the door and started the short walk home.

CHAPTER 7

With Suzanne's money in her purse, Jada walked the streets of New York. She had lied to Suzanne. There were no errands to run. She simply could not stand to be near her another moment, not in that theater close to those women. How could Suzanne have gone through with it and told people she was Spanish?

A cool evening wind blew against her and she pulled her shawl tighter around her shoulders. Her feet clomped hard against the city sidewalks, but the sound melted into those of all the other people around her.

To top the horrible day off, Suzanne had forgotten about her. Had she thought cleaning that horrible dressing room would take all day, or was Jada such an embarrassment that she couldn't have her onstage with her? If that was the case, why bring her to the theater at all? Why lie about her heritage to impress people if she wasn't going to show her off.

Jada clenched her shawl to her tightly as she rounded the corner and nearly walked into Sally.

"Jada?" Sally asked. "What's the matter with you?"

Wonderful to know the whole city could see her anger.

"I'm fine, Sally."

Sally glanced around at the others walking down the street. "Can I walk with you a bit?" she asked as she fell in step beside Jada.

Jada bit her lip. "I'm just off to get Suzanne a new pair of gloves."

"That's perfect. Miss Mitzi asked me to pick up the new fabric she ordered and I know that Miss Steel keeps a full stock of gloves for every occasion."

"I wasn't thinking of going to Miss Steel's shop," Jada said. That was the woman who started Suzanne on the idea that Jada's heritage was a bargaining chip in her quest for fame. She was not willing to forgive that woman now, or anytime soon. She was more than a pawn in Suzanne's career.

Sally slowed their pace until they had almost stopped walking. She motioned toward a small park across the street. "Want to talk? That Miss Steel is bad news."

Jada shook her head. "I'd just rather not see Miss Steel today. There must be another place to buy gloves."

Sally was silent for a moment. "We could go to Oliver's. It isn't much to look at, but his glove selection is wonderful."

"Give me his address and I'll go myself. I am sure you need to get back." Jada forced a smile to her face.

Sally smiled. "Miss Mitzi won't miss me for hours. I can take you. It's only a few blocks from here."

"I'm not going to go alone, am I?" Jada spoke her thoughts out loud.

Sally just laughed. "Of course you aren't."

"Are you sure you want to spend your alone time glove shopping for Suzanne?" Sally lowered her voice. "I'd like to spend my time making a new friend."

That thought had never occurred to her. "Really? You want to befriend me?"

Sally seemed shocked to be asked such a question. "You live a life most people like us only dream of. I've never imagined I'd get to travel, let alone leave a good job like Miss Mitzi's given me. But you . . . you have been all over the country and you are smart."

Jada had never thought of herself through another's eyes. The education Suzanne's family had given her was a huge gift. She had always been grateful for that. Mr. and Mrs. Haskins should have been grateful to her as well. Without Jada's tutoring, Suzanne wouldn't have learned nearly as much. They owed her just as much as she did them.

There were no words that would explain how Sally made Jada feel, so the pair remained silent. Jada linked her arm through Sally's and the pair started walking.

"Oliver's is just two blocks up this street." Sally pulled Jada down an alley. "Did Miss Suzanne's play close?"

Jada nodded. "We had our first rehearsal with the Follies today."

"Oh." Sally walked around a pile of horse droppings. "How was it?"

"You'd have to ask her." Jada tried to keep her tone light. "It sounded like she had a good day."

"I thought you two was close," Sally admonished. Jada gave her a glance and Sally's face reddened. "Miss Mitzi is always telling me I need to stay out of people's business. I'm sorry."

This woman truly wanted to be Jada's friend. The panic in her tone proved what any words could not. Jada smiled at Sally to show she wasn't upset and sped up their pace. It occurred to Jada that working at a place like Miss Mitzi's must be isolating. There were few employees and the guests were not those who would socialize with Sally.

"Suzanne and I are very close. But it is complicated." She glanced at the buildings around them. "We seem to have left the business district behind us," Jada noticed.

Sally turned a corner and the story-high advertisements were gone, as were the rows of storefronts. Instead, the street narrowed and the buildings turned into shorter apartment buildings and row houses.

Sally wrinkled her nose and looked away. "Yeah, Oliver is a friend of mine. He doesn't have a store."

"Sally!" Jada half laughed in shock. "I need to get these gloves for Suzanne and they have to be quality."

The pair stopped beside a wooden staircase that led to a boarded-up back door. If Sally weren't with her, Jada would never have stopped in this alleyway, let alone consider approaching one of the buildings. She wanted to trust Sally, but this place felt dirty and unbecoming. Hardly the place of a respectable business.

"I promise he will have an excellent selection. Far better than Woolworth's, and these are handmade." She turned toward the back stairs and seemed to see the condition of his home for the first time. "Please? He needs the money."

Jada glanced at the wooden back porch of the building. The windows had a layer of dirt on them and the door needed a fresh coat of paint. One section was boarded up, but perhaps Jada could overlook that. She closed her eyes and forced all prejudice from her mind.

"I will look. But I won't promise to buy from him."

Sally's face lit up. "Thanks, Jada!"

They walked up the rickety porch steps and Sally knocked on the door. "Oliver?" she called out.

The locks on the door were undone quickly and the dirty door opened to reveal a very tall, thin man. His skin was incredibly dark, but that wasn't what struck Jada as the most noticeable thing about him. It was the way he moved. She had read about fops in Mr. Haskins's novels, but this man was the embodiment of everything she'd ever read. His tan suit and pink shirt were pressed perfectly and matched the pastel hues of his décor so well Jada would have thought she walked into a painting set.

"Sally!" He held his hands out wide and she lunged at him in a huge hug. "And who is your friend here?"

Sally grinned. "This is Jada. She needs to buy some gloves for the lady she works for. She's in the Ziegfeld Follies."

"No!" Oliver exclaimed. "I hear those dancers are dropping like flies."

He motioned for them to follow him into the back room. The room was decorated in lilac shades with cherry furniture. He opened the top drawer of the desk and pulled out a white box. He placed it on the table and gestured for Jada to open it. Inside were dozens of pairs of gloves. White, off-white, cream, even some in a blush shade.

"These are wonderful," Jada said. She picked one up and slid her finger into it. The trim was so fine it felt as if it were made to fit her hand personally. "How much?"

Oliver smiled. "Twenty-five cents. They are all handmade from good fabric."

Jada pulled the glove off and reached into her coin purse. "Here is a dollar. I'll take one of each color. Thank you."

Oliver's face lit up. "Thank you," he said. He placed the four coins in his hand gently before walking over to the desk and depositing them into a box.

"Now, what number is your mistress in?" he asked. "My friend's friend works for Fanny Brice and I hear those girls aren't leaving because Flo is being too forward, if you know what I mean. I hear they are all leaving because they are scared."

Sally leaned forward. "Scared?" she asked.

Jada shifted uncomfortably. "What do you mean, scared?"

Oliver shrugged. "This friend overheard one of the girls telling Fanny that she was going home to Indiana. That the New York life was too much for her and she wanted to go home while she could. Fanny tried to talk her out of it, but her mind was set. You would've thought she'd have a stronger reason than that, but who knows; maybe there is a man she wanted to get back to." He took a deep sigh and fanned his face. "So, tell me. What is it really like there?"

"Um, well, they are all hard workers who want to dance. I haven't really been there long enough to know much else."

Oliver's face fell. "Oh. Well, if you hear something, you be sure you come see Oliver, darling." He handed her a small bag for her gloves.

"Thank you." She glanced at Sally. "I'd better get these back to Suzanne in case she changes her mind and decides to run off to that party tonight."

Sally stood up and kissed Oliver on each cheek. "Good to see you," she said to him.

"You too."

Once back on the street, Jada exhaled. "Who is that man? He's exhausting. I didn't know any men cared that much about such things as the Follies unless they were chasing after one of the girls."

"He is my best friend's brother. He doesn't leave the apartment much. I'm not sure he's gone out since before winter." She glanced at the ground. "I often give him what I can to help him keep food on the table."

"What about his sister?" Jada asked.

Sally looked away at the people across the street. "She died a few years back. Caught a fever and was gone in a week."

There wasn't much to say in response. "I'm sorry."

"It's over and done with. I help out Oliver when I can."

Jada looked into her bag. "Well, if Suzanne likes these gloves half as much as I do, then he'll have plenty of business once she tells the rest of the girls where she got them. Don't worry."

"Thank you," Sally stammered. "I never thought, I mean."

Jada swatted Sally's shoulder. "Of course you thought, you just didn't think it would happen."

"Exactly," Sally agreed.

"Suzanne is dying to give the other girls something to gush over. With his talent and frugal prices, those girls are going to fawn all over him." Jada grinned. "I suspect Oliver might like being the toast of the town."

CHAPTER 8

None of the rumors or society photos prepared Suzanne for the opulence that greeted her when she stepped out of her cab and into the Ritz. It felt overly decadent to hire a cab to transport only herself, but Suzanne could think of no other way to arrive at her first Ziegfeld affair. She took the valet's hand as she stepped onto the curb and pulled her blue silk shawl around her shoulders. She hadn't worn the shawl since they'd left Richmond, and it felt luxurious against her skin. If there was any night she needed to feel glamourous, it was tonight.

Ziegfeld girls were known for their style as well as their looks. Mr. Ziegfeld himself was the embodiment of class. He spared no expense with fitting his clothes to his frame so that they looked like a second skin on him. His productions were styled down to the detail on the stockings. Suzanne was sure the parties that he organized would be no less grand, and the Ritz did not disappoint.

"Welcome to the Follies," the gentleman at the entrance said as he took Suzanne's shawl.

"Thank you," Suzanne said as she took his arm and let him lead her to the ballroom.

One look at the other guests and Suzanne was

grateful she had chosen the light blue gown that evening. The salmon-colored walls and dark maroon carpet made her stand out in a way that others blended in with their pink and ivory dresses. She smoothed the front of her dress down as she thanked the hotel clerk for escorting her.

Everywhere one looked there was something to delight the senses. Along one wall was a table covered in chocolate desserts. In the far corner of the room an orchestra was playing for the dozens of couples on the dance floor in front of them. But Suzanne was mostly fascinated by the table a few steps to her right. The large, round table was covered by a pyramid of empty goblets at least ten rows high. A ladder stood beside it and a waiter climbed carefully to the top. Behind him stood another man with the largest bottle of champagne Suzanne had ever seen. A waiter stood on a stool, opened a bottle, and poured the gold liquor into the top glass. Instantly champagne floated down from one to the next. Suzanne stood transfixed by the golden waterfall.

"Would you like a glass?" the waiter on the ladder asked.

"Oh, yes, thank you." She sipped the fizzy liquid and forced herself farther into the room.

All around her, women she didn't recognize wore the latest fashions from Paris and none were without escort. Suzanne looked down at her dress and felt slight shame. She had chosen it for the embroidered beadwork that wound its way up from her toes to the bodice and looked like a Grecian staircase. It was her best dress, made by the best seamstress in Richmond, but it was at least two years old. She had worn it only twice before: once to her cousin's wedding and once the day she brought it home. It was the most beautiful dress she could imagine, but next to all the other girls' gowns, she suddenly worried she wouldn't measure up.

"Excuse me."

Suzanne quickly turned around and found herself face-to-face with her roommate. Lillian was wearing a muted green gown that made the red highlights in her hair shine. Her arm was linked with a tall blond gentleman's. His broad shoulders took up nearly the whole doorway, and the way Lillian looked up at him it was clear she was proud.

"Good evening, Lillian," Suzanne said.

Lillian looked over her shoulder. "Hi, Suzanne." She oozed charm. "Have you met my escort? This is Harry Handerson, of the Long Island Handersons."

The gentleman took Suzanne's hand. "Pleased to make your acquaintance."

He beamed as he took stock of who else was in attendance. Either Lillian was more important than Suzanne knew, or this was Harry's first

Ziegfeld soirée. He looked like Suzanne felt.

"And yours." Suzanne slid her hand back as soon as she could without being rude.

Lillian watched Suzanne as if waiting for a specific reaction. After a long pause she said, "That gown does look fetching on you. I wish that neckline would work on me, but my features are far too delicate. Oh, I see Fanny. Let's go say hello to her, Harry. Have a good evening."

It took every ounce of concentration Suzanne possessed not to look down at her gown to see what Lillian was referring to. She would not give that girl the satisfaction of making her feel uneasy.

"That girl," another girl hissed from beside Suzanne. Suzanne turned to find a statuesque blonde beside her. Her hair was shockingly bright, but it flattered her. The woman held out her hand. "I'm Laura. You're the girl Ann keeps gushing about. I hear you are a shoo-in for the Bert Williams number. Good luck. He gets the most press."

Suzanne smiled. "Thank you. My name is Suzanne."

"As if Ziegfeld would put any of us in danger. The very idea." She laughed a bit too much at her own jest.

"I don't think Ziegfeld would harm any of us, if that's what you mean." Suzanne took another flute of champagne from a roaming waiter.

Laura gave Suzanne an unreadable look. "Be

careful with that stuff. It'll go straight to your head."

"Oh, pishposh, Mother served champagne at my coming-out party." Suzanne took a slight sip and jumped at how the bubbles danced down her throat.

"Like I said, be careful. This room is full of men longing to conquer one of Ziegfeld's girls."

Laura gestured to a man across the room. He was leaning against a side table, gleaming at the girls as they talked. His eyes met Suzanne's and her whole body felt exposed. She knew she should look away, but his attention thrilled her too much to ignore.

"Who is that?" Suzanne asked.

"Craig Masterson. His family got rich a few years back mining coal in Colorado, I think. No one really knows what he's doing in New York this season, but he keeps turning up at our events."

"New money." Suzanne sighed. "Too bad."

"Too bad?" Laura repeated.

"I grew up with my share of the nouveau riche. They're . . . different." Suzanne broke her gaze away from Craig.

"I don't think I'd know one type of rich from another, to be honest." Laura laughed at herself. "Perhaps I'll be lucky enough to be new rich as well. Perhaps I'll even be brave like that Molly Brown!"

"Her story would make a terrific play. Country girl made rich by gold mines only to end up on the *Titanic*?"

"Such a tragedy." Laura shuddered.

Suzanne nodded, but refused to say more. She'd heard enough *Titanic* stories to last a lifetime. She'd rather entertain herself with finding a dance partner. If she was honest, she hoped to find someone more handsome than Lillian's Harry, but she'd make due with someone of equal stature. After getting involved with Elton too soon, she wasn't interested in roping in a suitor just for sport. She looked around the room at the dancing couples and dazzling décor, and gave herself a pat on the back. Surely she made the right choice for herself. She saved both her and Jada from horrible lives.

"Look, there is Ann!" Laura pointed over the crowd to a bright blue peacock feather that was strutting over the shoulders of dancers in their direction. The music ended and the partners separated. There was Ann, flouncing toward them in a tizzy of excitement. Her brown curls bounced on her tiny shoulders. Her dress had a slit on the side just high enough to showcase her dimpled knees.

"Laura! Suzanne! I am so glad to find you together. Isn't Suzanne a gem, Laura? I just knew you'd be fast friends."

"Where have you been, Ann?" Laura looked over her shoulder as if expecting someone to be following her. And there were several men who were standing close by, hopeful she'd look at them for a dance, but no one notable.

"Oh, you know . . . chasing away this suitor or that." She laughed a bit too quickly.

"No, not again." Laura took Ann's hand. "Is he chasing you again?"

Ann rolled her eyes. "Please, the misguided chase of one Florenz Ziegfeld is something I am well capable of handling."

Suzanne blinked. "Ziegfeld is chasing you . . . romantically? But isn't he pursuing Billie Burke?"

Across the room Billie's distinctive, high-pitched voice reached above the orchestra as she completed a joke and the group around her burst into laughter. Like her costumes in *The "Mind the Paint" Girl*, her gown highlighted her red hair and long neck with its rich color and wide neckline. She was able to captivate a room seemingly without effort. Suzanne looked away before Ann looked as well.

"Ziegfeld adores Billie, of course," Laura explained. "But there is nothing more attractive than the unobtainable. And Ann is good at playing hard to get."

Ann fingered the shiny broach on her gown. "Well, whatever keeps me on his good side."

Suzanne grinned. "A good number is worth a little flirting." Ann linked arms with her and started to pull them away from the crowd.

Laura refused to move. "It most certainly is

not. What about that man's feelings, or about your reputation. Girls, a career is one thing, but don't sell your bodies for it."

"Pishposh. As if any of us would do such a thing. Flirting is one thing, anything more is strictly off limits. Just ask Flo." She linked her other arm through Laura's. "Now, there are a few unattached gentlemen I'd like to introduce you to."

Laura held back for a moment, but quickly allowed Ann to lead them across the room. Suzanne finished her drink as they walked and took another from a roving waiter. She wondered if there was anything Ann wanted and did not obtain.

The trio walked across the room toward a small door at the other end. Lillian and her tall suitor were doing the turkey trot while Ruby and a short, paunchy man were watching. Ruby waved enthusiastically and Suzanne waved back before Ann pulled her into the smaller, more private room.

The air was thick with cigar smoke in the small room and as Suzanne's eyes became used to the dimmer light she realized they were in the gentlemen's room. In all the parties they had hosted at home, Father had never once allowed Suzanne into the back room where the gentlemen sat. Her status certainly had changed if she was being allowed in now.

"Ann, you naughty girl," one of the older

gentlemen coughed as he scolded. "You shouldn't be in here."

"Mr. Todd, you know perfectly well Craig and Martin have been asking to meet my friends. How can I ever fulfill their dreams if all you men do is stay locked up in here smoking your dreary cigars?"

Another cough exploded out of Mr. Todd. Craig Masterson appeared behind him to pat him gently on the back. "Don't overdo it, Uncle," Craig said. "Martin and I will join these young women outside."

"Thank you," Mr. Todd said gruffly.

Once outside the stuffy room, Ann started giggling. She didn't say anything as Craig and another gentleman were right on their tails.

"Laura," Ann said, grabbing her friend's hand. "This is Martin Vandergash. His family is from Springfield, Illinois, and he came three times last year to see you dance in the Follies."

Laura looked at the gentleman. He was of average height and slightly slim build, but his blue eyes were so intense they made up for whatever height he lacked.

"Pleased to meet you." Laura's voice shook slightly. For the first time, Suzanne realized that this girl was potentially shy. She squeezed her hand for confidence.

Martin offered his arm and led her to the dance floor. Ann grinned as she watched them.

"And this is Craig Masterson, Suzanne." Ann gestured to the tall man.

"Your reputation precedes you." Suzanne grinned up at the gentleman.

Craig's smile wavered. "I don't think I've been in the city long enough to gain a reputation. But, if you will allow me a dance or two, perhaps I can clear up whatever gossip you may have heard?"

He held his hand out for Suzanne. For a moment, Suzanne almost declined his invitation. But disappointing Ann, when she was being so kind to her, felt inconsiderate.

"Well, I doubt you could corrupt me with one dance," Suzanne said.

Craig laughed and said, "I will do my best."

She took his hand and he led her onto the dance floor, which was filled with twirling skirts and dapper-looking gentlemen. His hand gripped her back and held her against him just close enough to be scandalous, but with enough room to pass for appropriate. Despite herself, Suzanne's heart fluttered at his attention and how the other girls admired her dancing partner.

"The moment I saw you I knew I wanted Ann to introduce us." Craig looked down at Suzanne.

"Oh?" Suzanne let her eyes unfocus and gaze at the other couples on the dance floor. "I don't recall noticing you."

Throwing back his head with a chuckle, Craig said, "I saw your friend point me out to you."

Suzanne would not be baited. "Did she? There are so many eligible men here tonight. It is hard to remember them all." He spun her as they waltzed around the room.

"Ah, I'd think I'd be hard to forget. Heir to the Masterson coal mines, or did you not yet hear that?"

She hadn't, but she would never admit that to him. Instead, she looked up and met his eyes. "I've not yet heard of that company. Tell me, do you know the Alloway family? I believe they also have money in coal."

Craig's smile became stiff. "Of course I know the Alloways. A fine family."

He led her around the room in silence for a moment as the music swelled in a final crescendo. Suzanne didn't look at him, but she knew he had been lying. For one, the Alloways were from Winnipeg, not Denver, and to her knowledge, they had no children. Leave it to someone like him not to fess up to a lack of knowledge.

The last note was held out for a few beats and then the song was over. The couples all parted and applauded the orchestra.

"Thank you for the dance," Suzanne said. She took a step backward, hoping to flee to her friends. Perhaps he was good looking, but he wasn't as interesting as she hoped.

He grabbed her hand so she couldn't abandon him. "Look, I know I don't always say the right thing, but I think you are beautiful and, if you'll let me, I'd like to get to know you better." A piece of his dark hair fell into his face.

Around them, the couples were starting a two-step. Ann and Laura both had partners.

Suzanne looked down and shrugged coyly. "I suppose another few minutes wouldn't hurt anything."

CHAPTER 9

The kitchen was empty by the time Jada came downstairs for dinner. The other boarders were already gone for the night, thank goodness. The bread rising in the window gave the room a homey scent. Jada opened the cupboard to find the leftovers Miss Mitzi kept on the cheese plate. She cut a slice of bread and layered it with jam. It was lightly dry, but Jada didn't mind. The drab food fit her mood. She leaned against the counter and relished the silence.

"That you, Jada?" The question cut through the silence.

"Hi, Sally," Jada replied before taking another bite of bread.

"Why are you sitting alone in the dark?" Sally pulled out a chair across from Jada and plopped down.

"Just having a bite to eat. What are you doing?" Jada glanced about for Sally's basket or some other clue. Then she looked at Sally, who was dressed in a pale pink gown.

Sally's hand shook as she touched the collar. "I'm off to see my fella. He owns a nightclub in Harlem."

"Oh?" This girl was full of surprises. "What kind of joint?"

Sally stole a corner of Jada's bread and popped it in her mouth. "Why don't you come with me and find out? Pops doesn't like me traveling through the city alone. If you come, he won't be able to complain next time he visits."

The invitation was tempting. Jada yearned to see more of the city, but the compulsion to say no was strong. Sally grabbed her hands and pulled her from her chair before she could say anything.

"You won't learn anything sitting here. Come with me and see some of the city!"

"Very well. But I don't have an evening dress." Sally looked lovely in her gown. Jada couldn't go out in the same dress she'd laundered petticoats in!

"Could you borrow one? Surely that Suzanne has something that you'd fit in."

Despite herself, Jada grinned. There was one violet gown Suzanne hated, but Jada loved. It should fit.

"Just give me twenty minutes," she promised.

Jada leaned back in the rickety chair, letting the smooth notes wash over her. Sally had gone to get them drinks. The violet gown Jada had borrowed from Suzanne stood out in the small club, making her look delicate and dainty, but no one commented. Sally's own blush gown was faded from many washings, and its muteness made her blend into the landscape. The music pounded in Jada's chest and she was suddenly glad that she stood out. This was not a place she wanted to blend in. If anything, she wanted to be noticed here.

"Here you are, Jada," Sally said, offering her a glass of red liquid.

"Thanks." Jada's foot tapped to the beat. "Where is your beau?"

Sally laughed. "Roger is behind the bar. He'll come see us in a bit. He helps Jerry bartend until things settle down."

Of the two men behind the bar, it was obvious to whom Sally was attached. The first was tall and broad shouldered, but there was so much white in his beard he could pass for either girl's grandfather. The other man was shorter and of smaller build, but his friendly face and bright smile matched Sally's enthusiasm.

"He must be a hard worker to keep up a place like this." Jada took a sip of her drink and looked around. The room wasn't large, but it was packed with people. Every so often Roger threw back his head and laughed. His sparkling white teeth made his skin look even darker. Sally smiled as she looked at him.

"This place's his dream. His pops and him saved up for it." She knocked on the table. "So far it's a success."

Jada nodded. "They sure look plenty busy."

A chord trilled on the piano in the other corner

of the room and people congregated on the dance floor. "That's Danny. They just hired him. I've never heard someone play piano like him. I think he adds a lot."

The young man behind the piano was focused on the keys in front of him, but his music reached out to touch everyone in the room. The soulful tune encompassed Jada.

"Thank you for bringing me," Jada said. "I didn't know places like this contained such talent." Danny changed to a rag tune and almost instantly people were dancing.

Sally laughed. "Do you and that Suzanne live under a rock?"

"Of course not. But we've had to make it on our own for the last year and, well, money hasn't been easy. Not until she landed the part in *The Dancing Duchess* were we able to breathe freely. And now, on Ziegfeld's salary, we are able to live at Miss Mitzi's without worry." She took a sip of her drink and coughed. "What is this?"

"Oh, cranberry juice." Sally grinned. "With a little something extra."

Jada shook her head, but couldn't knock the smile from her lips.

"Hello there, lady."

"Roger!" Sally jumped to her feet and kissed the man's cheeks. "This is Jada. She is a new boarder. She's got talent too."

Jada winced at the compliment.

Roger stuck out a hand. "Pleased to meet you. Talented women are always welcome here at Roger's." He winked.

Jada laughed. "That is good to know. We tend to be welcome most anywhere."

"And what is your talent?" Roger asked. "Sally here makes the best corn bread this side of the Mason Dixon. Better than my mom, but don't tell her that."

Sally jumped in. "Jada is a singer. Her friend just took a spot in the Ziegfeld Follies."

"A Ziegfeld girl? Your friend must be very beautiful."

Jada pursed her lips. Talking about Suzanne felt out of place here. "She is very pretty. It is such a good opportunity for her. Perhaps me too. Just last week I met Bert Williams." The moment the words left her lips she didn't know why she spoke them. She wasn't one to brag about people she knew, like some of the people they had encountered on the circuit.

"Bert is a real class act. He was in here earlier listening to Danny tinkling the ivories." Roger looked at Jada and his eyes widened. "Wait a moment. Are you her?"

"Is she who?" Sally asked. She winked at Jada, clearly enjoying the excitement in Roger's face.

"He was talking about some girl who had refused to dance with him last week. It was a strange story. I mean, who refuses to dance with

Bert Williams?" Roger raised an eyebrow.

Jada felt her cheeks warm. "Who indeed? I don't know what happened." More like she couldn't upstage Suzanne. The thought made her cheeks even hotter.

Sally slapped the table. "You refused Bert? Jada, are you crazy?"

"Well, he was sure disappointed. Something about the way you held your shoulders made him think you would be a formidable dancer."

"Really?" Jada's heart fluttered as she sat a bit taller.

Sally looked pointedly down at her drink, but she grinned. Jada couldn't stop the smile that formed at her lips.

"Well, I better get back to work. It was very nice meeting you, Jada."

Jada nodded. "You too, Roger."

"And you." He nuzzled against Sally's ear. "I'll come back when I can."

"You better," Sally teased. "I didn't get all dolled up to sit with Jada."

"I promised you a dance." He kissed Sally's cheek and ran back to the bar. The piano man was there and the two quickly became animated in conversation.

"He's very nice," Jada said.

Sally grinned. "Kind, smart, and handsome. I don't know how I got so lucky."

They both took a drink. The piano man took

a glass of water from Roger and headed toward the small stage and his piano, just past where Suzanne and Jada sat.

"Hi, Danny!" Sally exclaimed.

"Hi, doll," Danny replied as he came over to their table.

He smelled of sawdust and vanilla. Jada leaned closer to him without realizing it.

"So, this is your new friend?" Danny looked at Jada as he held out his hand. "Pleased to meet you."

"Same," Jada said. "You are very talented."

"Well, thanks. I just play how I feel."

Sally snorted. "Oh, come on. Don't be modest. Roger says you are in here every morning practicing before going to the lumber yard. I hate it when talented people won't admit to caring if others appreciate them or not."

Danny laughed. "Cool down, girl. I do care if people like to hear me play."

"Well, good." Sally pouted. " 'Cause you are talented!"

"I've got to get back to it."

"The people are getting restless," Jada agreed.

A group of women were clustered around the piano. One ran her fingers over the keys and laughed. Jada wondered how it would feel to stand on that stage and sing to them.

"There's Selma. It was nice meeting you!" Danny nodded to Jada before dashing off.

A young woman walked through the tables and stepped up onto the stage. Her skin was caramel and her hair smoothed back into a bun at the nape of her neck. Over one ear was a beautiful rose that brought out the red flowers in her shawl. Selma let Danny take her hand and lead her to the piano's small platform. Jada leaned forward, watching the two closely. The woman turned and faced the audience, and Danny trilled an opening on the piano before the woman closed her eyes and started singing a song in a low alto voice: "You Made Me Love You."

"Selma is a singer?" Jada asked aloud.

Sally nodded. "What else would she do? Wait till you hear her peppier songs. 'When the Midnight Choo Choo Leaves for Alabam' is so much fun. Danny would like someone every night, but Roger hasn't found someone he likes yet. Selma comes when she can, usually Thursday and Sunday nights. I just wish she danced more. Standing still looks stiff, don't you think?"

As if she heard Sally's complaint, Selma swayed slightly as she belted out the love song. And Jada sat in silence for the rest of the song.

The audience clapped and Danny trilled the piano keys, announcing an up-tempo number. Dancers flocked to the floor as he started the intro for "Alexander's Ragtime Band." The small space in front of their platform was quickly filled with dancers. The woman's rich voice was reminiscent of the singers from Jada's church back in Richmond, and suddenly her throat felt tight. She finished the rest of her drink in one gulp.

"I think I've had enough." Jada had to shout over the dancing. "I'm tired. I should go home."

Sally bit her lip and glanced from the bar to Jada. "Want me to come with you?" she asked.

Jada patted her friend's hand. "No, you stay and enjoy your man. I'll see you at Miss Mitzi's tomorrow and you can tell me all about the night."

"If you're sure." Sally smiled in relief. "You know how to get home?"

Jada slid her shawl around her shoulders. "I'll be fine. You have a good night." She squeezed Sally's shoulder and walked toward the front door.

Behind her Selma started a slow, cool version of "Snooky Ookums" without accompaniment. Jada made a note to learn some songs like that. It would be good for Suzanne to know some songs that allowed her pianist to take a break if she were to ever sing in a nightclub. The very thought nearly made Jada burst out laughing. She could hardly see Suzanne in a bar, let along singing in one.

"Leaving so soon?" Roger asked. He glanced behind him at the door to the back rooms.

"Until next time, Roger. Sally is waiting for you to dance with her."

Roger grinned. "I won't keep her waiting long."

The door behind Roger opened and Danny jumped out. "Hey, are there any doctors here tonight?" he asked Roger.

Roger shrugged. "I don't think so. Want me to ask around?" His brow was creased in concerned confusion, but he didn't press Danny further.

"No, please don't make a scene." Danny scratched his head and glanced around as if hoping a solution would pop up.

Jada cleared her throat. "I used to help some back at the farm. Are you ill?"

Both Danny and Roger stared at her a moment. When Danny didn't reply, Roger said, "She is offering to help and you need to get back to the piano. Take her back."

Danny gestured for her to follow him through the back door. "It's not me." A few yards down the hall from there a doorway was lit from a candle inside a room. Jada followed Danny inside.

"Someone is here to help, Bert," he said.

The room was lit with only a small gas lantern on the table. A figure of a man was huddled in a chair in the corner, his head in his hands. Danny walked in and put a hand on Bert's shoulder. Jada tried to hide her surprise and alarm. Bert Williams was the man they wanted her to doctor? Hadn't she embarrassed herself enough around him for one lifetime?

"You brought a girl to help?" Bert asked gruffly.

"I brought who I could find. We don't need everyone knowing that *the* Bert Williams was attacked in the back alleys of Harlem. Do we?" Danny spoke as if they'd already discussed such things.

"Of course not," Bert said.

"What happened to him?" Jada asked, coming farther into the room.

"I was walking down an alley when someone rushed at me; he pushed me against a wall and punched me twice. Once in the shoulder, once in the gut. He threw some paper or something at me before running away."

Jada stood beside him and stared at his shoulder; a small red circle had formed on the white fabric. "Take off your shirt," she commanded. To Danny she said, "You get back to work. Have Roger or Jerry bring me some alcohol and some kind of bandage."

"The fewer people who know I'm here the better," said Bert.

"They will be quick," Danny promised. He met Jada's eyes. "Thank you."

Jada nodded in reply as Bert worked to undress his wounds.

Bert pulled his arm out of its sleeve and laid his hand in his lap. Jada touched the gash and pursed her lips.

"Was the man wearing jewelry of any kind? This seems like a deep cut for a punch."

Bert looked up at Jada for the first time. "You?" he accused. "You who wouldn't dance with me will clean this gash?"

"They are two very different talents." She pressed the gash again and was pleased when it didn't bleed much. "This is a deep cut. If I were back home and you were one of my pa's field workers, I'd insist you let me stitch this up. But since it isn't bleeding anymore, I'll leave the choice to you. If I don't stitch it up, it might scar."

"Stitches mean less range of motion, and I have to rehearse next week. I'll take my chances with the scar."

Jada's nose wrinkled at his choice, but she didn't say anything.

"We'll have to wait for Roger and the bandages."

She moved a bit so that she was beside him and blinked at the folded paper that appeared from under her skirt. She knelt over and picked it up.

"Mr. Williams!" she gasped as she read the writing. "Who on earth wrote such hate?"

"Miss Jada, I am sitting here half undressed—please call me Bert. And don't worry about that note. It isn't the first and won't be the last."

"Have you read it?" She sat down in the chair across from him and read aloud: *"Nigger filth doesn't deserve to live. Leave the Follies or die, scum."* She watched him for a response.

Bert leaned back and rubbed his neck. "If you have any interest in being an entertainer, you have to have a thicker skin than that. I am a black man in a white show. Of course people are going to send hate mail. They might even try to injure me. If they didn't, I'd be doing something wrong."

"Oh." Jada was silent for a moment. "I hadn't really thought of it that way. You must be really talented."

Bert winced as he chuckled. "That is what they tell me."

Behind her the door reopened and Roger reentered with Sally on his heels.

"I thought you went home, Jada!"

"No," Bert explained. "She got roped into my mess of an evening. You got the bandage in that basket, Roger? Let's get this over with."

Roger handed Jada the basket and she pulled the bottle of alcohol out and poured some on Bert's shoulder. He grunted in discomfort but didn't complain.

"Is your wife going to be upset?" Roger asked.

Bert shook his head. "I think she's been waiting for something like this to happen. There is usually some kind of mess before a show starts and this year with Ann onstage with me, I expected there to be a response."

A melancholy mood came over the entertainer. Instead of asking more questions, Jada took the roll of bandage and began rolling it around Bert's shoulder. No one spoke as she worked; even Sally was quiet. The faint sounds of Danny's playing were muffled with the door shut. After five layers, the bandage ran out and Jada tied the end in a knot.

Bert winced again.

"Do you have any more?" Jada asked Roger. He shook his head. "Very well. When you get home, Bert, you'll need to clean and re-bandage this wound. If that chest pain doesn't go away, you might have a cracked rib."

Bert nodded. "I'll have Lottie wrap it if it doesn't improve. Thank you for your help. I couldn't walk around the city looking like I'd been in a fight."

"Of course. You know you're always welcome here." Roger gestured upstairs. "Your room is always open."

Bert nodded. "I know."

Sally nudged Jada. "What?" Jada hissed.

"You should sing for him," Sally said.

"This is hardly the time or the place." Jada spoke as quietly as possible, but her words still carried in the small room.

Roger laughed. "You should sing for someone. Sally is a fan of yours and she doesn't like just anyone's voice."

Bert slid his arm back into the sleeve of his shirt. "I must get home. Rehearsals start early and I've been gone too late as it is. Lottie will worry." He turned to Jada.

Regardless of what he said, Jada knew that the attack had shaken the man. How could it not? That was the reason he ignored Sally's nudge. Jada ignored the doubt that settled in her stomach. Perhaps she had truly ruined her chances to perform for Bert.

"Are you able to make it home alone?" Jada asked him.

Bert clucked his tongue and said, "Such a question. Of course I can make it home."

Roger rubbed Sally's back. "Will you girls walk home together? The city feels a little less bright and a little meaner than it did earlier this evening."

"I don't like thinking that way." Sally shivered.

"Who does?" Jada said. "But I don't want to be out alone. Do you mind coming home with me?"

Sally looked from Bert to Roger and back to Jada. "Of course. Let me grab my shawl."

Roger watched her leave. "Make sure Sally gets home. She is my treasure."

"Of course," Jada replied.

"Take care of yourself too," Bert said. He winced as he stood up. "A woman who can sing as well as bandage is frightfully rare."

Jada made a motion to indicate she heard him, but nothing more. It was unclear whether he meant that in earnest or as a joke, and she wasn't sure she wanted to know.

"Seriously, though," Roger said as he picked up a few loose threads from the floor. "If you ever need a place to practice, my door is always open, especially to Sally's friends."

Out in the bar, Danny began a rag tune and Jada felt a slight thrill come over her. A place to practice would be nice.

"I'll be sure Sally gets home safely," she promised again before slipping out the door and meeting her friend in the hallway.

Selma stood just outside the nightclub, taking a long drag of a cigarette. Sally waved at the woman but didn't stop to say much. Jada forced a smile herself, but felt uncomfortable even looking at the singer. Her body curved against the building in a lazy way that was also confident and glamorous. Jada was not that kind of person. She was meant to stay behind the scenes.

Jada let Sally link arms with her and jabber about how Roger had saved enough for the nightclub, but she didn't really listen. Instead, she scolded herself for ever thinking she could be interesting like Selma.

CHAPTER 10

There wasn't an inch on Suzanne's body that wasn't screaming in pain. The girls sat about the stage stretching or massaging their various muscles. Suzanne slid into her dressing gown before sitting at a small table and rubbing her shoulder. What she wouldn't do for one of Mother's lavender baths. She could probably have Jada draw her one, but it wouldn't be the same. She sat and lifted her left foot into her hand and rubbed the ball of her foot. Hopefully she hid her discomforts well.

Bloody blisters bespeckled her feet, and her torso had hints of new bruises from her new corset. The only condolence was that she wasn't alone in her discomfort. Lillian was nursing her feet with foul-smelling soaks each evening, and Ruby was so tired she jumped whenever the dressing room door opened.

Jonathon walked around the stage offering glasses of water to the various clusters of women, while Leon and Julian spoke in low tones by the piano. More than once Suzanne had seen movement in the balcony, but if Flo himself had been watching rehearsals, she didn't know.

She pressed her thumb into the ball of her foot and rotated it like Jada had taught her. She was about to put her foot down when a shadow moved into her light. She looked up and Julian was looking down at her. He squatted in front of her. Behind her, conversations diminished.

"I expect a lot of you girls," he began.

Suzanne lowered her foot and gave Julian her attention. His eyes were so focused on her that she began to squirm. Had she done something wrong?

Please don't expose my faults in front of the others, she prayed.

"Ann wants you in the Bert Williams number, which I'm sure you know. The little I've observed of you, I understand her reaction. You are talented and beautiful. More than some of the others." Suzanne held her posture as strong as possible, hoping she looked professional. "Rehearsals start Monday afternoon. I expect you, Ann, and Ruby to be ready to work hard."

"Thank you! I can't . . . This is wonderful."

"You earned it. No thanks required." Julian extended his hand and Suzanne took it. "If you do well with them, we will be casting the two tango numbers. Flo is watching to see if it might be a good vehicle for you. Don't let him down."

So they were going to include a tango in the set for this year. She sat up straighter and forced any discomfort from her mind. This was what she had hoped for, a chance to shine.

"I will keep that in mind. Thank you, Julian."

Behind them, Lillian cleared her throat. "You know, Suzanne, I noticed this morning that you are consistently off in the finale. We are supposed to twist on three, not two." She put a hand on Suzanne's waist. "Sometimes the new girls need a little coaching."

Ignoring Lillian's tone, Suzanne replied, "I knew something felt off. I'll work to get it right. Thank you, Lillian."

"Thatta girl." Julian smiled and stood up. He strode to the other side of the room to the piano player. Within moments they were in a hurried conversation.

Lillian dropped her arm and turned her back on Suzanne. "Some people wouldn't know talent if it bit them in the ass," she muttered.

Ruby glanced at Suzanne, but didn't say anything in response. Everyone had assumed she was in the Williams number since she and Ann had been working longer hours together. With Ruby in the number, Suzanne had assumed she was out. She turned her back to Lillian and refused to let such a person diminish her excitement. Facing the wings, Suzanne saw Jada pacing back and forth. Her shoulders were slightly hunched and she held something in front of her in her hands. Again, Suzanne regretted not having Jada onstage with her, but it was never the right time. What made Jada think she should invade rehearsal like this?

Jada looked up and saw Suzanne. She stopped pacing and walked between the rows of curtains to Suzanne's side.

"This arrived for you," she said, holding out an envelope. "It's from home."

The telegram seemed to glow in Jada's hands. Despite their wealth, Suzanne's mother rarely sent telegrams. She preferred to take her time and write correspondence instead. She looked at Jada, unable to read her expression. What was so urgent that it warranted a telegram? All the jubilation melted from her as she realized the bigger question.

"How did she know where to find us?" Suzanne asked. The thin envelope felt heavy with implications to Suzanne. After not having any contact with her family since they left, something big must have happened to cause her to reach out. Was Father ill?

Jada shifted her feet. "I write to her. She deserves to know how we are doing." Her voice was barely above a whisper. "Please don't be mad."

Before either woman could respond, Lillian demanded loudly, "A telegram? Who sent you a telegram?"

"Probably Mr. Masterson," Laura offered before grabbing her towel and heading back to the dressing room. She called over her shoulder, "He's known for romancing the ladies."

When Suzanne didn't respond, Lillian snatched the paper from Jada's hand and tore it open. Jada made a move to get it back, but Lillian stepped away.

She read, *"Suzanne, darling. Stop. Please come home. Stop. Elton dead. Stop."*

All the color drained from Lillian's face. She glanced around at the crowd that was quickly forming around them. Her face went first pale and then flushed red.

"That was cruel," Ruby admonished her.

Lillian looked at the floor. "I'm sorry," she croaked.

"Give me that," Jada said, removing the paper from Lillian's hand. "Suzanne?"

What had Lillian just read? That couldn't be right. Elton had been ill for some time, but she never thought it was lethal. She searched herself, trying to find some emotional response, but all she had was disbelief. Dead? Lillian had to be mistaken. Suzanne glanced to Jada, hoping to see an angry expression. Instead, her friend had tears in her eyes and dread on her face.

"Elton's dead?" Her voice cracked on the last word. "Honest?"

Jada nodded and came to her side. She handed the telegram to Suzanne, whose shaky hands made it nearly unreadable. She took a moment to prepare herself and then looked at it.

Suzanne, darling. STOP. Please come home. STOP. Elton Dead. STOP. Suicide. Family asking for you. STOP. Await reply. STOP. Mother. STOP.

Suicide? How could Mother put that in a telegram? Lillian's pale face made more sense now. Her embarrassment wasn't for what she read aloud, rather it was about what she chose to conceal from everyone. Perhaps there was a heart in her after all. She glanced at the woman, who instantly looked away. Slowly, the rest of the stage came back into focus. A small group surrounded her, but most had dispersed to their own groups. Julian and the pianist talked quietly while other girls packed their bags for the night. There was noticeably less gabbing going on. Even Julian seemed to have one eye on Suzanne. She could not let this define her. She had just been offered a role in Ann and Bert's number, not to mention the hope of something more. Dedication was key.

"I can't go home. I am needed here. Mother must understand that," she said to Jada purposefully loud enough so that her words carried across the stage.

Jada took the telegram back from Suzanne. "But Elton . . ." She stopped herself from saying more. Quieter, she asked, "Are you sure?"

Visions of Elton's family surfaced in Suzanne's mind. They must be sitting vigil now, mourning gowns pulled out and pressed. His body would be delivered and they would prepare for burial. She shuddered. That was no longer her world. He had parted long before. She couldn't go back.

"I'll write to Mother. She will understand." The lump in her throat refused to leave.

Julian met her gaze and he looked like he was about to come over and say something when Ann appeared beside them, her face alight with excitement.

"Did I miss it? Has Julian told you?" she gushed. "Blast me and my appointment. I missed it, didn't I?" Her tone cut through the awkward stillness. Jada shifted uncomfortably, but Suzanne couldn't address her now.

Lillian rolled her eyes. "The Williams number? He told everyone." Her tone was flat. "You and Ruby and Suzanne. Congratulations."

Ann beamed. "Thanks! I'm so excited!" She glanced at Ruby. "Isn't it wonderful?"

Ruby nodded. "It really is."

Jada nudged Suzanne. "We should write your mother back. She's worried."

"We will," Suzanne promised.

"Suzanne!" Ann exclaimed. "I have to run and meet Fanny, but let's celebrate. Jody Mae's Sweet Shop in an hour?"

She felt suddenly light as a feather. Jody Mae's with Ann and Fanny? There couldn't be a more perfect way to celebrate her new part.

"That would be grand," she said. "Can we make it an hour and a half?"

"Of course. Don't be late!" Ann waved before she sashayed off the stage.

Lillian and Ruby retreated to the dressing room, whispering to one another. Suzanne hoped Lillian had enough discretion to keep the rest of the telegram a secret.

Suzanne shook the telegram from her head. She would not let the news of Elton's death bring her down. She grabbed Jada's hand and gushed, "Can you believe it?"

"No, I can't." Jada tone was even. "Elton must have been horribly ill." Her face flushed. "We need to write your mother."

Suzanne paused. Jada was right; she should write to the Plankstons, but what could she say? Elton was dead, but he'd really left them long before, when he first grew ill. There was nothing more to say.

"I need to court Ann's friendship," Suzanne tried to explain. "Mother can wait until tomorrow."

Jada didn't reply, but simply folded the telegram and placed it in her pocket.

Enjoying afternoon tea was a luxury rarely enjoyed by Ziegfeld girls. Suzanne had never really enjoyed such a watery drink. It was only good when it was really hot, and more often than not, it went cold too quickly. If let out on time, many girls headed down the street to Jody Mae's Sweet Shop. Not only did it serve a wonderful variety of tea flavors, but its open windows and upscale décor made it a wonderful place to see and be seen.

Suzanne had been hearing of the shop since her first day of rehearsals. Finally, she found herself sipping tea beside its distinctive rosy lace curtains. Despite asking for more time, Suzanne found herself sitting there thirty minutes early. The wait wouldn't have been so bad if Ruby and Lillian weren't seated at the table close to her. Leave it to Lillian to horn in on her celebration.

"I'm sorry he didn't choose you, but don't I get to be excited? This is a big break for me!" Ruby exclaimed. "I've worked hard and paid my dues!"

Lillian met Suzanne's eyes and turned quickly away, as if embarrassed to have even looked at her. "Of course you do." She took a sip of her tea.

Ruby leaned across the table and took her hand. "It's unfair. You've been with the company a long time too."

Inwardly, Suzanne rolled her eyes. If Lillian wanted to be in the number, she shouldn't complain about Bert Williams so loudly. Julian had made that point quite clear.

Lillian sniffed. "And *she* made it in. After being here only a week."

143

Unable to suppress the urge, Suzanne glanced at them. Ruby met her gaze with a look of apology before saying, "Ann gets what she wants. We both know that. And this year she wants Suzanne."

Whether insult or compliment, it stung just the same. Her success was more than one friendship!

Ruby finished her tea with a quick gulp. "We need to pick up your gown for the party this weekend. Perhaps Flo will rediscover your beauty."

Lillian put a few coins on the table before rising. "Perhaps he will." She looked at Suzanne.

"See you, girls," Suzanne said with a cheeriness she didn't feel.

"Don't wait for Ann too long," Lillian replied with the same false tone. As if she didn't realize Suzanne had heard everything they said.

Ruby cleared her throat and nodded. "Come, now, Lillian. We don't want to be late."

Lillian gave Suzanne a pointed look before they left the shop.

Glancing at the clock on the wall, Suzanne wondered at what point it was appropriate to leave.

Raising her cup to her lips, she suppressed the urge to make a face. Her tea was cold. In the time she had waited it had gone from burning hot to stale and cold.

Suzanne let out a deep sigh. Promise or no promise, she'd waited long enough. She threw a few coins on the table, picked up her handbag, and turned to leave.

"Pardon me," Jonathon said. "Did you drop this?"

Suzanne turned around and smiled. Jonathon stood behind her, staring down at her with clear green eyes. His smooth hair fell limply on either side of his part.

He repeated, "Is this yours?" He held out a sheet of paper, which Suzanne immediately recognized as her call schedule for the New Amsterdam.

"Thank you very much," she said. She held out her hand to take the paper from him.

"What is it?" Jonathon asked, a smirk threatening to break free. "Private correspondence?"

"It's nothing." Suzanne tried to grab the paper from him. What would he think if he knew she was so careless with her call sheet?

Jonathon held it tightly too high for her to get it from him without standing. As she watched, he turned it over and glanced at it. "The Williams/Errol number? I knew I heard your name batted around between Flo and Julian. You must be talented, but then, I saw you perform. You light up the stage."

"I remember, thank you." She held out her hand for her sheet. He didn't seem to notice.

"And have you been happy with our little family?" His face turned suddenly serious. "Any problems I should know about?"

Suzanne wrinkled her nose in frustration. "Can I please have my call sheet?" she asked as calmly as possible.

For a moment, it looked like he was going to continue to tease her, but instead he lowered the paper just enough for her to snatch it from him. Suzanne folded it neatly and shoved it in her bag.

"What are you doing here?" she asked.

"I came to have some tea with the beautiful people." He nodded around the café, which was filled with various people who looked like fellow performers. "Are you waiting for Ann?"

"As a matter of fact I am." She fiddled with the napkin in front of her. She didn't like being caught stood up. "How did you know?"

"She asked me to stop by and tell you she was running late." Jonathon's face lit up with his smile.

"But you said—"

"I said I came to drink with the beautiful people and you, Suzanne, are very beautiful." Jonathon gestured for a waitress to bring him a cup as Suzanne adjusted to his compliment. "Ann is a dear friend and is currently trying to calm down poor Fanny. Something about a stolen suitor."

"Never a dull moment," Suzanne said.

The waitress arrived with a new pot of tea and a cup and saucer for Jonathon. "Do you need milk or sugar?"

"Both, please," Jonathan replied. Once the

146

waitress was out of earshot, Jonathon turned back to Suzanne. "Will you be at Flo's party?"

"I wouldn't miss it. Is there a reason I wouldn't be?"

"I was onstage this afternoon. I didn't know if with your friend's passing, if you'd still come out and celebrate." He watched her carefully.

Suzanne looked away. "Life must move forward," she said. "I hadn't spoken to him for some time, years in fact. My life is here now."

"Well, I am sorry for your loss anyway, but glad you do not need to take a leave. Do you think—" Jonathon stopped and cleared his throat before continuing. "Do you think you could save me a dance at—"

"Oh, darling!" Suzanne turned to find Fanny Brice herself smirking at them. All thoughts of a reply flitted from Suzanne's mind. "Save you a dance? Do people still do that?"

Ann stood next to her friend. "Thanks for keeping Suzanne entertained, Jonathon. I hate being tardy, but it was unavoidable. Forgive me?"

Suzanne smiled. "Well, you did send this charming gentleman to entertain me." She winked at Ann. From the corner of her eye she saw Jonathon's cheeks redden.

Fanny took Suzanne's elbow and pulled her from her chair. "Flo wants us to take you shopping. You are in need of a *good* suit."

"This is a new suit." Suzanne gulped. She had

taken that woman at her word for what looked good. Her shoulders did stick out farther than normal, but that was the trend. Or was it. Suzanne suddenly felt foolish and out of place. "Is there something wrong with how I dress?"

"I think you're lovely." Jonathon took that moment to stand and take his leave. "Until we meet again, ladies."

Ann turned to Suzanne. "It isn't that what you wear is bad, or even ill-fitting. It just isn't tailored as well as it could be."

Fanny nodded. "Ziegfeld always said one well-tailored suit is better than ten ill-fitting ones."

Following Ann had only given her respect so far. Surely one more new suit would be well used. Jada could wait another couple hours for her, she assured herself. The telegram couldn't be sent until tomorrow and even then, she didn't owe Mother and the Plankstons anything.

"Very well." Suzanne took a last drink of her cold tea and stood up. "Lead the way."

CHAPTER 11

Nothing said "servant" quite like a handful of packages and armloads of bags. Jada's arms burned from carrying the heavy purchases, but she dared not put them down. A gentleman to her left offered his hand to a lady stepping off the curb, but he turned his back on Jada, who could barely see the step in front of her.

Suzanne's telegram to home crinkled against Jada's skin. She'd pressed it in her sleeve to be sure she didn't lose it. It had been hard to send. It was so impersonal! But, Suzanne had put her foot down. No need to miss rehearsal for someone she hadn't heard from in years. And yet, they'd known the Plankstons forever. It felt wrong not going, not doing something. She didn't even ask if Jada wanted to go. She hadn't asked Jada's opinion on anything since joining the Follies. It was as if she was actually just a servant!

Settle down, she scolded herself. It had only been a few weeks. Once Suzanne got used to the new schedule, things would go back to normal. This could be good for both of them if only she could let it happen.

Women in wide-brimmed hats walked alongside her, not noticing her as they gossiped about their terrible help and languishing staff. It seemed those who had hired staff from overseas were losing them as the tensions over there called some home, or at least pushed them into different professions. Jada wondered if anything could make her return to Virginia. Images of her parents swinging in the trees made her trip over the sidewalk. No, she could never return. Returning home only brought death.

"Miss?" A man's voice cut through her train of thought. "Miss?"

Jada kept walking.

"Are you Suzanne Haskins's girl?"

That made her stop and turn toward the speaker. The gentleman looked familiar. They didn't know many people in New York. He grinned as their eyes met and she realized it was Mr. Ziegfeld's assistant. The one who had first told them of the audition.

"Mr. Franks?" she asked.

The man was sitting in the back of a Model T automobile with a bowler cap tilted on his head. He looked quite stylish in his white suit and blue checked bow tie.

"Can I give you a ride?" He opened the door and gestured for her to get inside.

"Are you sure?" Jada glanced about her. A few of the men and women were now eying them with suspicion.

"Of course!" He jumped out of the automobile and took the packages from her arms. With a free elbow, he escorted her to the car. "Any friend of Miss Haskins. She may soon be a star."

Jada grinned as she settled into the bench. "Do you really think so?"

"Flo has a way with girls. You never know." He set the packages between them and jumped in beside her. "And Suzanne is special."

Jada heard the longing in his voice.

The driver tapped on the window and shouted, "Where to, Jonathon?"

Jonathon looked at Jada. "Where are you off to?"

"489 West Thirty-eighth Street."

"You heard the girl, Quincy!" Jonathon leaned back in the bench as the car putted into motion. The street was clear and Jada enjoyed the rest. They had gone about a block when Jonathon startled and declared, "Stop!"

He jostled the door open and burst onto the street. "Marie!" he shouted.

A woman in a pink gown slowed, but didn't stop. Jonathon called out again as he lunged forward and grasped her hand. She spun around.

Her dark brown hair framed her plump cheeks in such a way that her surprised expression looked almost comical. She reminded Jada of a cherub. Marie tried to push Jonathon away, but his grasp was firm. Jada slid over on the bench to be able to hear what was being said. From the little she knew of this assistant, brute force was not his style.

"Let me go!" she hissed. She sounded angry, but her eyes showed her fear.

"What happened?" Jonathon asked her calmly.

"I don't know what you're talking about."

"You disappeared! Something must have happened to cause your departure. Flo has been looking for you all over the city." He sounded concerned.

"Flo can keep looking! I will not work for a company that abuses women."

Any strength drained out of Jonathon's stature. "Abuses women? What are you talking about?" He dropped her arm.

Marie snorted and stepped back from Jonathon. "As if you don't know. You know everything that happens with the company. Please, don't play dumb."

"I really don't know what you are referring to." Jonathon looked over his shoulder at Jada, who shook her head in confusion.

Marie sniffed. "Next time you decide a girl isn't part of the group anymore, tell her. I've had enough harassment and fear for one year. It was cruel. Just plain cruel. Now, leave me alone."

"Marie, please!" Jonathon reached forward again and caught her sleeve in his grasp. "We never—"

A group of gentlemen stepped forward. "Is he bothering you, miss?" one asked. They were larger than Jonathon, who stepped back from them.

Once again free of Jonathon's grasp, Marie

took a few steps away. "No, we are done here."

The men glanced at Jonathon, who stepped toward the car. Jada slid over as he opened the door.

"Take care of yourself," he called after Marie, but she was already walking down the block. He settled next to Jada and nodded to Quincy to start driving.

After a long moment he said, "Sorry about that." He ran a hand through his hair.

"I hope she is well," Jada offered.

"Something strange is happening," Jonathon said aloud to himself. "Yes, she graced our stage last year. Then after lunch one day she declared she was leaving. She returned from her dressing room and told Leon she was done and walked off the stage. No warning, no explanation. Some of us, Flo included, thought it was a publicity stunt, but when she didn't return we knew it wasn't. Until today, we haven't seen her. We have money we owe her waiting at the office. She's never come to collect."

"Who would leave behind money?" Jada wondered.

Jonathon blinked as if he didn't realize he'd been talking out loud. "If it was only Marie, it might be explained as a fluke. But since then we've had half a dozen other girls leave. Some of our most promising talent gone in a fit of fear and anger."

"Sometimes fear breeds anger." Jada adjusted her seat as they went over a bump.

"True. You know, Mr. Ziegfeld has plans for Suzanne."

The hairs on Jada's arm stood up. Calmly she said, "He has been very generous."

"I hope you will let me know if she begins to have . . . doubts." Jonathon glanced out the window as the car stopped outside Miss Mitzi's. "She deserves to be a star."

"She does." Jada gathered her packages. When Jonathon didn't elaborate, she added, "Suzanne is a very hard worker. We—I mean, she rehearses every night."

"Of course she does." Jonathon smiled. "As her friend, please alert us if anything strange starts happening. We don't want to lose her."

Jada's spine straightened with pride. "I assure you, Mr. Franks. Suzanne is not going to let a little fear get in the way of her career."

"If there are any issues, please have her come see me." He opened the car door for her.

Jada took his hand while getting out. "Thank you for the ride."

With that she collected her packages and rushed inside. Suzanne would want to hear all that Jonathon said about her. She set the packages on the entry table and took off her hat.

"Jada!" Suzanne exclaimed. "What do you think?"

Jada turned from the hat rack to see Suzanne spinning around in a satin crimson dress with black lace overlay. Her hair was pulled high atop her head and her diamond comb was over her right ear.

"You look beautiful." Jada resisted asking where she got the dress. They made enough now that Suzanne could splurge now and again. "Who did your hair?"

"Oh, I asked that Sally girl to help. She isn't as good as you, but we made it work." She glanced out the window. "Listen, I know we were going to rehearse some of the new moves, but Ann asked me to come to a party. I think I can wave a leaf back and forth without too much trouble."

Jada raised an eyebrow, but didn't say anything. She picked up some of the packages and waited.

"Tomorrow morning," Suzanne said. "I have the whole day to work tomorrow." She kissed Jada's cheek. A car honked from the curb. "That's Ann waiting for me. Thanks, Jada!"

She was out the door and in the car before Jada could even think of what to say. She collected the rest of the packages and started up to their room. Since befriending Ann and Fanny, there seemed to be parties every night and they went later and later.

The next morning, Jada shook her head at Suzanne. "Don't you complain about a sore stomach to me. I didn't make you go to that party. You knew we needed to work today."

155

"I know, but I'm really tired," Suzanne whined. She rubbed her head. "I may have drank too much."

Instead of giving in, Jada grabbed the pitcher of water on the dresser and poured Suzanne a glass. "Here. Any better?"

After drinking the water, Suzanne nodded. "I guess."

"Good. Now, you need to stop leaping so high. You don't impress anyone by landing late."

Jada was fed up with excuses and being made to wait. If she had been forced to sit around waiting for her all morning, Suzanne would at least get her turns right.

Clapping her hands in a stern rhythm, Jada called out, "Five, six, seven, eight." She resumed her seat on the bed as Suzanne dipped and leaped gracefully across the room like the nymph Ziegfeld hoped she was. Jada's head kept the rhythm and her lips kept count as the routine was played out in front of her.

Suzanne leapt modestly into the air and landed on a bent leg and moved perfectly into a turn before stopping and turning toward Jada.

"Well?" she asked. Her chest was heaving, but her eyes looked hopeful.

Jada waited a moment before nodding. "That is exactly it," she said. "Keep your leaps modest, like you just did, and Julian won't have any further complaints." She tossed Suzanne a towel.

"Thank you, Jada. I don't know what I'd do without you helping me." She pressed the towel to her forehead and neck, dabbing away the sweat.

"Nor do I."

Suzanne kicked her playfully, before sitting down next to her.

"Shall we fix ourselves up and go get pastries?" Jada offered.

It had been a tradition since they first started rehearsing. Once Suzanne mastered something challenging, the two would pick up a rich dessert, go home, and have a night of giggling and sugar, usually chocolate. Jada felt it so special that she rarely ate chocolate except on such joyous evenings. Despite being tired, Jada knew Suzanne would jump at the chance. It had been too long since they enjoyed some time just the two of them without leaps to perfect or contracts to examine.

"Ugh, I am so sick of sweets." Suzanne held her stomach and plopped on the bed beside Jada. "Did I tell you about the chocolate fountain they had last night?"

"No, you didn't." Jada could only imagine such a dessert.

"I ate so much of it, the very idea of chocolate sounds foul." Suzanne turned so her back was to Jada. "Besides, I promised a few girls I'd be at Zarab's tonight. I'll have Miss Mitzi make me a

157

salad for lunch. I can't eat heavy all day if I want to keep my Ziegfeld figure."

"You'll need to get more sleep if you want to keep your beauty." Jada said it softly so it didn't sound too harsh.

"That was mean." Suzanne turned back around. "This is part of the job. Being seen."

Jada weighed her options. She didn't want to upset Suzanne, but needed to express her concerns. "Yes, you do need to be seen in society, but you also need to take care of yourself. You are sick this morning because of last night. That can't show at rehearsal."

Suzanne's face fell and suddenly she was the girl Jada grew up with again. Slightly insecure, yet determined. "I really didn't mean to drink that much."

"Really? You are better than that. You can say no to these gentlemen." Jada put a hand on Suzanne's shoulder. "Don't let them change who you are."

"Don't look at me like that." Suzanne shrugged off Jada's hand. "This is my chance to fit in to New York society."

Jada nodded, swallowing away her disappointment. "I understand that."

"Then you see why I have to attend these parties. It is important."

"I never said I didn't understand why you went . . ." Jada began.

Suzanne jumped to her feet, leaned down, and kissed Jada's cheek. "You're a peach," she said. "I'll make it up to you sometime. When I have a free night, we'll stuff ourselves with pastries. I promise."

"I wasn't really hungry anyway," Jada lied, but Suzanne was already out of the room and didn't hear her.

In the evenings, Miss Mitzi's parlor sank into the dusk haze with the warm red and yellow hues reflected inside. Sitting on the couch and reading the newspaper had become an evening tradition of Jada's. It was understood, of course, that she would leave should a group of gentlemen or ladies wish to use the space, but that never happened. The New York nightlife drew them away from the boardinghouse almost before the sun set. Lately, Suzanne had been joining them.

"Suzanne has so many nice friends," Miss Mitzi said as she entered the parlor and settled into her rocking chair. "Have you met no one to spend time with?"

"I don't know many people in the city," Jada replied. "Besides, this is the only time I have to enjoy the paper."

Miss Mitzi shrugged. "Suit yourself. Seems like a waste to me."

Jada chose not to answer. Instead she turned the page and began reading an article about the rising tensions in Europe. For a long time the only sounds were the crinkle of Jada's paper and the creak of Miss Mitzi's rocking chair.

"Excuse me, Miss Mitzi," Sally interrupted. "You are needed in the kitchen."

With barely a nod of her head, Miss Mitzi pulled herself up from her chair and left the room. Sally did not follow her. Instead, she came farther into the room and picked up a discarded section of the paper.

"You read this dribble?" she asked.

Jada looked up from her article and nodded. "Mrs. Haskins taught me to keep on top of the news."

Sally plopped onto the couch next to Jada and leaned over to see what she was reading. After a moment Jada heard a slight whispering in her ear. Without the slightest movement she looked down and saw Sally's mouth repeating the same syllable.

"Arch-Arch D—"

"You can't read," Jada blurted out.

The moment she said it, she regretted it. After all, wasn't it she who denounced those who thought coloreds weren't educated?

" 'Course I can read." Sally sounded a bit too shrill for Jada to believe her.

"I'm sorry, that was improper." Jada forced a pleasant smile and shrugged, hoping Sally would accept her apology.

Sally looked from Jada to the paper. "Truth?" she offered.

Jada nodded.

"I know my letters and all. Those papers, though! They use words I don't know and don't understand." After a moment's hesitation, she resorted to her usual demeanor. "Besides, why should I care what a bunch of stuffy white men have to say anyway?"

Jada stared at Sally for a moment, torn between shock and pity. "We could read a bit together and I could help you with the words you don't know."

Sally nodded slowly. "Do you think they published W.E.B. Dubois's speech?"

Jada nodded. "It's on the page you're holding."

Sally looked down at the crinkled paper as if it were covered in rubies. She unfolded it and began scanning the headlines.

"What's the big deal with him anyway?" Jada asked.

Sally nearly dropped the paper. "You don't know Dubois?" Sally pulled a few strands of hair behind her ears and adjusted her posture so she was completely facing Jada. "He speaks for us. Unlike other people, he is working to get us equality, not just rights. He stands up for what he believes. I wish I was more like him."

"I think you are well-spoken." Jada glanced at the paper.

Once she had brought home a pamphlet of

a speech Dubois made and was immediately chastised. Mrs. Haskins had insisted that "his kind" will only bring destruction and sadness to colored folk. That is what his violence will foster. But listening to Sally and hearing her passion, Jada wondered if it was fear or validation that Mrs. Haskins had felt.

Jada scooted away from Sally's gesturing hands and passionate words. Other than family and the theater, Jada had never felt so strongly about anything. She followed the news as she knew she should, but nothing had ever touched her soul. It occurred to Jada that there was little point in knowing about the world if she didn't care about it.

"I know you were raised alongside that Suzanne," Sally continued. "But that doesn't make you the same. You need to start a life outside of hers."

"I do know about life. Day after day tensions are rising higher in Europe, and picketing women are getting arrested every day in America. Women are working to get the right to vote." Each fact she stated made Jada feel more and more foolish. Nothing she said was specific, or even really involved her.

Sally handed her the paper and said, "Let's read. Perhaps I can teach you something as well."

CHAPTER 12

The trolley swayed back and forth as it made its way down Forty-second Street. A few packages sat on Suzanne's lap as she and Jada returned from an afternoon of shopping. Jada's shoulder bumped against hers annoyingly, but Suzanne didn't say anything. She was too tired.

"Look." Jada pointed out one of the windows.

The building ahead of them was plastered with theater sheets advertising productions opening soon. There, in between Cohen's new show and an unknown show, was a sheet for the Ziegfeld Follies of 1914. The red background accentuated the girl in blue, who was leaning over, looking at her face in the mirror, with her back end provocatively displayed toward the viewer. A few hatboxes dressed up the room, and the NEW AMSTERDAM THEATRE in bold lettering finished off the poster on the left.

"It is really happening," Suzanne said as the trolley passed by the building. "We are going to open and I'm going to be a real Ziegfeld girl."

Jada took the packages off Suzanne's lap as they came close to their stop. "Of course you are going to open. What did you think all the hard work was for?"

They got off the trolley and walked the two

blocks to Miss Mitzi's. Suzanne's feet screamed in the new shoes that had been gifted to her by a gentleman she met at a club a few nights ago. They pinched her toes but were too beautiful to return.

"Of course I knew we were going to open, but, I don't know, this just makes it feel real." Suzanne grinned.

"I can understand that," Jada said. She gestured toward the boardinghouse. "Looks like Miss Mitzi has a new boarder."

A car sat in front of the boardinghouse, the driver fiddling with the trunk on the back. The man didn't look up as the girls walked past him and toward the boardinghouse.

"Thank goodness! Maybe now she'll stop begging me to invite my friends to board there. As if Ann Pennington would leave the Ritz, or Kay leave her suite at the Boston Hotel. No, if any Ziegfeld girl were to move, it would be me for something far more glamorous than Miss Mitzi's."

"She has been good to us and perhaps once the show has been open for a while we can move, but it feels good to have so much money saved, doesn't it?"

Suzanne tripped on the sidewalk. "There is such a thing as too practical, Jada."

They turned to walk into the house when Jada froze. "Oh no," she said.

"What's wrong?" Suzanne glanced from her friend to the house and her face fell. Through the lace curtains the shadow of a woman could be seen. "Who is that?"

"You don't know?" Jada looked at Suzanne as if she were stupid.

The front door opened and Mrs. Haskins walked out. Her tall, thin frame was dressed in her tan traveling suit and ivory blouse with a wisp of baby's breath tucked into the lapel. It never ceased to amaze Suzanne how such a small woman could command such attention. Even the birds stopped chirping when she walked out onto the porch.

"Suzanne." She sounded both relieved and annoyed.

"Hello, Mother," Suzanne replied. Turning to Jada, she asked, "Did you know?"

"No," Jada insisted. "I had no idea."

"But you wrote to her."

Jada had no reply to the anger in Suzanne's face.

They stood in an awkward stillness before Mrs. Haskins glided down the stairs and embraced Suzanne.

"It has been too long, my dear." Mrs. Haskins grasped Suzanne's cheeks and looked into her eyes. "We must talk."

Suzanne didn't reply, but led her mother up the stairs and into the front parlor. Jada followed a few steps behind.

"Jada, darling," Mrs. Haskins said. "This Miss Mitzi person seems to be busy with something more important than my visit. Would you be a dear and get us some lemonade?"

Jada glanced at Suzanne and then smiled to Mrs. Haskins. "I'll put these upstairs for you and then check the kitchen for something for you to drink."

Mrs. Haskins nodded and turned her back to Jada.

"Thanks, Jada. I appreciate your help."

Jada raised an eyebrow as she left the room, but Suzanne refused to respond. Any acknowledgment of their friendship could set Mother in a direction of conversation Suzanne did not wish to pursue. Instead, Suzanne sat on the sofa and gestured for Mother to do the same.

"Why are you here?" Suzanne asked.

"Isn't it obvious?" Mrs. Haskins folded her hands together and stared at her daughter. "As the funeral happened in London, the Plankstons are having a dinner to celebrate Elton's life next week. They would like you to attend."

Suzanne could feel her muscles tighten. Mother understood nothing. "I sent a telegram. I am unable to leave at this time."

"And I am here to demand you reconsider."

"I can't, Mother."

"He is your fiancé."

"No, Mother. He was my fiancé two years ago.

166

When he chose to travel to London to see someone, we parted ways. I don't owe the Plankstons
anything." She knew she sounded harsh, but she
refused to let Mother change her stance on this
issue.

She expected Mother to reply with anger, but
instead, her shoulders slumped and she leaned
forward in her seat. She rested her head in
her hands for a moment before pulling herself
together.

"They lost their son, Suzanne," she said. "He
left for London in pain and chose never to return.
Do you understand what that might feel like?
Not only did their son choose not to live, but that
stigma, that embarrassment will forever follow
them. As their friends we must stand by them so
that others will know to do the same."

"His death does not change what happened."
Suzanne looked away. She had run away and
chosen not to return as well, though not in the
same way. "He chose to give me my life back and
I've made something of myself because of that."

"Why did you leave?" Mother asked.

"Me? You know all this. Jada and I left to
pursue my dreams." She gestured around her. "I
am going to be a star."

Mother rolled her eyes. "A star? You are joining
other women parading about onstage with little
between them and the audience. It is not what I
had planned for you."

"It is what I planned for myself. And I am happy. Can't you be proud of that, Mother?" Suzanne swallowed back a lump in her throat. She wasn't supposed to care about what her mother thought. That woman had made more bad choices than Suzanne cared to count, and yet she found herself hoping for her approval.

"I will always be proud of you, Suzanne," Mrs. Haskins began. "Disappointment is different. I raised you to be a lady, not to abandon the family who loved you so. I did not raise you to hurt a grieving family. You need to return to Richmond and say good-bye to Elton."

"You raised me?" Suzanne retorted. She stood up and walked toward the window. "Any values that were instilled in me came from Jada and her mother. Cicely is who I remember scolding me when I stole the neighbor's pie off their window when I was four, and it was Cicely who showed me how to do my hair for church when I was older. It was never you. You were the woman who I ate dinner with and who inspected the work Cicely did. And you never seemed to even like her, let alone respect her."

"Suzanne, stop. You are not being fair. I taught you to play piano and chose only the best schools for you. Cicely was just the help."

"Just the help?" Suzanne glared at her. "She died working for us."

Mrs. Haskins shifted awkwardly and avoided

Suzanne's eyes. "Her death was tragic. Had I only kept her inside that day? But your father and I fought and I sent her away. More than anything I regret that. I lost everything that day."

It was Suzanne's turn to look away. She never told anyone what she overheard her parents arguing over, nor the anger she witnessed in her mother. Some family secrets shouldn't be revealed.

"I lost everything too," Jada said. She stood in the doorway with a tray filled with cookies and glasses of tea. "I lost my family, my home, and my safety in one instant."

Mrs. Haskins went to Jada's side and took the tray from her. "I do know that you lost a lot that day."

"Do you?" Jada's reply was quick. "Because you never once wrote. I've tried to keep you in touch with Suzanne's career and not once have you reached out to us. I left forwarding information at every hotel that we stayed at hoping that you would try to find us, to find Suzanne. It's been almost two years; why now?"

Suzanne met her mother's eyes and waited for a response. She'd known about the letters, but not about Jada's hopes to be followed, nor how easy she'd made it for them to be found. Why hadn't Mother or Father come for her? Perhaps they were happier without her around. Then they both could go about doing whatever they wanted with whomever they pleased.

The tray clanged loudly as Mrs. Haskins placed it on a side table. "This is very unseemly, Jada."

"I'll tell you why it matters now." Jada was on a roll now. "It matters because suddenly it is your reputation that is on the line. You are worried that if Suzanne doesn't return to say good-bye to a man who deserted her that it will make you look bad. Embarrass *you*."

"She needs to be there," Mrs. Haskins repeated. "It is her duty."

"Is that the only reason you came, Mother?" Suzanne asked. Jada's anger had inflamed her own. "Two years of little contact and now this grand gesture all for Elton? Is that all I am worth to you, a husband?"

"Of course not. I came to bring you home." Mrs. Haskins went to Suzanne and tried to put an arm around her waist, but Suzanne stepped away and went to Jada instead.

"What Suzanne said is true." Jada glared at the woman. "Leaving now is nearly impossible. They open in Boston in two weeks. We have worked for this ever since we left home. She shouldn't have to risk all of that for a man who left her and a family who turned their back on her. Suzanne is unable to attend. We will send the Plankstons a letter and flowers if we are able."

Mrs. Haskins's glare hardened. "I had thought better of you girls. You were both raised to value family." She folded her hands together and waited.

Suzanne had had enough. "We've been over this, Mother. You have come a long way and I appreciate the effort, but you will not change our minds." And uneasy silence fell between the women. After a time Suzanne cleared her throat and offered, "Since you have come all this way, would you like to go out for dinner?" Suzanne tilted her head and smiled, hoping to charm her mother out of this horrible mood. "Perhaps I could show you around where I work."

Rolling her shoulders, Mrs. Haskins replied, "No, I don't think so. I have tickets back to Richmond that leave tonight. I promised Mrs. Plankston that I'd help make the suitable arrangements. I can't leave her alone at such a time."

"She has Mr. Plankston," Suzanne said. "Please, stay one night. You could come to rehearsal and meet my friends."

"I think not." Mrs. Haskins placed her hand on Suzanne's cheek. "You have made a life for yourself. You fought hard for it. I hope it is everything you wished it would be. I, however, should not be a part of it."

"At least let me take you to the train station," Suzanne insisted. "Jada, will you get my shawl and hat?" Jada happily left the room.

"You needn't trouble yourself," Mrs. Haskins sniffed.

"I want to," Suzanne insisted. "I've missed you."

"Your running away proves otherwise."

This visit wasn't about Elton after all. This was about finally having a reason to bring her home. Perhaps her mother missed her more than she realized. She was wrong in insisting that Suzanne return home, but perhaps she did deserve an explanation.

"That day, the day I ran away, it wasn't as simple as you probably think." Suzanne gestured for them to sit on the sofa. "Once Jada discovered her parents' bodies, she knew she had to leave. And I chose to go with her, but it wasn't just to avoid Elton and my failed relationship."

"No?" Mrs. Haskins looked skeptical. "What else could it be?"

"That afternoon, I was outside the door when you and Father fought. I know about him and Cicely. I know about their affair. You were so angry and said horrible things about her. I couldn't face you."

Mrs. Haskins's face was white and her mouth slightly ajar. "You know?"

"I know."

"All those years we tried to keep it from you. All those years of lying and you found out anyway." Mrs. Haskins shook her head.

"All those years?" Suzanne repeated. "I didn't realize, I mean. How long was it going on?"

Mrs. Haskins's cheeks darkened. "I've said too much."

"No, Mother. How long?" Suzanne had to know

the answer. "Cicely loved her husband. It doesn't make sense."

"Your father loved—loves—me too, Suzanne. But love is complicated."

"How long?" Suzanne repeated. She would not let Mrs. Haskins derail the conversation.

"I don't know."

"A few years?" Suzanne pushed. When her mother shrugged she pushed further. "Longer?"

Mrs. Haskins got up and walked across the room. "It was on and off. I knew it started before I had you and then started back up five years ago. Please don't make me explain the details, Suzanne. It is between me and your father."

Before she was born? Suzanne swallowed a sour taste in her mouth. "I'm sorry, Mother. No wonder you were so upset. I had no idea. Were they in love?"

"I said I don't want to discuss it. It is over now and your father is better for it. Some women just don't know when enough is enough."

"You don't seriously mean Cicely ran after Father?" The very idea seemed comical. Cicely was a beautiful woman and Mr. Haskins pudgy and distempered. Suzanne loved her father, but he was no Casanova.

"Who knows what those animals do." The anger in her mother's voice put Suzanne's hair on end.

"Mother," Suzanne whispered. Jada would be

back any moment and she didn't need to hear any of this.

"Well, it is true. What that woman did to get a better position was disgraceful. If she hadn't come to an ill end, I would have acted myself."

Suzanne's nostrils flared. "There. That is why I had to leave. That anger in your voice. That blame. I couldn't live near it. Not knowing what happened to them. I'd always question the truth of what happened."

Mrs. Haskins glared at her. "You think that I could hurt Cicely? She was a friend of mine for at least two decades. She helped me settle into married life. I'd not let anything bad happen to her."

"Those are just words. And perhaps you believe them, but I don't."

"I don't have to listen to this." Mrs. Haskins grabbed her clutch from the side table. "When you are finished insulting me, feel free to write."

She pushed past Jada, who was standing in the doorframe, a shawl and birch hat in her hands. Suzanne prayed she hadn't been standing there long. She didn't need to know about Cicely and Mr. Haskins.

"Your mother left?" she asked.

"Yes, she is gone." Suzanne flinched as the front door slammed shut. "On second thought, I believe I will go out with Ann tonight. Is my green dress pressed?" she asked.

Jada blinked. "I will pull it out for you."

"And the ivory gloves that friend of yours made. I just love the rose buttons."

As Jada rushed off to get her outfit ready for the evening, Suzanne pulled back the curtain and watched Mrs. Haskins climb into her cab and drive away. She hadn't meant for that conversation to go so horribly wrong, but now that it was out, she knew there was no other way it could have gone. She'd write to her mother, soon, but for now, she'd take care of herself. And that meant dazzling New York society.

CHAPTER 13

After an hour of dressing and redressing Suzanne's hair, Jada finally closed the door and found herself alone in the front parlor. She waved dutifully from the window until Suzanne's driver pulled away from the curb. For the first time she was grateful for the endless evenings of parties. Spending the evening with Suzanne after what she overheard was too much.

Over the years she had heard her mother crying in the evenings and, occasionally, her father raging on about the cost of working for the Haskinses, but she never understood what they were referring to. She assumed they worried about her closeness with Suzanne or the little time they were together as a family. Never did she think it was about Mr. Haskins forcing himself upon her mother. And that is what it had to be. Jada's mother and father were in love, more than most couples Jada knew. And Mr. Haskins, although always kind to Jada, never presented himself as a suitor to her mother.

Despite Mrs. Haskins's departure hours before, the parlor still smelled like her lilac oil. Jada dropped the curtain and stepped back from the window. This was no good. She needed to not think for a time. Without another thought she grabbed her handbag and slipped out into the night.

There was only one place that could make Jada forget what she overheard between Suzanne and Mrs. Haskins: Roger's nightclub.

"Jada!" Roger exclaimed from behind the bar. "Is Sally coming tonight?"

"I'm on my own for now, I'm afraid," Jada called back. "Sally might come later."

There were three gentlemen leaning on the bar, chatting together. They turned and tipped their hats to Jada as she spoke with Roger. She smiled back.

"What brings you in here so early tonight?" Roger wiped the bar dry with a rag.

Jada gestured toward Danny, who was warming up at the piano. "I needed to clear my head."

"Here, on the house." Roger filled a glass with one of the beers from the tap.

Jada took the glass. "Thanks, Roger."

"If she doesn't make it tonight, tell Sally I missed her."

Suzanne nodded and walked toward the booths she and Sally had sat at. Most of the booths were empty. Two men sat at a table playing cards, and at another two women sipped beers and laughed at each other's stories.

"Jada! Darling, come over here!" In the farthest booth, Oliver sat waving his hands and gesturing for Jada to join him.

"Oliver, hi!" she replied as she sat across from

him. "I didn't think you liked to come to such places."

"Sally been buzzing in your ear, I see."

"She adores you." Jada glanced around to be sure Sally wasn't there somehow. "She only mentioned it because she worries about you."

"Well, I make an exception to my rules for Roger's place." He took a sip of a pink drink. "It doesn't help that business is booming. All thanks to you."

Jada raised her drink to him in a mock salute and took a drink.

"Is Danny due for a break anytime soon?" She smiled at Danny, who was swaying boldly to the song he was playing.

Oliver followed her gaze and leaned back with a smirk on his face. "Finally someone seeing that man for what he is. Danny is a peach."

"Oh, no, nothing like that. I'm not here because he is handsome." She clenched her hands and cursed her big mouth. "Not that he isn't handsome." *Stop talking,* she scolded herself.

"You, Miss Jada, are wonderful," Oliver said as he chuckled. His blue eyes shone with bright tears. "I didn't think you were searching for a man, come on. Some of us have more important things to think about. But it doesn't hurt to watch him."

Jada relaxed and smiled. Oliver understood. Danny ended the peppy tune and started a slower piece that reminded Jada of "Let Me Call You

Sweetheart." Once the introduction was over she winked at Oliver and started to sing with Danny quietly so as not to bother anyone. Oliver's eyes widened as she sang.

> Let me call you sweetheart
> I'm in love with you
> Let me hear you whisper
> That you love me too
>
> Keep the love light glowing
> In your eyes so true
> Let me call you sweetheart
> I'm in love with you

"You've got the voice of an angel. Anyone ever tell you that?"

"One of the women at my church back in Richmond tried to get me to sing the lead solo, but I never took her up on it. It felt better to work on blending in with Mother and the rest of the choir instead."

"And now?" Oliver leaned back in the booth.

"Now? Well, Mother is gone and there is no one to want to sing beside. I would be happy to belt out a worship song until everyone had fallen to their knees in prayer." She grinned. "Singing always brings me peace, no matter the venue or audience. It does something no other form of expression can do."

"Then that is what you should be doing with your life. Darling, do you think someone handed me scissors and asked me to design fashion? Gracious me, no! I've been hunting for my own future and am all the happier for it. You need to fight for yours too."

"Thank you." She took another sip of her beer.

Oliver's eyes were stuck on her and soon Jada found herself squirming under the pressure of the silence.

"If I tell you a secret, will you tell me one in return?" His question was sudden.

"I'll try," Jada replied.

Oliver leaned forward. "You saved my life."

"What?" Jada leaned forward to meet him. "How? I hardly know you."

"Your friend shared my name and suddenly my little business is a success. I've had requests for fifty gloves last week alone. Her friend showed off the beading on the gloves I made her at some party downtown and now these hands are in demand." He held up his hand and wiggled his fingers.

"I had no idea Suzanne even listened to me explain who you were or where I found you. I am so glad!"

"I've never been so happy. Miss Fanny Brice herself came to see me. That woman has no fear. She requested a crimson pair with black beads up the side. I am having so much fun working with Mr. Ziegfeld's women. They are the cat's meow."

He rolled his *r*'s like a purr and Jada laughed.

"They are interesting and unique women," she agreed.

"Your turn." Oliver finished his drink and waited.

"Okay." Jada exhaled. "I wish I were onstage instead of Suzanne."

The words felt sweet on her lips. However often she had had that same thought, she'd never spoken the words out loud. Now that she had, she felt lighter.

"Girl, what is stopping you?" Oliver gestured toward Danny and the small stage. "Go get onstage."

Danny finished the last few notes of the song and stopped. "I'll be back in ten minutes," he announced.

"It's complicated," Jada said. "Please, don't ask any more questions. I played the game. I told you my truth." The usual panic rose in Jada's throat. Opportunities to perform didn't come often, but she froze every time. She pushed that thought away.

"Hi there, Jada." Danny leaned against Oliver's booth and looked down at Jada. "What brings you in tonight?"

Jada smiled up at the piano man. "Just clearing my head."

"It should fill up in the next half hour," Danny said. "Can I join you for a drink?"

Oliver scooted over. "You can sit right here." He patted the seat beside him.

"Thanks, let me just get a drink." Danny winked at Jada and walked away.

Oliver nearly bounced with excitement. "He is flirting with you, girl."

"He is just being nice."

"You clearly don't know men." He whistled.

Danny reappeared with Sally and Roger. "Look who I found at the bar."

"Move over, Jada!" Sally exclaimed as she sat and scooted over so Jada had no choice but to move. "Oliver, I'm so glad to see you out!"

"Milady," he said with a grin and tip of his hat to her.

"Did you see that Arthur Conan Doyle arrived in New York yesterday?" Danny asked Roger.

Jada's ears perked up. "Yes," she exclaimed. "Did you read his comments on the condition of our prisons? I believe he is quoted in the evening edition."

Roger raised an eyebrow at her. "You read Sherlock novels?"

"Why wouldn't she?" Oliver puffed his chest up as if building for a fight. "She's a smart girl with too much time on her hands. A good mystery is hard to resist."

"Too true," Danny said. "I haven't gotten to the late edition yet."

Jada, however, had stopped listening to Danny

and Roger discuss the latest Sherlock novel. Oliver's words had set her mind in motion once again. He knew there was something going on at the New Amsterdam Theatre. His comment was meant to nudge her. A quick glance at him confirmed it. His bright eyes were watching her intently. Someone was sending those notes, but who and why?

"Danny asked you a question, Jada." Sally leaned and knocked shoulders with her.

"Hmm?" Jada asked.

"Have you read 'The Mystery of Black Peter'?" he asked. Gesturing back to the piano, he said, "I just finished that story. If you haven't read it you are welcome to borrow my copy and we could discuss it next time you visit?"

"Oh." Jada fought the swarm of happy butterflies that filled her stomach. "I don't have much time to read these days. Perhaps another time?"

Danny looked surprised, but replied, "Of course. I understand." Then to Roger he said, "I should get back to playing. Thanks for the drink." He returned to the piano.

Oliver and Sally stared at Jada.

"How could you!" Sally exclaimed at the same moment Oliver clucked his tongue in disapproval.

"I don't have time. And even if I did, I can't take his book. I don't know whcn I'll be back."

"But you know me! I could pass the book back

183

to him through Roger." Sally gestured at Roger, who was now sitting next to Oliver.

"I don't think I've ever seen him express interest in someone." Sally glanced at Roger for confirmation.

"He doesn't have much time himself."

Oliver simply glared at her with his lips in a "you knew better" pout.

"Next time I'll accept the book," Jada promised.

CHAPTER 14

For the first time ever, Suzanne was late to rehearsal. Head pounding, she slipped into the back of the rehearsal room, hoping no one would notice her sudden appearance. She glanced around and found quite a few girls were missing. Ann had still been dancing when she left the party the night before, but it never occurred to Suzanne that she might miss rehearsal.

Laura was on the opposite side of the room, her foot perched on the barre as she leaned over it, stretching. She moved so fluidly, Suzanne wondered if she even had joints. Despite the absence of Leon or Julian, Suzanne didn't want to draw any more attention to her tardiness and instead put her bag against the wall and started her warm-up routine.

Lillian and Ruby sat about a yard away. Ruby was working out a knot in her shoulder while Lillian rubbed lotion into her feet.

"Looks like Suzy isn't so popular without her beloved Ann," Lillian sneered, loud enough for Suzanne to hear.

"Oh, leave her be," Ruby said. "She's always been nice to you."

It took extra concentration for Suzanne to keep her focus on her warm-ups. Her back was straight, her sit-ups were sharp movements, and she held her stretches for exactly eight counts.

"I know. Someone should tell her she's a beat ahead during that one number."

Even though Suzanne knew Lillian only mentioned it to intimidate her, she still felt her face flush from the embarrassment. She was ahead, but in what number? Suzanne would have to discover that for herself.

As Suzanne finished her warm-up, the side door slammed shut. The girls all froze in place. Julian ambled across the room until he stood directly in front of the mirrored wall.

"Good morning, girls. I'm glad to see you all are here. For those who are not here, the rehearsal has been closed and they will not be in the running for the new quartet that we need to cast."

An excited murmur slowly filled the room. Suzanne thanked her lucky stars that she had arrived just in the nick of time!

"We need four women to make a cohesive unit onstage as they will represent the petals of a rose. With that in mind, instead of normal rehearsal, we are going to put you through a series of exercises to see how you move together. Let's get started then, shall we."

It wasn't a question.

Within seconds the girls were standing in rows following the dance director in a series of movements that involved rolling their heads around and swishing their hips from side to side.

Somehow in the shuffle Suzanne had ended up right in between Ruby and Lillian.

"Ann wouldn't be a star if it wasn't for her good looks," Lillian said. "Same goes for Suzanne. She wouldn't be here if she wasn't pretty."

Ruby shook her head. "Same goes for all of us. Do you think Mr. Ziegfeld hired us because we could pose well? No, we're pretty. So stop blaming people for that."

Suzanne grinned at the look that came over Lillian's face.

When she saw Suzanne's amusement, Lillian snapped, "No one invited you to listen."

Suzanne laughed out loud. It wasn't like she had a choice to listen or not. "Ruby is right. We're used as scenery. It doesn't take that much talent to hold a branch in midair. If we are lucky we have more talents that can be used onstage."

"And you could do more?" Lillian's tone was full of daring.

"I believe I've already proved that." Suzanne rolled her shoulders back as she followed the director's moves. Suzanne's feet throbbed every evening, but she wasn't about to give Lillian the satisfaction of knowing how tired she had been of late. Instead she said the most impressive thing she could think of. "I'm dancing with Bert Williams."

Lillian leaned toward her slightly and whispered, "I'm not talking about some monkey dance. I'm talking about real talent."

"Lillian, focus!" Mr. Mitchell exclaimed from his seat up front. Immediately, Lillian snapped her head back to attention and lunged to the left.

Ruby looked past Suzanne and met Lillian's eyes. "You have to stop saying that kind of thing, Lillian. It's holding you back."

It was hard to read Lillian's expression, but she didn't look pleased.

Suzanne let a small smile slide across her lips as they rolled into a standing position. "Sometimes it is better to swallow your own trepidations. You won't get anywhere telling Flo he's wrong. It isn't always about who you know, but who you accept."

The dance director clapped his hands. "All right, everyone. We are going to call you up in groups of three to see how you look together."

Suzanne pressed her back to the wall and slowly lowered herself to the floor. To her disappointment, Ruby and Lillian sat beside her.

"I see why Ann likes you so much now," Lillian scoffed, quickly regaining her composure. "You're driven, just like her."

"You truly hate her," Suzanne said. She rubbed her head, trying to press the last of the pounding out.

"She isn't half as talented as some of us girls, and yet Ziegfeld fawns all over her. Just because she's got a cute smile and dimpled knees."

"You said yourself, there are more important things than talent, and Ann has those qualities in abundance, not to mention her dancing ability." Suzanne defended her friend. "I'd like to see you two dance the Tangorilla or the Black Bottom with her charisma."

"Ann *is* very gifted at keeping a level head," Ruby admitted. Suzanne had a feeling she might have said something else, but was silenced by Mr. Mitchell.

"All right, now, everyone take a book," Julian called out.

Jonathon came into the room, pushing a library cart full of books. He stopped the cart beside Julian and then proceeded to the back of the room, where he pulled a wide platform out from under a table and placed it in the center of the room. From under that he pulled another platform and placed it on top of the first so that there was a square riser in the middle of the room. Once it was completed, Jonathan tipped his head to Julian and left the room. Suzanne stared at the door from where he left, confused. He hadn't so much as winked at her. What had changed between them?

"Ruby, Lillian, Mary, and Suzanne, you will be first." Julian gestured toward the cart. "You will place a book on your head and walk in a large circle about the room. The book must balance atop your head as you walk up and down these stairs. Do you understand?"

All four women nodded.

"Wonderful. Please come take a book, girls." Julian stepped back so that Ruby, Lillian, Suzanne, and Mary could have access.

Suzanne fell in line behind Mary and was about to pick up her book when someone whispered in her ear, "It's not as easy as it seems."

Lillian had her arms pulled out wide and was already balancing a book on top of her head, her jaw jutted slightly to the left. It was a challenge Suzanne couldn't refuse.

"I can handle anything, don't you worry about me," Suzanne replied.

"Bet you can't keep your book in place the whole rehearsal." Lillian's dark eyes were glistening with competition.

Suzanne followed Lillian's gaze and saw Ruby and Mary struggling to walk up the high steps without jostling the book too much. Every few moments one of them would lift a hand to their head, panicked, to catch the book before it fell to the floor. Jada had made Suzanne walk with a book on her head for days before she premiered her Lady Ann act. This should be simple.

"It can't fall once, not until Julian says we're done." Suzanne amended Lillian's dare.

Lillian's eyes widened a bit, showing the doubt in her mind. But she just said, "Loser buys lunch."

"Deal."

From the corner of her eye, she saw Julian watching them, nodding with approval, but she didn't care. This wasn't about impressing Julian.

With a wave of her arm, she motioned for Lillian to go first. Lillian placed the book on her head and began the long walk up the staircase. Suzanne followed her every move, careful to catch any twitch in her arms. It wasn't until Lillian reached the top platform and was about to come back down did she fumble. Forgetting to keep her eyes straight ahead of her, she glanced down at the stairs and the book slid straight off her head and hit Mary's back, causing her to drop her book. The loud thud as the books hit the ground echoed throughout the theater. Suzanne couldn't help but allow a smirk to tug at her mouth. Regaining her composure, Lillian placed the book back on her head and walked the rest of the circle without any more trouble.

Suzanne reached the top platform and glanced across the circle at Lillian. She glanced around the room at the remaining girls until her eyes landed on Laura, who was sitting by herself watching them. Once their eyes locked, Laura's face lit up and she gave Suzanne an encouraging nod. Using Laura as her visual focus, Suzanne stepped on the stairs. She held her stomach in, as if she were doing multiple pirouettes, and concentrated on keeping her neck long and her head relaxed. A moment later her foot landed on solid wood floor. She turned slowly around to give Lillian a knowing smile, but nearly jolted when she saw Jonathon standing next to Julian, both of them watching her. When had he returned to the room? Their eyes locked for a brief moment, but Suzanne forced herself to pull away and flash Julian Mitchell a dazzling smile. Two could play hard to get.

Meeting his eyes, she was surprised to see him staring at her intently. Without thinking, she put one foot behind the other leg and lowered herself in a deep curtsy, keeping eye contact with the director the entire time. He nodded as she stood up and continued to follow Ruby around the circle—all with the book neatly atop her head. From the corner of her eye she saw Jonathon lean against the back door, still watching her intently. That amused smirk still tugged at his mouth.

"Very well, ladies, I've seen enough. Let's try Laura, Emmaline, Claudine, and Charlotte."

Suzanne handed her book to Laura and grinned. "Just don't look down and you'll do great."

"Show off," Lillian whispered. Suzanne's smile turned into a dazzling laugh; she made five trips up and down the steps and not one fumble.

"I can't help it if I'm naturally coordinated." Suzanne meant it as a joke, but Lillian didn't think it was funny. She linked arms with Ruby and moved across the room to sit with some of the other girls, leaving Suzanne to sit alone.

"All right, girls, that's all for today!" the director called out. "Would the following girls please stay onstage: Ruby Booth, Mary Schider, Lillian Darmin, and Suzanne Haskins. The rest of you are free to go home—but such a short rehearsal will rarely come your way twice, so enjoy your time off!"

"This will be fast," the man said. "Ruby, you know what I am going to say."

"Put on some weight?" she asked guiltily.

"Exactly!" he exclaimed. "We want the audience to desire you, not desire to feed you."

"Yes, sir," she said, smiling. "I'll work on that."

"Good. Mary, we'd like you to work on your posture. You dropped your book often, and from what I could see, it was due to a lack of support from your abdomen."

"Yes, sir," Mary promised.

"Now, the four of you impressed me today. Not only did you strive to do your best, but you found ways to push the other girls in your group to be better than they are. That shows leadership skills."

"Thank you, sir," Suzanne and Lillian said.

"Flo is impressed with you as well."

"Mr. Ziegfeld?" Suzanne repeated. "He has been watching me?"

"Yes—why else would Jonathon be here but to check up on rehearsal for Flo? We'd like to have you, Mary, Ruby, and Lillian work together to complete this vision of a rose that Flo has in mind."

Suzanne grinned. Such an honor was worth more time with Lillian. "When do rehearsals start?"

"I'll have Jonathon add the time to your call sheets. Congratulations, ladies. Keep up the good work."

Julian walked away while Mary and Ruby clasped hands, their faces filled with wide smiles. Suzanne nudged Lillian with her shoulder. "If this doesn't warrant a lunch date, I don't know what does."

Lillian nodded curtly. "I couldn't agree more."

"Could I borrow Suzanne a moment?" Jonathon asked, offering his arm to Suzanne.

"Of course." Lillian gladly let Suzanne go. "Shall I meet you in our dressing room?"

Suzanne glanced at Lillian. "Yes, I don't think I'll be long." She accepted Jonathon's arm.

Once Lillian had walked away, Jonathon leaned over to Suzanne and whispered, "Julian or Flo are going to tell you soon, but I wanted to see your face when you heard the news."

"What?"

Jonathon put a finger to his lips and led Suzanne out into the hallway. "After seeing your dedication, outside of your tardiness today, Flo has asked Julian to choreograph an entire production number around you. The Tango of Brazilian Dreams."

Suzanne swayed where she stood. "A whole number around me?"

Jonathon nodded.

"I don't know what to say." It was what she had wanted, a chance to make her mark. But knowing that Flo had requested this specially for her . . . it was too much to handle.

Jonathon put a hand lightly on her back. "Should I not have told you?"

The news slowly sunk into her consciousness. "He is building a whole number around *me!*" She leapt at Jonathon and hugged him.

"Oh!" Jonathon said as he was almost forced to wrap his hands around her as well to stop from falling over. "I'm glad you are happy."

"I should get home. I should find Ann and go celebrate tonight. I believe the Ritz is having another party. I'll send her a note." She stopped. "Oh no. Lillian."

Jonathon smiled at her contagious excitement. "Go to lunch with Lillian. I'll deliver a note to Ann for you and then will come back to drive you home."

"You must have better things to do, Jonathon."

"Better than driving around the next toast of New York?" Jonathon grinned. "I think not."

CHAPTER 15

With a flick of her wrist, Jada broke the thread from the garment she was sewing. She leaned back in the kitchen chair and admired her work. Several times she glanced from the magazine picture she'd stolen from Suzanne's bed stand to the dress in her hands. She had never made anything quite so intricate before. There were four layers of fabric, each overlapping the next and with a different hemline. The bodice had a calla lily embroidered across the neckline. Jada worked hard to replicate the look of the petals, but it wasn't as good as hoped.

Mr. Ziegfeld was taking the show to Boston for an opening run, and Jada knew there would be more parties for Suzanne to attend. Suzanne wanted to be noticed, and Jada hoped this dress would help make that dream come true. Ann's personal tailor was making Suzanne a suit, but Jada knew that she'd need a new gown for the evening events.

"That is beautiful, Jada." Sally admired the gown's silky fabric.

Jada smiled. "Do you really think so? It's a surprise for Suzanne."

"It will look wonderful on her," she promised. She sounded so sure of herself. Jada folded up the magazine sheet and slid it into her pocket. From here she would design by heart.

"Thank you," she said.

"Could I ask a favor of you?" The formal way Sally spoke made Jada give her full attention as she nodded. "Roger is coming to visit this afternoon and Miss Mitzi will be gone. She don't like to have anything improper going on here. Would you mind sittin' with us while he visits?"

"You want me to chaperone you and Roger?" Jada asked. She'd never been anyone's chaperone, not even when Elton courted Suzanne.

"If you wouldn't mind. It's an odd thing to ask, but there isn't anybody else." Sally looked from her hands to Jada's eyes. "I don't want to upset Miss Mitzi."

"What do I have to do?"

Sally laughed. "Nothin' much, don't worry. Just sit with us."

"I can do that for you," Jada said with a smile.

After putting her sewing back in her room, Jada walked down to the sitting room and found Sally sitting on the window seat, staring out intently. If Jada knew how to paint, she would have wanted to capture this moment. The sun came around Sally's frame, shadowing her in rays of hope. Jada stood in the doorway for a long moment before coming into the room and interrupting the peace.

Sally glanced over her shoulder and smiled at

Jada. "Thank you for this, Jada. I know you have better things to do with your afternoon."

"Nothing is better than helping a friend." She sat on the sofa. "How long have you known Roger?"

"I suppose it's been five years now. But only well the last year that we've gotten close. He used to deliver Miss Mitzi's grocery items. That's what he did each morning before the lumber yard to help save for his nightclub."

Jada nodded. "He is a good man."

A soft knock rapped upon the door. Roger had arrived.

Immediately Sally pinched her cheeks and pulled her skirt down in the front. Her frizzy hair was pulled back in a slick braid that was twisted around into an intricate bun at the base of her neck. Her drab servant dress had been replaced by a blue sundress that made the natural pink in her cheeks appear more vibrant. If only Suzanne could see her now, Jada thought, remembering Suzanne's nasty comments about Sally's appearance.

"You look beautiful," Jada said, coming over to place a calming hand on Sally's shoulder.

"Thank you," she said as the doorbell rang. "Could you get that?"

Without another word, Jada walked out of the parlor, into the entryway, and pulled the glass-fronted door open, revealing Roger. He wore a black suit and red bow tie with a bowler hat atop his head. Outside the bar, Roger appeared more mature and yet also younger than he did as the owner. Jada smiled and stepped backward, allowing him to enter the house.

"Hello again, Jada. I'm here to see Sally. Is she available?" he asked crisply.

"She's in the sitting room," Jada replied. With a motion of her hand, she led Roger to his girl. As he stepped into the room, he removed his hat and turned it in his hands.

Sally had positioned herself in front of the fireplace and was examining a bouquet of flowers intently. As they entered the room she turned around and allowed the smallest of smiles to cross her lips. Jada could feel Roger's excited energy fill the room, but Sally did not make a move. Jada watched the two eye each other with admiration. If she ever found a man she was as interested in as Sally was in Roger, she wouldn't be able to act as coyly.

"You look beautiful, Sally," Roger whispered.

"Thank you. I like your hat, is it new?" Sally asked.

Roger nodded and the two stood in awkward silence for a moment. Without all of the activity of the club surrounding them, they were two different people. Jada turned away from them and tried to examine Miss Mitzi's collection of novels. From the corner of her eye she watched as Sally gestured to the sofa. Sally stepped backward and her elbow knocked the corner of the flower vase, sending it to the floor.

"Oh no!" Sally exclaimed. "Clumsy!"

"It didn't have much water in it," Jada said. She knelt to the floor and started collecting the flowers by the stem. "Miss Mitzi will never know."

Roger righted the vase. "I can get new flowers if that would help."

"No need." Jada placed some flowers in the vase. "I'll add new water and it will be as if it never happened."

"I'm so sorry," Sally said again.

"Don't worry. I'll clean this up. You two enjoy your time. Really."

Roger mouthed, "Thank you" to Jada before seating himself on the sofa by the window. Sally paused a moment before joining him.

Sally grinned at Roger. "Imagine meeting someone as special as her here."

Jada's whole body warmed at the compliment. The only other person who gave her such respect was Suzanne. She had to agree with Sally. Never would she expect to meet a kindred spirit here at a boardinghouse.

Jada collected the large pile of discarded leaves in her hand. She moved to throw them into the waste basket when something poked her palm. Looking down, she saw a small, white, rectangular piece of paper mixed in with the leaves. She dropped the leaves in the waste basket and unfolded the small card. When she read what was written on it, she gasped.

Dance with the Nigger and you'll be sorry.
I know the things you don't want shared.

Jada reread the message a few times, letting it sink in. Had these flowers been sent here, or were they some of the bouquets Jada had taken home from the theater. She looked at the pink roses and couldn't remember.

She read the card again.

"Jada?" Sally asked. "Are you ill?"

Shoving the card into her bodice, Jada forced a smile. "No, I'm fine."

Sally smiled and turned back to Roger.

"Hey, do you know when these were delivered?"

Sally took a moment to think before replying. "I think they came on Thursday . . . so three days ago?"

"Ah, thanks."

The pair went back to their conversation as Jada picked up the last bits of leaves. These flowers were delivered the same night Bert was attacked. Could that be a coincidence? No, she thought, that was impossible. Suzanne couldn't have angered someone so quickly.

Jada walked over to the window seat and

settled herself onto the edge. The morning paper was laid out there haphazardly, and Jada picked up a section, trying to give Sally and Roger some amount of privacy and herself space to think.

On cue, the couple turned to one another and began speaking in low voices. Out of duty, Jada kept them in her sight, but she need not have bothered. Roger was more than content to sit holding Sally's hand while they discussed the latest movies or politics. Jada could hardly keep a smile off her face as she watched them. Every young couple should be so content.

Giving up her vigilance, Jada leaned back against the wall and looked out the window at the street. There was something very soothing about watching people walk back and forth in front of the window. As she followed a young boy and his mother's quick run to the building next door, a black Model T automobile slowed to a stop in front of the house.

Jada sat up a bit straighter as Jonathon opened the door and escorted Suzanne to the curb. After adjusting her armful of packages, she took his arm and the two walked toward the house together. Jada's mouth fell open. Had Suzanne mentioned socializing with Jonathon?

"I'll return in a moment," she said as she hastily stood up and went to meet them at the door.

"Everything all right?" Sally made a movement like she might join Jada, but Jada silenced her with a wave of her hand. Sally settled back into the sofa next to Roger.

"I'll only be a moment," Jada repeated.

She walked to the entryway just in time to see Jonathon open the door for Suzanne. She crossed her arms and positioned herself such that they could not enter the house without moving her out of the way.

"Jada!" Suzanne said, obviously surprised.

"Suzanne," Jada replied.

"I-I didn't think you'd be here," Suzanne fumbled.

"I'm chaperoning." Jada gestured to the parlor.

Suzanne raised an eyebrow. "You chaperone the help?" She sounded so much like her mother.

"Evening, Jada." Jonathon tipped his hat to her as he piled Suzanne's packages onto a side table.

"Hello, Mr. Franks," she replied.

He returned his attention to Suzanne. "Perhaps I'll see you at the theater tomorrow."

"Perhaps you will," Suzanne replied with a smile.

"Until then." He tipped his head to each of them and exited the building. Suzanne's eyes followed after him until he had climbed into the Model T and was driving down the street.

"Were you ever going to tell me about you and Jonathon?" Jada asked, walking back into the parlor. She had left Sally and Roger alone long enough.

"There isn't anything to tell," Suzanne replied, removing the pin from her hat and setting it on the table in the center of the room. "He offered me a ride home."

"It looked like more." Jada noticed Suzanne's flushed cheeks.

"No, I don't think so." Suzanne shook her head. "He's Flo's assistant. Hardly the type of man I should be seen with."

Jada glanced at Sally and Roger and mouthed, "I'm sorry" to Sally, who just shrugged and returned her attention to Roger.

"And what is in all these packages?" Jada asked, lowering her voice.

"My new skirts and blouses, of course," Suzanne replied. "Oh, and my new gown!"

Jada's heart fell to her feet. "New gown?" she asked.

"I have to look stylish. Ann took me to a shop and we had a few items made for me. Her prices are so reasonable even you'd say so! And I have to have something new to wear in Boston."

Jada thought of the carefully crafted gown hidden in her trunk and swallowed her pride. Her craftsmanship would be nothing compared to the items Ann had picked out.

"I've been working on a few new things for you as well," she admitted.

"Now you don't have to waste your time," Suzanne said cheerily. "You can find more important things to focus on. Isn't it wonderful?" Without another word she collected her packages into her arms and walked up to her room.

Jada's mouth dropped open as she watched her friend sashay away from her.

"I had probably be going," Roger said from the front room. "Jada, thanks for everything."

Jada returned her attention to her friends, who were standing in the doorway. "Anytime."

"I'll see you soon," Roger whispered to Sally, and he kissed her cheek. Then, nodding his respect to Jada, he let himself out the front door.

"Why didn't you tell her?" Sally asked. " 'Bout your dress."

"She would still wear the one Ann chose," Jada explained. "She's happy. That's what matters."

Sally didn't have a clever retort. Instead, she stood in silence as Jada walked upstairs to her room.

CHAPTER 16

"The Williams rehearsal starts at three this afternoon," Suzanne said as she walked down Forty-fourth Street while reading her call sheet. "Can you slip into the balcony and watch it?"

"It would be easier to observe from the stage," Jada explained. "I may not get all the small details that Julian or Bert wants."

Suzanne bit her lip. There was no easy way to say this. "I don't know if you and Bert should be too close around the other girls. I mean, what if Ruby sees you two and realizes you aren't Spanish? Think of how embarrassing that would be."

"I don't think Ruby notices me unless something is untidy."

"Ruby doesn't mean to be inconsiderate."

"That doesn't make it acceptable."

Suzanne flinched at Jada's words. There was a time when she worked hard to make sure everyone knew how to treat Jada with respect.

"You're right, it doesn't." Suzanne stopped walking. "I will talk to her so she treats you with respect."

Jada held up her hand, stopping Suzanne's train of thought.

"Don't do that. Please. It will only draw attention to me and make her and Lillian hate me more."

An automobile passed them as the wind rustled their skirts.

"No, it won't. And they don't hate you, they just don't see you. Not like I do."

"Suzanne, please. Just don't."

"Very well. I don't like you feeling mistreated."

Jada rolled her eyes and continued to walk. "If you felt that way you wouldn't make me pretend to be someone I am not. My heritage is important to me. It is all I have left connecting me to my folks. It wasn't right of you to ask I put on such a pretense."

An automobile drew closer to the curb and slowed down.

"I should never have lied about you. It makes everything more complicated." Suzanne kicked at a pile of grass as she spoke.

Jada rolled her eyes. "Of course you realize that now."

The automobile pulled over at the end of the block. A gentleman stepped out and took off his hat.

"Well, fancy meeting you here." Mr. Masterson grinned at Suzanne. "My beautiful Ziegfeld girl."

Suzanne flushed and stepped in front of Jada, effectively cutting her out of the conversation. If anything would upset Jada more, it would be Craig Masterson. He was everything she despised in men: arrogant, pretentious, and scandalous. Under all of that, Suzanne saw a charm that she hoped to draw out. Perhaps the rumors were wrong about him and he wasn't looking simply to "bag a Ziegfeld girl." No matter what, who she spent time with was her affair. Jada didn't need to comment on her choice in gentlemen callers.

"Hello, Mr. Masterson." She stood a little straighter. Inwardly she squirmed. She never worked this hard to impress men back home, why was she for this person?

"May I escort you to the theater?" He held out his arm for her to accept.

"How'd he know where we are going?" Jada whispered from behind.

Mr. Masterson looked over Suzanne's shoulder at Jada with a look of disdain. "I make it my business to know such things." His tone was dismissive. "Shall we, Suzanne?"

The gallantry and power he exuded were too much to ignore. A thrill vibrated through Suzanne's body. She couldn't turn her back on such a reaction. A tall, rich gentleman was interested in her. She had to see where this led. Hopefully Jada would understand. They would finish their conversation another time.

"Thank you, Mr. Masterson," she said coyly. To make herself feel important, she added, "That will be all, Jada. I'll see you this afternoon."

Something was almost audible from Jada before she said, "Thank you, Suzanne."

Suzanne wondered if she should feel guilty, but Jada deserved the morning off. She was really doing her friend a kindness. Even knowing that, she couldn't bring herself to look over her shoulder at her friend. She knew there would be hurt in her eyes. Instead, she looked up at her escort.

"Meet us at the New Amsterdam, Frank," Craig directed his driver. He took her hand in his and said, "Knowing you girls, the walk will warm you up for rehearsal."

It took a lot to keep the disappointment from her face. Arriving in Craig Masterson's automobile would have been quite a coup. She had already heard the jealous whisperings from the other girls in her mind, but she didn't want to argue with the man. She didn't want him to think she thought about him at all. Instead she looped her arm through his and pointed out a bakery a few storefronts down from them. "Did you know that little bakery has the best muffins? I sometimes stop on my way home from rehearsal."

She glanced over her shoulder to see if Jada was still visible, but her friend had already turned a corner and was out of view. They passed the bakery without comment from Craig, despite her gushing about their quality.

"I must admit," Craig said. "You made quite an

impression on me. I've barely been able to think of anyone else since we met."

Suzanne laughed. "It wasn't intentional, I assure you." How exciting to captivate such a man!

Mr. Masterson stopped in front of a billboard outside the theater. The sheet promoted the 1914 Follies by showcasing Ann Pennington and Bert Williams, as well as a chorus of beauties. He tapped along the headlining performers. "Your name belongs here."

"Thank you." Suzanne stared at Ann's name. "But there are many girls, and we all have talent."

Craig's dark brown eyes looked down at Suzanne. "But none of the others sparkle like you when they move."

Suzanne couldn't put her finger on it, but there was something about the way Craig looked at her and the grin that tugged at his lips that made her feel exposed. As if one blink from the man could unravel the thread that held the dress fabric together. Warmth flooded Suzanne's body from her toes up. Perhaps she shouldn't have sent Jada away.

Craig stepped into a small alcove beside a tailor's shop and leaned against the wall. Suzanne stood beside him, her arm still linked with his. They were very close suddenly. Suzanne placed her hand on his chest to keep a set distance between them. This was beyond scandalous, this felt improper.

His hand moved so that it was around her waist. Her stomach flipped in a warning motion of excitement. Men and women passed by them on the street, with more than a few giving them a raised eyebrow of surprise and a disappointed shake of their head. No one stopped to ask if she was all right.

"Flo won't appreciate my tardiness, no matter how well I move," Suzanne said. She intended to be firm, but jovial, but once spoken her words sounded flirtatious.

"Tell him you were with me." He smiled. "Flo will understand."

"No, Mr. Masterson. Flo does not tolerate *any* tardiness." Suzanne pressed her hand against her chest, trying to keep the distance between them. Today of all days she had to be on time. She held out her other hand for a handshake. "Until we meet again?"

Instead of shaking her hand, Mr. Masterson leaned over and pressed his lips against Suzanne's long fingers. "I'll be sure it won't be long."

Oh my! If Jada had seen him, Suzanne would've had an earful. She promised herself to keep this private. They chose to join the Follies. Letting dashing millionaires court her was one of the perks that Suzanne intended on enjoying.

He led her out of the alcove and down the alley toward the back entrance of the theater. The small staircase was empty. In a short while it would be busy with girls arriving for rehearsal and caterers arriving with food.

"Thank you for the walk." Suzanne oozed polite formality.

Craig winked and held the stage door open for Suzanne. "The pleasure was all mine," he said.

She slipped inside before he could say anything else. The door shut behind her and she leaned against the wall, taking a deep breath. Next time she'd either insist on being driven or she'd keep Jada with her. Now that Craig was gone, she wished she hadn't dismissed Jada for the day. What had she been thinking? She needed her eyes for the new choreography. Craig Masterton was not worth all that.

Echoes of raised voices came down the hallway.

"Francine, please!" Jonathon exclaimed. "You can't leave the show!"

Suzanne ducked into a narrow alcove. Francine had barely spoken two words to her since rehearsals began, the last thing she needed was to interrupt something she shouldn't. She got the impression that Francine was very private. She had been rumored to be up for a solo number, but never heard past that. Suzanne pushed herself as far into the alcove as she could squeeze and waited for them to pass her by.

"Jonathon, enough. I have never been so ill-treated." Francine stopped and turned to

212

face Jonathon. Her skirts brushed the edge of Suzanne's, but she didn't notice.

"Ill-treated?" Jonathon looked baffled. "We haven't even finished casting the show. There are at least two numbers we've yet to cast. Flo has many plans for your beauty."

Francine snorted. "As if that matters! I will not stay somewhere I am not wanted, no matter the part. Please tell Flo good-bye for me." Her words were soft, but her cheeks flushed with emotion.

"But you are an asset to our production!"

Suzanne pressed herself against the wall as Francine reached into her handbag and pulled out a clump of papers.

"Well, someone doesn't want me here," she hissed. "And I am not about to find out who." She threw the papers at Jonathon and stomped out of the building.

Jonathon bent over and picked up the crumpled mess. The small bits of paper had landed all over the floor. A few were mere inches from Suzanne's dress. She would surely be found any moment. He reached toward her and, instead of letting him discover her, she knelt down and handed him the few pieces near her.

"Suzanne!" he jumped back. "How long have you been standing there?"

"I heard you arguing with Francine and had only just come inside. I didn't want to get in the middle of anything."

Jonathon pocketed the paper he had picked up. "That is probably for the best."

"What sparked that?" she asked.

Jonathon thought for a moment. "I don't know. She came to Flo's office to say she's leaving. I tried to convince her to stay, but you saw what happened."

Suzanne picked up one of the papers and smoothed it out. She glanced at the scrawled words.

"What is it?" Jonathon stood and read the paper. Instantly they opened other sheets she'd thrown.

"They are all the same," Jonathon said.

"No wonder she left. These are horrible. *'You are an abomination to women everywhere.'* Who would say that of Francine?"

She read through the notes in her hand:

One false move and you'll be sorry.

Dance your life away, dear Francine.

The time has come for you to die.

Leave the Follies or you'll be sorry.

"None of them are signed." Jonathon turned the papers over.

"No one would sign such notes," Suzanne

scoffed. "But these alone aren't enough to make her leave the show."

"Something more must be happening," Jonathon said.

The stage door opened and Ruby stepped inside. Despite the heat, her face was pale and her blouse wasn't fitting well. Many girls lost weight during the stress of rehearsal, but Ruby was already so small it was disconcerting. Ruby stared at the pile of notes that covered the floor and her face went even paler.

"What is this?"

"It's nothing," Jonathon said. "I just spilled some garbage."

Ruby looked to Suzanne and then walked quickly past them.

"Great, I've lost my advantage of being early." Suzanne handed Jonathon the notes she picked up. "I've got to go."

Jonathon took Suzanne's hand for a moment. "Please don't tell anyone about this."

"Of course," she agreed. "It would only upset the other girls."

Rehearsal, if you could call it that, had been dull. Not what you'd expect from performing with a great comedian. Bert barely spoke. He sat in the audience and watched as Leon and Julian placed the girls in different positions to get a feel of how to balance the stage. They were representing a forest while Bert and Ann sang about life at a ball. In the middle of the number they would come alive and move around Ann and Bert to symbolize the frivolity of love. At the end of two hours, Julian declared, "Thanks for your time, girls. Suzanne, you look pale, get some rest. And, Ruby, try to eat more."

Ruby and Suzanne walked back to their room in a silent buzz of fatigue. The dressing room was quiet. Jada stood to one side, collecting the strewn garments Ruby and Lillian shed. She hardly looked up when Suzanne entered. A wave of guilt hit Suzanne and she was frozen for a moment. This was not what she meant when she told Jada she'd see her later. She didn't want her cleaning up after Lillian and Ruby all day.

"Jada . . ." Suzanne started to say, but when Lillian looked up she didn't know how to finish.

"I was there, just like I promised," Jada said as she hung up a blouse.

Lillian cleared her throat. "I think I've been in the wrong. I am sorry if I made either of you feel bad about the Williams number. I will try to be happy for you from now on. We should all be supportive of one another."

Jada turned toward Lillian, a look of surprise on her face. Suzanne rubbed some lotion into her skin as she asked, "What brought this apology on?"

"It's just, Ruby is my friend and I should be

supportive of her. And while I don't know that I like you, we share a room and I'd rather not have you as an enemy, or have you thinking that way of me. Ruby deserves better than what I've been doing."

Lillian turned, clearly expecting Ruby to say something in response, but she was silent. A small bouquet sat on the table in front of her, the card in her hand.

"What's wrong?" Suzanne asked as a slight dread filled her stomach. She gave Jada her blouse to hang up.

Lillian laughed. "Didn't you tell Joe to stop sending you flowers?"

Ruby still didn't reply. Casually, Jada passed behind her and glanced at the card.

"Suzanne," she said instantly. "Suzanne, the card."

Before Ruby could toss the slip of paper, Suzanne took it from her hand.

She read aloud: *"One more move like today and you'll be dead. Eat up, dear."*

Lillian dropped her powder puff. "What on earth?"

Just like with Francine's the note wasn't signed. Suzanne looked on both sides. "Do you know who sent this?"

Ruby shook her head, refusing to look up. "It came with this." She handed Lillian a box from her vanity. Lillian lifted the lid to reveal a small assortment of chocolates each painted with a different design. As the overly sweet scent filled the room, Lillian went to her friend and hugged her.

"This is so wrong," Lillian said. "You are beautiful just as you are."

"Is this the first card?" Suzanne asked.

Jada met Suzanne's eyes and shook her head. When Ruby didn't reply, Suzanne asked, "What do you know, Jada?"

"There have been at least two others."

"Two?" Lillian gasped. "Why did you tell her and not me?"

"I didn't," Ruby said.

"I found them while cleaning." Jada gestured around the room.

"And you never said anything?" Lillian's tone was accusatory.

"Who would write such awful words?" Jada's question hung unanswered.

Lillian plucked the card from Suzanne's hand and stared at it.

Ruby's shoulders slumped. "I don't know. Who cares that much about me? I'm nobody here."

"That is not true," Lillian said. She dropped the card on the table. "You're a Ziegfeld girl!"

Ruby snorted. "If I can't gain weight I may not be for long."

"That's it!" Suzanne snapped her fingers in excitement.

Jada took the card and read it again. "Yes, whoever sent this must have been onstage when Julian spoke with you about Bert's number. 'Eat up, dear.' Your declining figure was his only criticism."

"You think someone from the company did this?" Ruby asked. "Who hates me so much they want to scare me?"

Lillian's face flushed as Ruby wiped a tear away. "Ruby is upset. Let's do tea another day."

"No," Suzanne decided. "Julian told you to gain weight and we shall help."

"I agree," Lillian said. She slipped her arms into a violet blouse. "An early dinner and then early to bed. Whoever this is won't ruin you."

"Thanks." Ruby's voice sounded as small as she was.

As her roommates got dressed, Suzanne stepped over to Jada's side. Jada held out the jacket to her suit and Suzanne slid her arms into the sleeves.

"There were truly others?" she asked in a low tone.

"Not as strange, but yes. And perhaps more." Jada shook her head. "She is sweet and hardly a threat. Why her?"

"I don't know."

Jada took Suzanne's hand. "Suzanne," she said, then faltered. "She isn't the only one who has gotten notes."

"I know. Francine left the show this morning.

219

She received so many notes that she couldn't take it. They drove her out."

"What?" Jada asked.

"Francine. She's really quiet. Big brown eyes. She left the company over stunts like this."

"Is that their goal? To push girls out of the Follies? That takes a lot of emotion. There are a few girls with that kind of jealousy."

Suzanne locked eyes with Lillian's as she helped Ruby button up her skirt. There were a few people jealous enough to hurt Ruby. A few people who wanted special treatment enough to torment someone out of the show. Given Lillian's history and her sudden role reversal, Suzanne wondered if Lillian could be one of them.

CHAPTER 17

The note was still sitting on Ruby's vanity. Jada pocketed it and finished cleaning the room. Suzanne and the others had gone to dinner. The box of chocolates was left behind untouched on the vanity. Jada sniffed them and shuddered at the sweet scent. When combined with the card, the threat seemed too real. She had to tell someone. Someone who might be able to do something to help Ruby. She glanced at the clock. It was barely five. Perhaps Jonathon was still working. Would Jonathon take these notes as seriously as she did?

Don't be such a ninny, she instructed herself. *Jonathon wants to know why girls are leaving. He'll thank you for the information.*

Jada peered into the hallway. To her relief it was completely empty. The others must've bolted just like Suzanne. An evening of fun after a day of work. Jada's thoughts floated to Harlem. If she had a choice, she'd be back there listening to good music and laughing with Sally. Had the note not been pressed into her palm, she may have run off right then. But this was more important.

The door to the stage was open. She slid through, half hoping to hear voices. Instead, she felt her way through discarded set pieces and assorted hanging ropes and pulleys until she found herself on the stage. The lights still blazed life into the space, but it was empty. The wood gleamed beneath her feet and the rows of empty chairs beckoned her.

Her hand rested on the velvet trim of the curtain. Pulling back the curtain, she peered around into the house. Although the lights were on, she was still able to see back to the top of the balcony. The vines and wreath details of each box seat nearly reached out to Jada, inviting her to perform for them especially. The cream ceiling with its Greek-inspired details gave the theater an even brighter appearance than a normal theater. Small grapes climbed up the walls and highlighted the stage shape as well. Jada had never seen such decadence in a theater's décor. Despite her best efforts, jealousy nudged at her stomach.

You'll just tell them Suzanne said to meet you, Jada promised herself. Thoughts of finding Jonathon fell from her mind.

She took a few steps over the wooden floor until she was far enough onto the stage she had to drop the curtain from her hand. The warmth of the stage lights were fuel for her soul. She stood for a minute bathing in that warmth, before walking to the center of the stage.

As she and Suzanne had done as young children, she glanced down to where the conductor would be standing and nodded her head as if telling him she was ready to perform. That afternoon she had watched Julian and Suzanne start working on the tango number that would close act one. It had potential to be the best number in the show. It was Suzanne's number, but Jada knew she could perform it without any direction. With grace, she rose to her toes and swung and dipped herself across the stage. Her arms did not exude as much strength as Suzanne's, nor did she express enough confidence to become the smoldering temptress who Suzanne tried to emulate in her dance. But the fluidity of her moves and the smile on her face made her feel beautiful.

After performing Suzanne's number, she stood in the far right corner of the stage, working to catch her breath. The stage was so large she felt like an ant in a lush green field. Over and over she ran to the far stage left corner and ran across the stage to the front stage right making a grand leap in the middle of the stage. She felt her legs extend to the point that her skirt's slit tore to accommodate her extension.

Turning back to the center of the stage, she inhaled deeply. The smell of grease paint and velvet seats filled her nostrils. Without thinking, she cocked her hip out and rolled it over to the other side.

"Dat Jim Crow. He don't know nottin'." She used her strongest coon accent. "Says no darkie is going to dance again. I be showin' him wrong."

She placed her feet in fourth position, lifted up, and turned around in a complete circle, not lifting a single toe. Letting her body flow in the pattern she knew too well from watching rehearsal, she took three steps forward before lifting up again and turning around in a pirouette.

She was going to continue, when she heard the distinctive sound of one of the house seats snapping back into its upright position.

She froze.

Her eyes scanned the audience for the offending spy, but the air felt as still as if no one stood in it. No new shadows appeared, no footsteps sounded or doors opened. It wasn't until a figure appeared in the far aisle that Jada was positive she had heard anything. As the man stepped farther toward the stage, Jada realized why he had blended into the shadows so well; it was Bert.

He had sat in silence, watching Jada perform. She had to know what he thought of her.

" 'Lo," he said once his foot landed on the wooden stage.

"Hello," Jada replied.

"So you can dance as well as mend cuts."

Jada grinned back at the compliment. "How is your shoulder?"

Bert rolled his shoulder back. "Almost healed."

Jada came to the front of the stage beside him.

"It looks good. Why were you sitting in the house?"

Bert rubbed his neck. "I like to sit out there and imagine what the different numbers will look like onstage. Something is missing from my number with Ann. The girls add a nice element, but it isn't how we thought it would look."

Jada looked down at the man. "Maybe it just needs time. You only started rehearsal."

"Perhaps. What are you doing dancing across the stage, Jada?"

Jada felt heat pulse throughout her body as if searching for an excuse. It would've been so simple to say that she was waiting for Suzanne, but she couldn't bring herself to lie to Bert Williams. Instead, despite all better judgment, she told him the truth.

"Rehearsal was out early and the theater was empty. I didn't think anyone would mind if I took a turn or two across the stage." She shrugged, and added, "You won't tell anyone, will you?"

Bert shook his head. "It'll be our secret." He winked.

The two stood at the corner of the stage in silence for a moment. Jada smoothed her skirt down in the front as she tried to find something interesting to say.

Bert walked upstage. "Your friend and Ann are good friends. She's caught Flo's attention. You must be pleased for her."

Jada nodded. "Thank you for allowing her to dance with you. I never thought she'd have such luck her first year."

"We both know that my choices were limited." Bert stiffened. "I won't force anyone into an uncomfortable situation."

"Oh." Jada glanced out into the back of the audience. Opening night, all those white faces would be looking at Bert. The stage suddenly felt very large and lonely.

This melancholy man was not the same man she saw onstage, nor the man who asked her to dance for him. As the silence grew, Jada suspected that this was the true Bert, the one behind the stage persona. As that dawned on her, it suddenly felt too personal to stand so close to him. Too awkward to try to discuss Suzanne or anything about the Follies with him.

"Do you know where Jonathon is?" she asked.

Bert shrugged. "If he isn't outside Flo's office, he's probably gone home for the night. I hear there are some parties tonight. I suspect he may be invited to those."

"I'll look for him at the office then," Jada said.

"Jada? I don't know you well, but I know what Sally and Roger say, and they don't lie. I'm usually the last to rehearse here at night. My offer is always open."

"I will think about it," Jada promised. "But now, I should go see Jonathon."

Jada left Bert sitting on the stage, looking out over the empty seats, quite alone in his thoughts.

Mr. Ziegfeld's office was a few flights up, above the theater. Jada stopped at the top of the stairwell to collect herself. Jonathon might be upset that she had held this information back for so long, but she couldn't correct the past. Only move forward in the future. She made her way down the hall to the grand office.

"Mr. Franks?" she called out as she stepped into the room.

The fire was still blazing in the fireplace and papers were strewn across Jonathon's desk. Jada stood in the center of the room, wondering where the gentlemen was and how long she should wait for him before it became improper.

"We are leaving in a week for Boston. These arrangements should have been done by now!" Ziegfeld's voice carried from down the hall.

Oh no, thought Jada. *I don't want to be caught in the middle of a disagreement.*

"Of course, sir. I won't leave until they are complete. Travel, hotel, and theater arrangements will be double-checked and complete. Do not worry, sir."

The out-of-town trial was starting so quickly. Jada had her own preparations to make for Suzanne.

The two men entered the front part of the office. Mr. Ziegfeld glanced at Jada before walking into his office without a word. Jonathon dashed behind his desk and started sorting papers.

"Hello, Jada." Jonathon's head didn't look up from his work.

"Hello," Jada said. "You said you were available if I were to need help." She clenched the note in her pocket.

Jonathon stopped what he was doing and looked at her. "I did. What's happened?"

She pulled out the note and handed it to him. "Ruby and Suzanne have been receiving notes like this since rehearsals started."

"Notes?" Jonathon raised his eyebrows. "You think people are leaving the Follies . . . the Ziegfeld Follies over some notes?"

"It isn't just notes. Someone sent Ruby chocolates, possibly poisoned."

"Possibly poisoned?" Jonathon shifted in his chair.

"Look, here is the note that accompanied the chocolates. 'Eat up'? It is a threat that implies poison, if nothing else." She swallowed. "I threw them away just in case."

Jonathon reread the note. "How could something so short cause so much fear?"

Frustrated, Jada walked around the room. "When you put it like that it sounds silly, but you didn't see Ruby's face when these cards came."

"No, I didn't." Jonathon rested his head on the back of his chair for a moment before getting up.

"Suzanne told me about Francine. I don't want to see Ruby leave too."

"We agreed that the notes were not what pushed Francine over the edge. These notes were not enough."

Suzanne hadn't mentioned that when she and Jada spoke. That did change the perspective. Jada couldn't think of anything to say.

"I am very behind in making plans for our Boston opening and even if I had the time, I'm not sure where to start looking for an answer to this problem."

"I beg to differ," Jada said, hoping he would listen. "Whoever is sending these cards is a part of the theater. They reference things that happen onstage. Ruby was told to eat more by Julian today and not an hour later those chocolates were in her dressing room. Suzanne was given a part with Bert and soon after was sent a card saying not to dance with that . . . with Bert. This person is in the company."

"In the company? That feels like a large leap. Look at Ruby, anyone can see she needs to eat more. And many people knew about Suzanne's promotion. I think it might have been in the paper even. I don't think one of our own would scare her friends in such a manner."

"I disagree," Jada stated firmly.

"I really am sorry." Jonathon went back to sorting his papers. "If you find proof of a specific

229

culprit, let me know. Otherwise, I'll keep my eyes and ears open and will have the company manager inspect deliveries from now on so more girls aren't upset by this mess."

"I really think it could be one of the girls. Suzanne agrees."

Jonathon clenched his hands into a fist. "I told you what I thought. I have a lot of work to do. Please, Jada. Another time."

Jada sighed. "Very well, thank you for your time." She did a poor job of masking the bitterness in her words.

CHAPTER 18

Trying to slip out of Miss Mitzi's boardinghouse unnoticed was like walking through a den of wolves. No matter what time Suzanne went down for breakfast, Miss Mitzi was always there, waiting to accost her about her celebration tea. With the trip to Boston less than a week away, she was now calling it an opening night celebration. It seemed she was hell-bent on having a houseful of Ziegfeld girls, and nothing Suzanne said changed her mind.

Suzanne had come in so late from the party at Mary's house that she'd hardly slept at all. But it was their first production rehearsal and she wanted to be the first at the theater if possible. Jada didn't stir as Suzanne picked up her shoes and slipped out of the room. Ever since they discovered the threats against Ruby, Jada had been in a bad mood. She kept starting conversations with Suzanne, only to end in the middle of sentences and then sulk. Suzanne was perfectly happy to leave her behind.

As she came down the staircase, she found most of the floor was still dark. The only light came from the kitchen. Even a conversation with Miss Mitzi was worth the toast and oranges she knew awaited her in the kitchen. She hadn't planned on stopping a moment before she was handed her food, but when she heard her name spoken, she paused to listen.

"But she only holds back because of Suzanne. If it wasn't for her, Jada might be auditioning for Ziegfeld right now!" Sally whined.

Of all the remarks Suzanne could've imagined, Jada auditioning for Flo was the farthest from her imagination. What had Jada been telling Sally about their theater life? Surely she'd never met Ziegfeld; even Suzanne had only spoken with him a handful of times and she was in the theater every day. Yet, she'd never known Jada to tell a lie.

"It doesn't pay to meddle in other people's relationships, Sally," Miss Mitzi said through the sounds of shuffling coals. "Jada made her choice and you should respect that."

"But it was Bert Williams! How can she keep working for that Suzanne girl when Bert keeps throwing possibility in her face?" Sally slammed something on the table. "This is her dream, why is she pushing it away?"

Miss Mitzi clucked her tongue. "Just because she can do it well doesn't mean she dreams of being on the stage. Maybe she is happy with Suzanne."

Sally snorted.

Suzanne leaned against the wall and tried to absorb all she heard. Jada had met Bert Williams and hadn't told her. It should have been her introducing Bert and Jada. Suzanne clenched her fists in frustration with herself. If Sally was right and Jada had given up the chance to dance with Bert Williams, Suzanne would have to find some way to thank her.

With that thought, Suzanne walked straight into the kitchen, purposefully interrupting their conversation. If anything else had happened to Jada, she didn't want it pressing on her mind.

"Good morning," she said. She hoped no one noticed how her voice trembled.

"Good morning, Suzanne." Miss Mitzi sounded warm and inviting. Sally, however, took one look at Suzanne and clomped out of the room muttering something about laundry. "Don't you mind her. She gets irritable easy."

Suzanne watched Sally go before asking, "Is there any toast made yet? I have an early call this morning."

Miss Mitzi lifted the cover from one of the baskets on the small table revealing a pile of freshly warmed bread. Suzanne immediately lunged forward and grabbed two pieces from the basket and leaned back against her chair as she ate. Her corset dug in uncomfortably, forcing her to sit up a bit straighter. She'd have to adjust the laces once she arrived at the theater. As she adjusted herself, she caught Miss Mitzi raising an eyebrow in her direction.

When Miss Mitzi finished stoking the stove fire, she walked over to the table and sat across from Suzanne. "I'm going to speak plainly to you, Suzanne."

Suzanne swallowed her mouthful of bread before she croaked, "Very well."

"I'm sure you overheard what my Sally was saying before you came into the room; she was speaking too loud for you to have turned a deaf ear. Now, it is none of our business what goes on between you and Jada, but I would like to remind you that she's a good worker and deserves your respect."

Suzanne's mouth went dry at the woman's words. Her heart beating in her ears, she wet her lips before she replied. "You're right. This is none of your business. My relationship with Jada is not for you to understand or to judge."

Immediately, she jumped up from her seat, grabbed an apple, and headed toward the door. Before she got there, Miss Mitzi grasped her arm. It was the kindness in her touch that made Suzanne turn around and look at her accuser.

"Suzanne. No one questions that you care for Jada. That is evident in how you are with each other. I know how busy your life can be and wanted to make sure that you remember that Jada has talent beyond washing clothes." Miss Mitzi's brown eyes bore into Suzanne.

"I can't let her . . . I need her."

Miss Mitzi's mouth fell open in surprise at the compassion in Suzanne's words, but before she could say anything Suzanne pulled her arm away and was running toward the front door.

Even with her brief delay at breakfast, Suzanne was one of the first people on the stage that morning. Although she walked across the stage nearly every day, it looked larger that morning. Perhaps it was because they were finally going to be performing on the stage, or it was because the houselights were all on, revealing how deep the seating actually went.

Suzanne shook the impending stage fright from her mind and sat in the center of the stage and began her stretches. In the past few days she had made an intense routine for herself and had the tendency to get lost in the movement. She breathed in the smell of dust and grease paint and let the red velvet chairs fade together into one large red mass as she focused on her body.

The next thing she knew Suzanne was surrounded by her costars and the sound of dozens of voices melding together. Ann was standing in the corner intently talking to Leon Errol and didn't see Suzanne's wave to her. In the back of the balcony Suzanne could see Ziegfeld looking down at all of them. Although she couldn't see any details, she was sure it was Mr. Ziegfeld, as that is where it was said he liked to watch rehearsals. Immediately she opened her legs in a wide split and leaned over them. She had to be more prepared than ever today if Ziegfeld was to be watching them.

"Ruby," Laura whined. "Ruby, give me back my sweater!"

Suzanne turned around and saw Ruby and Lillian tossing a lavender cardigan back and forth over Laura's head. She rolled her eyes at Ruby and Lillian's silliness. Poor Laura!

Pulling herself to her feet, Suzanne walked behind Lillian and pulled the sweater from her hands. "At least try to be mature, Ziegfeld is watching," she hissed as she handed Laura back her sweater.

"Thanks." She held up the sweater before giving Lillian a glare and walking toward the front of the stage.

"Well, la-di-da," Ruby said, still giggling.

"I know," Lillian said.

"You two can be so childish," Suzanne said, trying to hide the annoyance in her voice.

"Give it up, Suzanne. You know it was funny. Laura is almost four inches taller than me and she couldn't get her sweater back. What a joke." Lillian glanced toward where Laura was standing and shrugged.

Suzanne forced a smile on her face and shook her head. "You guys better get warmed up. I expect we'll be starting soon."

Without another word Ruby and Lillian sat on the stage and began stretching their legs out. Suzanne took a few steps away from them and raised her arms above her head, working out a tight spot on her side.

Suzanne glanced up to find Laura and Ann sitting next to her, deep in their own stretches.

"Thanks," Laura said again.

"No problem. You'd have done the same for me," Suzanne replied. "They didn't mean anything by it. They are just immature."

Ann rolled her eyes. "They choose to behave poorly."

Suzanne agreed, but didn't want to discuss them anymore. To Laura she asked, "Do you see your beau often?"

Laura rolled her eyes. "Not as much as others. He is a busy man."

"Oh, I see." Ann giggled. "Is he busy or are you busy?"

"It's always the same thing," Laura replied. "Bottom line is I don't want to be tied down. There are too many men out there."

"Shall we go out tonight and see some of them?" Ann asked.

"Didn't you mention a new hot spot?" Suzanne asked Laura.

"Oh! The Club!"

Ann perked up. "I haven't been there yet. Tonight?"

"Tonight," Suzanne and Laura agreed.

Laura stood up and began her tendus. Suzanne moved closer to Ann to accommodate Laura's long legs.

Julian clomped across the stage. In a few moments the entire theater was silent. He stood before them, his hair greased back in an oddly stiff fashion. Finally he broke the silence.

"Good morning, ladies and gentlemen. I believe we'll start with the Open Rose this morning and then move into the finale."

Laura raised her head. "Are they so early in the show?"

"No," Julian didn't explain further.

"But this was to be a full rehearsal. I thought Bert and Ann started the show."

Julian gave her an exasperated look. "The Rose number has had the least amount of rehearsal and the finale has not been performed without mistakes yet. We will run through those numbers before we start the full rehearsal. Is that to your satisfaction?"

Properly embarrassed, Laura turned from Julian and stalked off the stage. Suzanne tried to catch her eye once she was seated in the audience, but Laura didn't look up once.

Ann nudged Suzanne. "What's wrong with Ruby? She looks awfully pale."

"She probably overpowdered her face or forgot to rouge her lips. She was just playing keep-away from Laura. I'm sure she's fine." Suzanne glanced at Ruby, however. She continued to glance around as if someone was behind her.

Julian clapped his hands. "Clear the stage, people."

Instantly, the girls parted and Ruby, Mary, Lillian, and Suzanne were left alone on the stage. The pianist sat at the piano and readied himself to play. The girls took their places. Suzanne licked her lips. This was it.

Suzanne shifted her posture and raised her arms into fourth position. Lillian was offstage awaiting her and Ruby was behind her. The piano began and Suzanne started her motions. The music was fluid and sensuous, and she felt the audience inhale with the beauty of her movements. Ruby moved from behind and took her hand as Mary burst onstage and took her other. The three moved as one for eight counts until Suzanne dipped back and headed offstage.

But instead of letting go of Suzanne's hand, Ruby made a wild grab to keep grasping tighter and suddenly both Suzanne and Ruby toppled to the ground. Suzanne felt the wooden floor bruise her hip but managed to keep her head from landing on it as well.

Mary stopped dancing and turned to Suzanne on the floor.

"Are you hurt?" Mary asked.

Suzanne sat up and untangled herself from

Ruby. Her hands felt slick and she wiped her hands on the floor, but the feeling wouldn't go away. She looked down and saw a line of grease shine through one of the cracks in the floor. The stage hands must have been working on the stage last night and forgot to clean up. And now the grease was all over her. She glanced at her practice skirt, and sure enough a small yellow stain streaked against her left side. Jada would not enjoy getting that out of the white fabric.

"I'll be fine once I change clothes," she said. "Ruby?"

She turned toward her friend and frowned. Ruby remained on the floor, her arms limp and her leg at an uncomfortable angle. She scowled as she rolled her head toward Suzanne.

"Owww," she moaned.

"Ruby is injured!" Lillian exclaimed as she ran in from the wings.

From the back of the balcony Flo shouted, "Don't move her. Jonathon will bring the car around and take her to the hospital. Jonathon!" He left the balcony in search of his assistant.

Julian and Leon jumped onto the stage and were quickly at their side.

"What on earth happened? We've rehearsed that a dozen times and no one has even so much as tripped."

Ruby moaned again and Lillian grasped her hand. "It will be fine, Ruby."

"I don't know," Suzanne said. "I went to exit and she didn't let go of me. She slid and then pulled me down with her."

Jonathon appeared from the wings. "Was Flo calling me?" he asked. His eyes landed on Ruby. "Oh no." He crossed the stage in a matter of seconds.

Carefully he knelt beside her and cradled her neck and knees in his arms. "Hold on to my neck, Ruby. We are going to get you to a hospital."

Mary glanced between the two girls. "Suzanne fell as well. Should she be looked at too?"

Jonathon stopped and looked back at Suzanne. "Are you injured?"

"Take care of Ruby. I may have a few bruises tomorrow, but I'll recover."

Jonathon looked Suzanne up and down before relenting. "If you are sure."

"I am, go."

"Very well. Hold on to my neck, Ruby."

As Jonathon lifted her from the floor, Ruby shrieked; then in a moment they were gone. Leon looked down at Suzanne and offered her his hand. It had all happened so quickly that Suzanne hadn't even stood up. Her hip was a bit sore from where she fell, but other than that she seemed to be unharmed.

Julian clapped his hands and recalled everyone to his attention. "Jonathon will take good care of Ruby. In the meantime, we need to press on with rehearsal." He waited for his words to sink in. "As I believe we need to lighten the mood, we will preview the new Williams/Errol number. I do not believe anyone here has seen it yet. Please hold all comments until the end."

Suzanne followed the others into the house and took a seat in one of the red velvet chairs. The moment she sat, one of the girls declared, "How scandalous. Think he'll hop off the stage and attack one of us?"

Suzanne's face burned in embarrassment at the comment, but even more so to the giggles that answered it. Suzanne certainly had no interest in taking up with a common Negro, but she had enough sense to know they didn't go into heat like dogs either. She thanked fate that Jada had chosen to stay home that day. Suzanne didn't want to defend her new friends twice in one day. Nor did she want to have Jada and Bert in the same room.

A few moments later a pale Negro with large lips walked onstage to a mix of tepid applause and stoic faces. He nodded to Leon and the two fell into their skit. Bert's entire demeanor changed from the gentleman who had first walked in to the stance of an uneducated coon. The comedy was not her taste, but Suzanne could not stop laughing nor take her eyes off of him.

Julian didn't even wait for the applause to end before he walked to the couple and began giving them his critique. In the midst of their discussion a secretary burst into the theater with a folded piece of paper in her hand, which she handed to Julian. The room became silent as he read the brief note. Suzanne was certain that every girl noticed how his shoulders slumped.

He passed the paper to Leon before standing up and facing the house. "As it is clear Ruby has an injury that might keep her out of the show for some time, we are going to choose another dancer to learn her part. Please take a five-minute break while we discuss this."

After he finished his announcement, the girls all stood up and moved into groups to talk or stretch. Suzanne moved closer to Lillian's group, but her concentration was on the stage. Leon and Julian were standing in a tight circle, whispering to one another. Suzanne was sure they were batting around names for the replacement. That thought was confirmed when Mr. Ziegfeld came down from the balcony and joined their circle.

"After brief debate we are going to have Lillian step into Ruby's part. Marie, you will step up as an alternate just in case."

"The three of you should go downstairs and get Lillian up to speed," Leon said. "I'll be down in a bit to work with you."

Julian clapped his hands. "Very well. Let's get back to work."

CHAPTER 19

With Ruby in the hospital, Jada expected Jonathon to come asking about the notes she'd mentioned, but he didn't seek her out.

Lillian and Suzanne were spending another evening rehearsing with Laura, hoping to get her up to snuff before they traveled to Boston. Jada had not been asked to attend. Most of the house staff was out finishing errands before the evening meal needed to be served. Jada had no errands to run and no chores to finish. She was seated in her favorite spot: the rocking chair in the front parlor. Beside her the clock ticked its way past five PM. Five-thirty was quickly approaching. Given the rehearsal time Bert mentioned, Jada knew five-thirty was the latest she could leave for the theater without missing her chance. Soon she would have to decide—meet with Bert or not. If she wasn't needed, why shouldn't she pursue her own dreams?

A stab of guilt hit Jada. Suzanne gave up her life to help Jada—needed or not, loyalty belonged with Suzanne. If not for her, Suzanne would be married and content in Richmond. She'd still speak to her parents and she'd have the life she grew up wanting.

Sally walked up the front steps with a basket

of bread on one arm. She opened the door and came directly into the parlor. "You still here?" she asked.

Jada blinked and looked from the window to her friend. "I don't know if I should go."

"We've talked about this. Don't give up." Sally put her basket on the couch and picked up the dishes left haphazardly on the side table. "This is your chance, girl. Bert William wants to see *you* dance. What is holding you back?"

Jada stood and helped Sally stack the dishes on top of the large serving plate. "I just don't know if it is the right thing to do. Suzanne—"

"Don't you go talking about loyalty to Suzanne again. Whatever happened, she don't need you now. She's got us to clean her room and mend her clothes, a slew of friends at the theater and directors for dancing help. You should meet Bert before you begin to feel as useless as you are."

Jada took the plate and walked back into the kitchen.

Sally followed. "You need to do this," she repeated.

Jada thought about that big stage and her stomach burst with excited butterflies. Meeting with Bert would be worth it just to dance across that stage again.

"It is just a dance. It doesn't mean anything will happen." She set the tray on the sink and turned to Sally. "I'm going."

Sally nearly jumped up and down with excitement. "Yes!"

Jada slipped into the theater through the house doors to avoid seeing any of the girls leaving rehearsal. Although she hadn't really thought of what she expected to find in the theater, it wasn't the comedy duo knee-deep in their act. If anything, she'd hoped for a bit of time to collect herself before approaching them. Only the door closing behind her propelled her to completely enter the theater.

For a moment she stood by the back row of chairs watching the two men clown about onstage. Bert's pale lips were outlined with his burnt cork makeup, and Leon Errol was pasty white with painted rosy cheeks; it made Jada smile just to look at them.

Leon was pantomiming restocking a store and Bert, playing the ignorant coon, stood behind him asking questions. They weren't projecting, so Jada didn't hear every word, but Leon's character showed his frustration so clearly, Jada soon found herself laughing out loud anyway.

"Who dat laughin'?" Bert called out in his coon accent. Breaking character, he squinted and looked out under the houselights.

She summoned extra confidence and walked down the aisle and out of the shadows of the balcony. "It's only me," she called out. "Jada."

"Jada?" Leon raised an eyebrow at Bert.

"You came." He practically bounced with excitement. "Come on up here."

"With both of you?" Jada asked, tentatively approaching the stage.

"I don't bite," Leon promised. His makeup made him look like a very old baby doll.

Bert reached out a hand and helped Jada up the stairs and onto the stage.

"So you're the talented girl Bert's been bragging about." Leon grinned. "I was beginning to think you didn't exist. Had I known it was Suzanne's girl, I'd have gotten you up here sooner."

"Well, she's here now in the flesh." Bert's smile went from ear to ear.

"Let's see what you can do," Leon said, walking to the edge of the stage, then squatting down so he was looking up at her.

She glanced from Bert to Leon, waiting for one of them to give her instruction or some detail on what they'd like her to perform. When neither of them flinched, she turned to Bert and asked, "What should I do?"

"Can you cakewalk?"

Jada smiled. Instead of answering, she loosened her body with one quick shake of her limbs. She stepped into the syncopated two-step that mimicked the movements of formal dances. Mama had taught her the movements when Suzanne wouldn't teach Jada "proper" dances.

"All dancing is, is putting movement to music," Mama explained. Jada had thought it the most marvelous thing ever created.

Bert stood back and watched her for a moment, but before Jada could worry if he liked her interpretation, he clapped his hand and joined in with her. His legs were like rubber as they flung themselves inside and out. It was hypnotizing to watch. Only his occasional clap or holler reminded her to keep dancing herself.

As Bert and Jada fell into a rhythm together, a loud whelp escaped Leon's lips. The older gentleman became alive with joyful jeers and rhythmic pounding of his feet. "She's a gem, Bert. Has Flo seen her yet?"

Bert clapped his hands to the left and right as he walked around Jada in a figure eight pattern. "Not yet, but he will."

Jada's heart flew away from her just then. Suddenly the stage felt larger, the lights warmer, and the world more inviting. She closed her eyes and let her body fall into the sweeping patterns Bert and her had made together. Nothing in her whole life had ever felt so right.

She was so wrapped up in the moment, she didn't hear clicks of heels on the wooden stage, nor the giggles that came shortly after.

"Isn't that your girl?" Lillian demanded.

Jada opened her eyes to face Suzanne's friend. The entire mood of the theater had changed.

Leon's smile had melted into a flat line, Bert had stopped dancing, and both stared at Suzanne and Lillian. The dancing had forced some hair from her bun. It was a negligible amount, but it made her feel exposed before Suzanne and her friend.

While Lillian whispered under her breath, Suzanne had taken a few steps forward toward Jada. Her head was slightly tilted to one side, as if asking what was going on. Her eyes betrayed nothing, but the silence spoke volumes.

"Why didn't you tell us about Jada?" Leon asked. "She's very talented."

Suzanne nodded once. "She is, but she had other things to attend to." Her tone was flat. "I never realized you would be interested in a girl like her."

Jada and Suzanne had never discussed Jada performing. The shock and hurt of it radiated off Suzanne.

Bert and Leon glanced from one girl to the other, clearly unaware of what was happening. Jada stood between the men, her eyes locked with Suzanne.

She wanted to say that she had planned on telling Suzanne of the meeting with Bert. This wasn't how she meant for Suzanne to find out.

"Jada." Suzanne's tone was more a confirmation than a comment.

"What is she doing dancing here? And dancing

with that Negro," Lillian asked loudly. "She's a servant, not a dancer."

"She used to perform at church." Suzanne sounded flat, as if her mind was occupied elsewhere. Still, Jada was relieved to hear herself defended.

"Then she should stick to church singing and get back to work!"

Jada had had enough of Lillian's attitude. "I am dancing with an acclaimed performer who happens to be of the same race as me."

Lillian glanced at Suzanne. "But you said she was Spanish."

Suzanne's face flushed. "Does it really matter, Lillian? She's . . . Jada."

In the following silence, Bert stepped closer to Jada. "This girl is very talented, Suzanne," he said.

"I plan to introduce her to Mr. Ziegfeld," Leon added. The fact that he used Mr. Ziegfeld instead of "Flo" told Jada she was not the only one who felt uncomfortable. Thank goodness.

"But she's a no one." Lillian addressed her words to Leon, as if he was the only one of importance in the room. Jada tried hard not to flinch at the word.

Bert's lips tightened. "She will meet Flo if I have anything to do about it." He put his hands on Jada's shoulders and pulled her back toward him.

"You have nothing to do with it. You shouldn't even be in this show."

Leon stepped between the two. "This attitude has already cost you one number. Do not anger me further."

Lillian's nostrils flared and her face turned red, but she didn't say another word.

Bert turned Jada toward him and asked, "Do you want to be a member of the Follies?"

Jada looked into Bert's eyes, ready to exclaim that of course she wanted to be his partner. She glanced once more to Suzanne, whose face was stone cold and cheeks were red, and the words died on her lips. She never intended on hurting anyone.

Jada locked eyes with Suzanne and felt all the determined joy run out of her body. The excitement she felt in Bert's confidence was nothing compared to her friendship with Suzanne.

She turned back toward Bert and opened her mouth to reject his offer, but she couldn't do that either. His brown eyes urged her to accept his offer, and it made Jada sick to know she couldn't. Tears threatened to overcome her as she struggled between her desires and responsibilities.

After a time, Leon stepped forward, and asked, "Jada, shall I send for Flo? It's your choice."

Jada's throat tightened to the point she feared she'd lose her breath. When she felt strong enough to speak, all she could say was, "Excuse me." Then, with heavy feet, she clomped across the stage and out the stage door.

It wasn't like Jada to run away from anything. Of the two of them, Jada was the fighter. Suzanne watched the hem of her friend's skirt disappear behind the curtain. Behind her, she could feel Lillian's indignation simmering. She knew she should follow Jada, but her feet were glued to the stage. How would it look if she rushed off to follow a servant? Not just any servant, but one who was trying to take a role onstage beside her? The very thought of Jada in the Follies made Suzanne's stomach flip in an uncomfortable way.

Bert made a move to follow, but Leon held him back with a single hand on his shoulder. "She has to want this, man. No one would survive who didn't. We can't force her."

"I suspect she wants it more than she is letting on." Bert met Suzanne's eyes. "I suspect she's wanted this for a long time and hasn't been allowed to show it."

Shame and embarrassment flooded through Suzanne's body. She couldn't deny what Bert said, and she wouldn't lie to either of the men. She respected them too much to do that. But Lillian was a different story.

"Just a minute. You can't talk to Suzanne like this. She did nothing wrong. That upstart girl is trying to take over our stage." Lillian's chest heaved with emotion. "She does nothing but lie to get ahead. First she lied about her race, and now she shows up here when she should be home getting Suzanne's gown ready for tonight's soirée."

Leon took a small step toward Lillian as Bert walked off the stage and into the house. He sat down in one of the first-row seats and rubbed his head.

"Stop, Lillian," Suzanne said. "Enough."

"What?" Lillian asked. "But—"

"It's over. Jada has left the theater and the rehearsal is over." Suzanne took a steadying breath. "I trust, Leon, you will not pursue Jada unless she requests another meeting?" Her heart pounded as she heard her words. *Thoughtless, mean friend,* she scolded herself. But she couldn't help it.

"Unless she contacts us, I will respect her distance," Leon said. In the audience, Bert grumbled something inaudible.

"Thank you." Suzanne turned to Lillian. "I need a private moment with Leon."

Lillian's eyes peeled to slits. "Of course you do," she said, but she did as she was asked and stalked off the stage.

Suzanne waited until she was sure Lillian was out of earshot. She turned to Leon. "How good is Jada, really?" She raised her voice to be sure Bert could hear her.

"You honestly don't know?" Leon asked.

Bert looked up from his seat. "She's the girl who has been helping you learn the choreography all spring, isn't she?"

"We work together . . . sometimes. It is always beneficial to have someone watch you rehearse to point out where you are offbeat or letting go of a part."

"Then you know how talented she is." Leon's normally cheery voice had an edge to it. "You don't need to ask if she is talented, you've always known."

"I don't know if I did," Suzanne muttered.

"You would have another number offered to you," Leon promised. "You would not lose the status you've worked so hard to obtain this year."

That was it. Leon had nailed it on the head. Even Suzanne didn't know why Jada joining the Follies or even being friendly with Bert bothered her, but Leon's promise pointed out perfectly what would happen. If Jada joined the Follies, Suzanne would no longer be needed in Bert and Ann's number. Even Ann might be dropped. And whether she really cared about racial rights, she still liked the idea of being a part of history.

"Of course," Suzanne managed to get out. Her throat felt as if it were swelling shut.

"Thank you, Suzanne. This is big of you." Bert extended his hand to shake hers, but she found she couldn't take it. She couldn't shake and promise this man that she'd help ruin her career. She couldn't promise anyone the moon but herself. He put his hand down. "If Jada would like to talk, I'll be at Roger's tonight in Harlem."

"I'll see you at rehearsal tomorrow," she said to Leon and raced off after Lillian.

Leon's and Bert's voices followed her down the hallway and toward the exit. Suzanne placed a hand on the door and stopped. She couldn't leave without at least talking to Jada. She turned down the hallway and slunk back to her dressing room.

Her heels clicked loudly down the dressing room hall. Everyone had gone. Given the early dismissal and the multitudes of party invites, it was hard to imagine anyone staying for private practice. She should be staying. Before she joined the Follies and determined to out-impress the other girls, Suzanne and Jada would have been practicing every night until her moves were perfect. She had only stayed a few nights for extra practice and never with Jada.

"Stupid Suzanne," she scolded herself.

Their dressing room door was shut. The white wood of the door shone in the slight light of the hallway. Suzanne put her hand on the doorknob. What if Jada was inside? She pulled back and knocked a few times before slowly opening the door.

"Jada?" she called out in what she hoped was a soothing voice. "Jada, we need—"

She stepped into the room and went silent. It was empty. Everything was exactly as she and Lillian left it. Jada hadn't returned here.

Suzanne swallowed nervously. If Jada wasn't waiting for Suzanne to apologize, where did she go? No answer came to Suzanne's mind. She had to admit that she knew little of Jada's life outside of where it intersected with her own. The realization did not make her feel good. When had she forgotten her friend?

Behind her the door rattled. "Suzanne?" Lillian's whine was painful.

Suzanne turned around. "Sorry, Lillian. I got distracted."

Lillian walked into the room and took her arm. "Why did you lie about your girl?"

No more lies, Suzanne promised herself. "I wanted you to like me, and having a fashionable servant seemed to impress you."

Lillian shook her head. "Ruby and I never cared about anything other than not having a messy room. I should really be mad at you, but she is the one I can't handle."

"Jada?"

"She is ungrateful for trying to steal our place. But what else can you expect from a nigger."

The spite in Lillian's words made Suzanne's skin crawl.

"She isn't trying to steal our place. Flo doesn't even know she exists." Suzanne wished she could defend Jada more, but the words stuck in her throat.

"Hopefully Flo knows better than to bother with such a person." Lillian shuddered. Her head cocked to one side and her eyes lit up. "Forget about her. Come to Craig Masterson's party tonight."

"I don't know. I already told him I couldn't make it. If I make an appearance now it will be strange."

Lillian put her hand around Suzanne's waist and led her through the dressing room door. "Or will it be romantic?

"You can borrow one of my dresses. I live right around the corner from Craig Masterson's penthouse."

Suzanne's arms tingled with excitement. "If you are sure you don't mind."

"You'd do the same for me," Lillian replied. "I think I have the perfect gown. How do you feel about yellow?"

Suzanne allowed Lillian to guide her out of the theater as she described the yellow fabric. Suzanne's mind was already floating toward the release such a party promised. A diversion like Mr. Masterson was exactly what Suzanne needed.

CHAPTER 20

Jada couldn't decide whom she was angrier with—herself or Suzanne. That indecision only fueled her anger further. How could she walk away from Bert and Leon? And how could Suzanne not support her in front of that horrible Lillian? When did they even become friends?

She stood at the door to Miss Mitzi's, unsure of what to do next. The idea of going to their room left Jada with a sour taste in her mouth. There was nothing she could say to Suzanne to fix what happened, but much could be said that would make it worse.

There was only one place Jada knew Suzanne would never go. She opened the door and walked into the boardinghouse.

Sally's room was in the attic. Jada slipped up the servant's staircase and knocked on Sally's door. It opened instantly.

"Jada?" Sally asked. She glanced over her shoulder into the hallway. "What's wrong?"

"Thank goodness you're here. Can I come in?" Instead of waiting for a reply, Jada stepped into the small room.

The room was surprisingly bright, even with the slanted attic walls. Sally's small bed was pushed against the wall, which was covered in ads from various colored papers promising lighter skin, smoother hair, and brighter smiles. The other wall had a trunk and a dresser tucked into the small space.

Sally leaned back against the closed door. "What happened?"

Jada was again surprised to find a deeper level to Sally.

"Bert and Leon seemed to like me, but Suzanne showed up and . . . it was awful. She didn't support me at all."

Sally shook her head. "That girl doesn't see you. She just sees herself."

Jada's throat tightened. "It wasn't always like that."

There was a long pause. "Let's go out tonight. I haven't been to Roger's for a while. A break from all this is just what you need."

Despite herself, Jada smiled. A night of smooth jazz and good company sounded perfect.

"That sounds like the best medicine. Thanks, Sally."

"Roger will be so happy!" Sally frowned. "But you can't wear that drab brown dress."

Jada looked down and laughed. Sally would find this gown dull. All she wore were bright colors when she could. It matched her room: bright and warm.

"I can't go to our room. I don't know what I'd

say if Suzanne was there." Jada glanced toward the door.

"You are welcome to try something of mine, but I don't know if anything I own will fit you."

Jada glanced from Sally's small frame to her own. Sally was probably correct. "What time do you expect we can leave?"

"I hope to be ready by nine." Sally thought for a moment. "Perhaps a bit later. Mr. Franklin just left and I'll need to put his room right before I can start getting ready."

"That gives me a few hours yet. Perhaps Oliver has something that will work for me."

"Yes," Sally exclaimed. "I know he's been working on a few new gowns. You should go see him." She pulled out a pen and paper, and jotted down the address and directions. "If I don't see you here, I'll find you at Roger's."

Jada knocked on Oliver's door. The smell of backed-up sewers was strong in the air. If Oliver was truly doing as well as he claimed, hopefully he'd be able to move to a better neighborhood. Jada felt dirty just standing on the porch. Inside, a shuffling sound moved closer to the door.

"Jada, darling!" Oliver hooted when he opened the door. "What a surprise. Come in!"

"Greetings," Jada replied. "I am in need of a dress for tonight."

"You don't beat around the bush, do you, girl?"

He grinned. "What happened to that pretty lavender number you wore the last time I saw you."

"I, um, I can't . . ."Jada fell over her words.

Oliver held his hand up. "It don't matter. I've been working on a blue gown that will look amazing on you."

Jada exhaled in relief. She took the arm Oliver offered and made her way through the mess of an apartment. She nearly tripped over a pile of fabric and headfirst into a basket of bobbins.

"What is going on here?" she asked, stepping around another pile of fabric.

Oliver glanced around him as if the mess had always been there. "Oh, yes. I am trying something new. Since those Follies girls keep buying my gloves, I thought I'd try designing a gown. Something new and perhaps a bit scandalous." He wiggled his eyebrows.

"Can I see?" Jada asked.

"For you, anything." Oliver opened a closet door slightly before slamming it shut. "But, if you don't like it or think it is garish, please don't comment."

"I am sure it is beautiful."

Oliver opened the door. Inside were three finished dresses hanging in a row. Jada reached in and pulled out a blue satin gown. It was unlike anything she had seen before. The bodice had no sleeve; instead, the fabric came up over the shoulders to connect behind the neck. The waist was embroidered with flowers and pearls.

"This is beautiful." Jada slid off her glove and felt the fabric. "Can I try it on?"

Oliver's eyes lit up. "Would you?"

Jada glanced around the small space. "Where can I change?"

Oliver unfolded a fanned partition and gestured for her to change behind it.

Jada had never worn anything like it. Suzanne's clothes were tailored to highlight Suzanne's best assets. Jada had never thought about what she would choose in a gown for herself. But even without a mirror, Jada knew she had to own this dress. She fiddled with the satin-covered buttons in the back but was unable to reach the last two.

"Oliver, can you help me button the back?" she asked.

"Coming," he sang from the kitchen. In a moment he was beside her, his hand raised to his mouth. "Jada, that dress was made for you."

His hands were cold on her back and he fiddled with buttoning the top two buttons. After retying the neck and examining her once more, he pulled open a panel on the wall and turned Jada to look at her reflection in a mirror. Oliver stepped back and watched Jada look at herself.

"You shine in this dress." Oliver nearly bounced with enthusiasm. "A star is born."

Jada hardly heard his words as she looked

at herself. The back of the gown was lower than Jada was used to, only covering her up to her shoulder blades. The top of the bodice tied behind the neck, with the rest of the long ribbons falling down her back. The neckline came to a V in the front, and the dazzling blue color made her skin glow. Even showing so much skin, the dress looked glamorous. It highlighted her small waist and curves while making her caramel skin look smooth and luxurious.

"Can I wear this tonight?" she asked.

Oliver grinned. "It's yours."

Jada beamed and shooed Oliver away so she could change back into her day dress. "Will you come to Roger's with Sally and me tonight?"

"I think not. Once people see you in that gown, I'll have more orders coming in. I have to get a head start." He winked at her.

Jada buttoned up her blouse, picked up her shoes, and walked over to the couch where Oliver was laying her dress into a box.

"I love how hard you work to achieve your dreams."

"What about your dreams?" Oliver asked.

Jada raised an eyebrow. "Suzanne is going to be a Ziegfeld star. I'd say we accomplished our dream." She pushed her foot into her boot. Just saying Suzanne's name upset her.

Oliver's face fell. "But Sally said—I mean. Don't you have a dream?"

Jada stood up. "My dream is to wear that dress at Roger's tonight. What do I owe you?"

An uncomfortable silence filtered into the room. Oliver's typically jovial personality diminished until he just stared at her. Jada looked away and waited.

"That dress will bring you luck," Oliver said. "It is a gift. I couldn't see anyone else wearing it but you."

"Thank you." Jada leaned over and kissed his cheek. "I'll tell everyone who designed it."

Oliver's face lit up. "I'll be sure to have my face on for all the adoring fans."

Three hours later, the streets of Harlem were dark except for the random streetlights. Jada and Sally linked arms as they stepped out of the elevated train and walked down to the excitement of the nightclub scene.

"I can't believe Oliver made that gown." Sally watched the skirt flutter in the wind. "Who would've thought he was that talented?"

"You are the one who introduced me!" Jada half laughed.

"Well, yeah, but I didn't look at those gloves and think dressmaker. Did you?"

Jada opened the door to Roger's and smirked. "No, I was surprised too."

The tavern's rag tunes filled Jada's ears. Sally's body was already moving in movement to the sounds, as if every pore was anticipating the music's enchantment. Jada ran her hand down the side of her dress. The smooth texture invigorated her. The night was young and the nightclub was filling up with men and women in an assortment of navy, olive, and brown ensembles. The indigo gown stuck out like a sore thumb, but that just made Jada smile wider.

It took a moment for Jada's eyes to adjust to the sparse lighting. The smoke from the gaslights gave the tavern a romantic fog coating. Jada stood still for a moment, taking everything in. A faint smell of alcohol wafted from the bar through the tavern while the dance floor sent the happy scent of sweat throughout the room.

Sally gave Jada's arm a tug. "Let's go sit in that booth."

"Lead the way," Jada said.

Sally led Jada deep into the tavern to a booth in the back of the room right across from where Danny sat tinkling the ivories. The piano man winked at the girls and nodded to a booth across from him.

"Roger's been missing you," Danny called out.

"It's good for him!" Sally shouted back, as she pointed out their booth to Jada.

Sally plopped down on the leather bench and began to tap her fingers on the table with the rhythm of the tune. Had Jada not known her better, she might have thought Sally was playing an imaginary piano. Jada sat carefully down onto the bench opposite Sally and smiled across the table. The benches were not made for straight-back, prim and proper seating, but gave plenty of room for swaying and moving to the music.

"How are we doing today, ladies?" Roger winked at Sally. He leaned over and handed her a daisy.

"How sweet!" Sally took a sniff before placing it behind her ear. "Danny's really going to town tonight!" She nodded toward the piano.

"He's just warming up," Roger replied. "What would you two like to drink?"

Jada was about to ask for a tea when Sally said, "We'll have two beers and two glasses of water."

"Great." Roger walked over to the bar.

"Beer?" Jada whispered harshly at Sally. "I can't drink that!"

"You've gotta live a little, Jada. Suzanne won't know if you have a few drinks. Heck, what do you think she's doing now?"

Probably drinking champagne and dancing with millionaires, Jada thought. Or maybe tripping over someone's leg. Ruby's accident came to mind and Jada shivered. No time to even joke about such things.

Roger reappeared with the drinks and slid in next to Sally.

Jada lifted her bottle and declared, "To life!" She took a swig.

"Attagirl!" Sally exclaimed before taking a drink herself.

Roger's sarcastic comments kept Jada in stitches for the better part of an hour. She'd never really considered dating before, but as she watched the closeness Roger and Sally shared, she yearned for someone like that; someone she could share every secret with. Even Suzanne didn't claim that level of confidence.

Then, as if reading Jada's thoughts, Sally nudged Roger in the side and said, "We should get Danny to come sit with us."

"Oh, yeah?" he asked, as he threw an arm around Sally's shoulders.

"The way he looks at Jada. We could all go out on the town."

Roger glanced at Danny, who was in fact looking at Jada. "I'm here every night, as is Danny. Perhaps you two ladies should go out on the town and then tell us all about it."

Sally pouted. "Well, at least get him to ask her to sing. Her voice is the tops."

"So I hear." Roger squeezed Sally's shoulders in a quick hug.

"Sally exaggerates." Jada had come for a fun night out. Images of Bert's and Leon's disappointed faces filled her mind. This conversation was taking an uncomfortable direction.

"I do not!" Sally shifted so she was looking at Roger. "Bert Williams wants to hire her."

"I think I remember Bert mentioning something about that." Roger glanced over at the stage. "Selma won't be here tonight. Would you like to sing with Danny?"

Jada glanced at the stage. Singing was easier than dancing. She wouldn't choke like she did dancing with Bert. She knew exactly what song to sing and what key to ask for, but this was not the night for such things. She felt beautiful and wouldn't jinx it with tempting herself with things she could not have.

"Danny is fine on his own," she said.

"He'd be better with a singer." Roger glanced at the bar. People were starting to come in, but it wasn't yet too busy.

Sally reached across the table, knocking over an empty bottle. "Do this for me. Give yourself a chance, girl."

"I tried and I failed. And in front of Bert and Leon. No, I'm better where I am, on the sidelines helping Suzanne." Jada watched Danny sway to the notes.

"Loyalty is wonderful," Roger began, "but you have to take care of yourself too."

"You don't understand." Emotions from her earlier fight with Suzanne were threatening to flood Jada. She swallowed and cleared her voice. "Loyalty doesn't begin to cover it."

"From what you said it sounds to me like she owes you everything," Roger said, taking another swig from his bottle.

They didn't understand. Jada shook her head at Roger's declaration. Suzanne had given up everything to save her.

"I'm with Roger." Sally patted Roger's hand. "Just because she's a pretty white girl doesn't mean she controls you."

Jada glanced from Roger to Sally. She had never told anyone about what happened. They'd left so quickly after it all, she never had a chance. She and Suzanne rarely spoke of it. Even Mrs. Haskins didn't know the whole truth. It never felt right to divulge such information to that woman. For all she knew, people assumed she had died with her folks.

"It isn't a black-white thing. Suzanne saved my life," Jada began.

Roars of laughter from a nearby table and the piano overpowered the voices at their table as everyone took in what Jada had said. Scents of cigar smoke and alcohol wafted above their heads, encouraging Jada to lean forward and take another sip of her drink.

"Saved your life?" Sally asked. "We are talking about Suzanne, right?"

"It's hard to explain." Jada grabbed Sally's bottle and took a long slug. She needed something to give her strength to speak.

"We'll listen," Roger promised, pulling his arm off Sally's shoulders and folding his hands on the table in front of him. Sally nodded her affirmation.

Jada cleared her throat. It had been a long time since she'd spoken about that day. She thought for a moment about where to begin.

"A few years ago, I was walking home after a storm and I came upon my parents' bodies. They . . . They were hanging from a tree."

"What?" Sally asked.

Jada cleared her voice. "They'd been lynched."

A pause settled as Roger and Sally absorbed Jada's words.

"That sounds like something that happens to other people's families, not people I know. Certainly not you." Sally shuddered. "Oh, Jada. How horrible."

Roger leaned back. "Do you know who did it?"

"I have my suspicions, but I don't know. Not for sure." Jada forced the grocer's face out of her mind. She'd never know what happened, and there was no point in dwelling on vengeance unanswered.

Sally leaned forward and took her friend's hand. "That is horrible, Jada. But what's it got to do with Suzanne?"

Jada looked at the wall and tried to swallow the flood of emotions that washed over her. Her parents were gone, which she'd known for a long time, but talking about it . . . trying to explain what that meant to her . . . she didn't have words for that. Her inarticulateness was overwhelming in its symbolism. If she couldn't even mention the event without tears, how did she expect to discuss it with people?

Roger shushed Sally. "Give her a moment." They waited until Jada was able to speak again; then he asked, "What did you do?"

"I did the only thing I could think of. I decided to run away. But when I said good-bye to Suzanne, she insisted on coming with me. That two would be better than one. We left that night. Packed what we could in two bags, grabbed the secret wad of bills from the hallway vase, and fled. Suzanne was planning a wedding and she left him behind to save me. She knew a man who ran a theater in Philadelphia and so we took the next train north. She managed to convince the man to give us a chance onstage. And from there, we made it on our own."

Sally was quiet for a moment. Jada could almost see her trying to form what she wanted to say. Roger met Jada's eyes, but didn't hold the gaze. She reached for her water and took a sip.

"I don't understand. That Suzanne girl got her dream. She's happy."

"She is now, but it was a hard road getting here. Long hours of training after booking jobs on her looks alone. It was rough. And she did it all to start over because of me. There are days I wonder if she wouldn't be happier as some rich gentleman's wife instead of working every day and living at Miss Mitzi's."

"That girl thrives on attention. She was born to be onstage. I'm sure you saved her just as much as she did you," Sally said.

"Not that she didn't make a huge sacrifice for you, Jada," Roger said.

"Of course," Sally jumped back in. "What she did was noble, but she didn't have to join you. She could've stayed behind or gotten you settled with a new position somewhere and returned to her old life.

"If she hadn't agreed, you would have run on your own. I may not know you well, but I know you wouldn't have sat back and let some Klan member kill you," Sally insisted.

"Well, no," Jada replied, her head swimming with questions. The knowledge that Suzanne had saved her life had pushed her through hundreds of troubling rehearsals and sentimental outbursts. If she hadn't owed Suzanne so much, she wondered if she'd have stayed at her side that first year.

Sally and Roger let Jada's mind wander for a time. Roger filled their glasses with water and ice before Sally said, "Jada, honey, just because Suzanne saved you from one fate, doesn't mean she can take the rest of your life." Sally glanced at Roger and nodded toward Jada. "She should be onstage."

Roger nodded in return and smiled like a proud papa. "I don't care where you got your talent, as long as you have some."

Jada pulled herself from her thoughts and looked at Roger. "What do you mean?"

"Just that, if you'd like to share your talent, my stage is open to you. Danny needs someone to sing with him. Selma is only available sporadically." Roger turned and looked at the empty space onstage next to the piano. "If you'd like to audition, the stage is yours."

Sally leaned against Roger's chest, a smile beaming on her face. "Roger's got that big old stage just waitin' for you. We both said so after your first visit here."

Jada was about to argue that Sally had no right to expect her to perform, but her eyes drifted to the stage and the words fell from her mind. Shaking her head, she said, "All right then."

"Great!" Roger jumped from the booth and took Jada's hand.

The two meandered their way through the tables until they were at Danny's side. Danny quickly improvised an ending to his song and looked up at the pair.

"Danny, Jada is going to sing for us this evening."

"What would you like to sing?" Danny grinned as he offered his arm.

Even though calmed by his manners, her mind went suddenly blank of song suggestions. Sally stepped up beside her and grinned.

"How about 'Let Me Call You Sweetheart'? I bet you know that one," Sally offered.

Jada wanted to glare, but found herself smiling instead. Suzanne and she sang that tune often enough that she knew the words by heart. Danny was staring at her, waiting for an answer. "I do know that one," she admitted. Her cheeks warmed as he winked at her.

"All right then," Danny said, beginning an intro to the song. "Let's do this.

Before Jada had a chance to argue, Sally pushed her onto the platform and walked back to their booth. Next to the flat back piano, Jada nervously twisted her hands around and around.

Danny finished his intro and then declared, "Ladies and gentlemen! An impromptu surprise for you. The mysterious Jada!" And with that he sat down at the piano and began her introduction.

Suddenly, a wonderful feeling of confidence washed over Jada and she lit up with such a breathtaking smile that men in the audience began to whistle at her before the song even began. She tapped the piano, giving Danny the tempo she wanted, and then walked to the center of the small stage, which was really only a few feet away from the piano.

At first she only loosely bent her knees and swayed back and forth to his tunes, waiting for her cue. But as the intro went on longer than she remembered, she slowly shuffled her feet and kicked her legs until she was full into a dance that filled the room with energy. An instant later she licked her lips and began to sing, " 'Let me call you sweetheart, I'm in love with you. . . .' "

The song came to an end in what felt like an instant, and every person in the audience stood up and cheered for her. Sweat dribbled down her back and the sides of her face, but for once, Jada didn't mind. Her heart was light enough to fly. When the song ended, Danny segued into another melody, but Jada didn't dare leave the stage. She dived right in, singing lyrics she didn't know she knew and dancing steps she made up on the spot.

Performing with Danny was different from working with Suzanne or even auditioning with Bert. It was easy. There was no hesitation, no self-conscious wonderings if she was doing something right. He played and she sang and it felt wonderful.

When closing time came, the bar was still packed and the customers stayed on the dance floor until Danny and Jada finished the last note.

"Thank you. It is time we were all heading

home now," Danny said. "But come back again tomorrow to see the mysterious Jada and I perform again!"

The crowd roared with applause before slowly dispersing to gather their belongings and exit.

With the bar empty, Danny locked the door and turned to Roger. "That must be the best night we've ever had."

Roger grinned as he handed a glass to Sally to dry. "If Jada will have us, I believe she is the missing piece to our little establishment."

Jada didn't hesitate in her answer: "I'd love to join you."

CHAPTER 21

Craig Masterson leaned down and whispered in Suzanne's ear, "You look divine." His breath was warm and wet against her cheek. He was drunk, though he hid it well.

Suzanne took an uneasy step away from him. "Thank you," she replied.

The orchestra was playing loudly and couples were dancing in the parlor. Suzanne took another step toward the door, but Craig stopped her. He grabbed her elbow and pulled her close. "You don't really want to dance to that old rag music, do you? I took you for a modern woman."

His fingers dug into Suzanne's skin, burning with pressure. This was not what she had in mind when she accepted a dance with Craig. Instead of charming, he was overbearing and boorish. For the first time in a long time, she wished she'd stayed home.

"Laura!" Suzanne called, waving her free hand. "Laura, hello!"

"Hi, Suzanne." Laura glanced at Craig and smiled. "Your house is massive. I got lost just following the music."

Craig chuckled. "Thank you."

"Is Ann here yet, Laura? I wanted to ask her about the Williams number." Suzanne hoped that

Laura would understand and take her away from Craig.

Laura instantly rolled her eyes. "Suzanne, tonight is about fun, not work." She laughed. "Has she been discussing the show all night?"

Craig placed a hand on Suzanne's back and stepped closer. "We have much more interesting things to discuss."

This closeness felt all wrong. Even if he had drunk too much, his hand was holding her too tight and his comments were too intimate. She should have followed Laura's advice before and left Craig Masterson alone.

"Oh!" Suzanne cringed as Craig's hand lowered slightly. She had to get away. "I see Flo in the other room. I must go say hello. You will both excuse me, I'm sure."

"But, Suzanne . . ." Craig's voice had an odd tone. She didn't reply, but took her exit into the dance room.

Behind her Laura said, "Let her go. It's important for all of us to be on Flo's good side."

Luckily, Flo was standing just a few feet inside the door. His date, Billie Burke, stood beside him. The dark red in her dress contrasted nicely with her red hair, which was piled into a bun on the very top of her head. Her tall neck gave her a stately quality that her pale skin only amplified.

"Hello, Flo," Suzanne said. Her voice was

much quieter than she meant it to be, but still Flo turned to include her in his circle.

"Suzanne, my darling. So lovely to see you tonight. That gown does not do you justice." Flo took her hand and kissed it.

Billie hit him with her fan. "Florenz Ziegfeld, that dress is stunning and you know it." Her famed high, trilling voice wavered between annoyed and amused. Then to Suzanne she held out her hand. "Billie Burke, pleased to meet you."

"Likewise, I'm sure," Suzanne replied, taking Billie's hand.

"You were in *The Dancing Duchess*?" When Suzanne nodded, Billie continued. "My friend Albert had a small part."

"Bertie? He was a good sport. He knew the whole script and kept feeding the other gentlemen lines when they forgot. Has he found another show?" Suzanne stepped closer to Billie.

"He went back on the circuit. I tried to get Flo to hire him, but there are few spots for men in his amazing Follies." She laughed.

Flo frowned. "Perhaps I should have hired him. He might have proved useful this year."

There was a sullen pause that made Suzanne nervous. Flo's face sparked with life all of a sudden. Both Billie and Suzanne followed his gaze to the door where Ann had just walked in, as usual without an escort. All over the room people started to comment, and several gentlemen went to offer their arms for a dance.

"Excuse me," Flo said, releasing Billie's hand and walking over to his star.

Instantly Ann's face lit up in a display of charisma and charm. She took Flo's hand and let him lead her about the room.

Suzanne looked over at Billie, whose face had lost some of its light.

"How dare he!" Billie whispered. Then to Suzanne she demanded, "How dare *she* when I am here."

Ann and Flo were in the center of the room dancing the fox-trot. As always, Ann looked radiant in Flo's capable arms, and she made him look like he could dance. A few people stepped to the side to watch them move across the dance floor.

When Suzanne didn't answer, Billie pursed her lips and then said, "But enough about that. I have been wanting to speak with either you or Lillian for the last week. Flo said your friend was injured."

"Ruby, yes." Suzanne could feel her face heating up.

"What do you know about it?" Her sweet voice was flat and firm. She expected answers.

Suzanne swallowed. "She fell during rehearsal. Her ankle was injured. It is unlikely that she'll be back to dancing before we open."

Billie stepped closer to Suzanne so that no one else could hear their conversation. "Why did she fall?"

"What?"

"Is she known for such mistakes?" Billie asked.

"Well, no."

"Did anyone ask why she fell?" Billie asked. "I hear she had been reprimanded for losing weight. Is she healthy?"

"Ruby had lost some weight, but she was in good health. Dancers trip sometimes. I'm sure even you have had a tumble once or twice." Suzanne smiled as Billie laughed at her honesty.

Now that Billie had pointed out the question, Suzanne's mind wouldn't stop racing. She had landed in a spot of grease. She'd never really questioned its presence, but Ruby wasn't one for tripping or losing her balance. Why *had* there been grease on the stage?

"Someone should think about it. Flo won't hear anything against you darling women, but the few times I've overheard him and Jonathon arguing, I am pretty sure I know something is not right at the New Amsterdam."

The letters. If Billie knew about the letters, she would *know* something is not right at the New Amsterdam. Suzanne swallowed. She should have known that Ruby's accident wasn't an accident. An uneasy feeling filled her stomach.

Across the room Lillian's shrill giggle exploded

as Henry Darling ended a story. The friend hadn't been to see Ruby since the accident and had managed to be cast in all of Ruby's parts. Suzanne bounced on her toes. Could Lillian be the reason such things were happening? Her laugh flitted through the air again as she lay her hand on the gentleman's arm. Suzanne turned away in disgust.

"Oh!" she exclaimed as she bumped into Jonathon.

"Hello," he said, jumping back to give her room. "Lovely to see you again, Suzanne."

He looked very sharp in a top hat and tails. Looking down at her, he fiddled with his white necktie. Suzanne hid an amused smile. It was charming to see him nervous and, if Suzanne was honest, rather flattering.

"I'm glad you came tonight," Suzanne said.

"Would you—that is, could I have the honor of this dance?" He extended his hand and bowed slightly as he awaited her answer.

"Oh my, Jonathon. I thought you'd never ask."

She slid her hand into his and let him lead her onto the dance floor. His hand rested lightly on her back as he guided her around the dance floor in a smooth fashion.

"I never knew you were such an accomplished dancer." Suzanne looked up at him with admiration.

Jonathon's cheeks flushed. "I don't normally

attend such soirées, but Flo insisted. I admit after your friend was injured I have taken any opportunity available to observe the company together."

"Yes, I quite agree. Something is not right."

"I'm sorry I didn't have time to talk to your girl before." He stepped back and spun her before coming back and guiding her to the other side of the dance floor. "It was a bad time and I was woefully behind with work. Can you tell me more about the notes Ruby received?"

"What?" Suzanne asked. Jada had been to see Jonathon and hadn't told her. That didn't sound like her. Jada told Suzanne everything, especially when she was going to speak with someone from Suzanne's world. What made her keep such a secret from her?

Jonathon looked at the other dancing couples around them and shook his head as if to say, "Not here." Instead, he took her elbow and led the two of them into a back room off the main parlor.

Despite Craig's lack of interest in anything intellectual, the room was filled with books. Every wall was a bookcase featuring anything from Charles Darwin to Jane Austen. Suzanne wondered whom he paid to cultivate such a collection. The round room had only a short bench and leather chair for seating and a fire that contained a small flame that warmed the room.

"Before the accident, Jada came to me with a note Ruby had received with a box of treats." He walked over and set his elbow on the back of the chair.

"Yes, I know about that. She'd gotten more than one note, but the chocolates put us all on edge. The notes were usually accompanied by a flower arrangement or some other nonsense. Don't feel bad. I didn't really give them much credence either. I mean, the words were threatening, but not violent." Suzanne perched on the edge of the bench, giving her feet a small rest.

"Threatening, but not violent," Jonathon repeated.

"But with Ruby's accident, they have been on my mind more and more."

"Did you tell Flo about the notes after the accident?"

"Tell Flo? No, why would I?" Suzanne stood up and moved closer to the fireplace. "I hardly see the man, let alone consult him on such affairs."

"Well, an unusually graceful girl was injured after being threatened. Shouldn't someone take action? How are we supposed to keep you girls safe if you don't confide in us?"

Suzanne's head snapped toward Jonathon. "Safe? Keep us safe? I wasn't aware that was one of your duties. I didn't know that we needed protecting. Perhaps that would have been good to know when I found you slinking after me all about the city!" Her voice had gone shrill, but she didn't care.

"Slinking after you? Is that what you thought?" Jonathon's voice was soft. "I wasn't aware I was such a nuisance. But that doesn't matter. What matters is the accident, if we are still calling it that."

Suzanne thought for a moment. If Jonathon hadn't been following her for Flo, then why was he always around? Temptation to pull at that thread nearly overcame her, but she was better than that. There were more important issues to be examined.

"Did anyone notice that I fell into a small spot of grease that day? It stained my bloomers and stockings."

"Grease? Really?" Jonathon walked around the room. "There were so many people onstage that week, it wouldn't have been easy to put a grease spill onstage, but it wouldn't have been impossible. Perhaps someone wanted Ruby or one of you to fall?" He stopped pacing and sat on the chair.

"I don't really know. I had wondered if Lillian would go so far as to hurt her friend just to get ahead."

"Get ahead?"

"She has been in the Follies before, and yet it was I who joined Ruby and Ann in the production with Bert. And it was I who was in the tango trio with them as well. If you look at it from her perspective, it doesn't seem fair."

"And she was chosen as Ruby's replacement." Jonathon nodded as he spoke.

"But just because she was chosen to be in the show doesn't mean she was behind it. Lots of people had access." The music from the other room stopped.

"I didn't think you liked Lillian." Jonathon raised an eyebrow.

"I don't particularly. But I don't like a lot of people, that doesn't make them criminals." The music started back up again.

Jonathon nodded. "Just the same, we should keep an eye on her for a few days."

"We?" Suzanne asked.

"Of course. You share a room with her, who better to do it? I thought of asking Jada to help as well, but after the way I treated her, well, I wouldn't help me."

"Jada help you?" Suzanne's voice was soft now. First Jada met with Bert without her knowing and now Jonathon.

"It seemed a great rouse. She is nearly unnoticed as one of the help and she has access to all the dancers. But I ignored her warning about the notes and now we have lost another woman. I wouldn't be surprised if she was upset." He was visibly upset with his own ignorance. "So, will you help me?"

Lillian would be at all of her late-night rehearsals. There really was no one else as well equipped to do this as she was.

"Very well," Suzanne agreed. "But I don't want Flo or anyone knowing what we are doing. I don't want to risk the special treatment such involvement would provide. Both good and bad. No one can know. Is that clear?"

Jonathon slid closer to her and held out his hand. "We've got a deal."

Someone jostled the handle on the door.

Jonathan and Suzanne both snapped their heads toward the sound. Suzanne grimaced. What would Ann say if she and Jonathon were found in a room alone? The idea was a little thrilling, but also concerning. Her reputation could be ruined in one moment.

The door jostled again.

"No one can know?" Jonathon confirmed.

"No one," Suzanne repeated.

"I am sorry about this," he said.

The door handle turned and the door started to open. Jonathon reached toward Suzanne, cupped her cheek in his hand, and kissed her. His lips were firm and his touch gentle. She gasped in surprise.

Jonathon pulled back from Suzanne and the two looked toward the door.

"Do you mind?" Jonathon asked with a fake sneer.

"Suzanne?" Craig sounded almost hurt. His dark hair was unkempt and he swayed ever so slightly on his feet.

"Yes?" Suzanne replied. Hurting Craig hadn't been something she meant to do that evening, but perhaps it was better this way. If his ego was hit hard enough, perhaps he would stop pursuing her.

Craig didn't enter the room, but stood and looked down at her and Jonathon. His gaze made her feel unfit in a way she'd never felt before. His frustration and distaste for Jonathon ignited an anger in Suzanne. This man didn't own her, nor had she pledged her hand to him, or even accepted a date. And yet, with the way he was glaring at them, she knew he felt like he had lost in some strange game.

"I believe we wanted to be alone, right, Jonathon?" She laid her head on his chest and looked pointedly at Craig.

Jonathon inhaled sharply in surprise, but didn't move away. Instead he pulled her close and agreed. "Yes, we had come in here for privacy. Surely you understand, Masterson."

The millionaire looked at both of them. Suzanne knew him well enough to know that he was weighing his options. His pride had been hurt, but not badly, but the alcohol from his breath could be smelled from across the room. His cheeks became redder before he declared, "No, this is inappropriate. I'll not have it in my house. Please leave. Now." His voice was firm, but you'd have to be a fool not to hear the undercurrent of rage that accompanied it.

Jonathon glanced at Suzanne.

"Let's leave, Jonathon. No point staying where we aren't wanted." She stood in a huff and waited for Jonathon to follow suit. "Please do not call upon me again," she said to Craig as she brushed past him.

"I wouldn't stoop to such a level. Enjoy your dalliance with the help."

Suzanne spun on her heel, the back of her dress slapping against Jonathon's ankles. "I think I'll do better with the ear of Flo's assistant than a flashy drunk like you."

They stalked out of the room, through the hall, and out the front door. Suzanne was palpably aware of the eyes on her and promised herself it would only add to some mystery quality she hoped she possessed.

Once on the street Jonathon stopped her. "I'm sorry for such an indiscretion. I just knew that would cover our conversation."

Suzanne shrugged. "I was looking for a way out of his attention anyway."

The clock behind them struck the hour. "Can I escort you home?" Jonathon asked.

"Thank you," Suzanne replied, taking his arm.

CHAPTER 22

The air was crisp and cool as Jada and Sally walked back to Miss Mitzi's. Jada's throat was warm from singing and her fingers tingled with excitement. Danny wanted her to sing every night and was willing to pay her to do so. The very thought brought tears to her eyes.

"You want to borrow a nightgown?" Sally asked as they keyed into the back door.

Jada glanced at the clock. 12:10 AM.

"No, I want my own things. Suzanne won't be back this early. Those parties go all night. I'll meet you upstairs."

"There is a couple in the room across from you. Don't wake them," Sally reminded her.

"Of course," Jada replied. Jada clip-clopped up the stairs. Fatigue fell upon her as she walked.

"See you soon," Sally singsonged from behind her.

The house was dark and quiet except for the creaks of the house settling and people sleeping. Very different from the chaos during the day. Jada made sure to walk quietly so as not to disturb anyone. In her head she made a list of what items she needed to grab to get through the next few days.

The room was surprisingly clean. Suzanne

had rehung the dress she wore that day, and her vanity table was still in passable condition. Jada swallowed a sudden wave of guilt. If she had kept the room this neat, she probably hoped that Jada would return that night and didn't want to spark more anger. She felt a moment's hesitation, but a small voice inside her forced her to grab a pillowcase off a pillow and pack what she'd need. Perhaps she would go back to Suzanne or at least reconcile, but if she didn't stand up now, she would forever be her servant.

Her trunk was in the far corner of the room, stacked under several hatboxes. She placed the boxes on the floor and opened the lid of the large trunk. The wooden smell immediately sent her back to Richmond and that horrible night. It smelled like home and of Mother and suddenly, Jada was overcome with emotion. They had come a long way and no one had tried to find them, thank God. Where would her life have been had none of that happened?

"Jada?" Suzanne pushed the door open and tiptoed in, her skirt rustling against the furniture. "Jada, are you here?"

"What are you doing back so soon?" Jada demanded as she stood up in her corner.

Suzanne jumped as Jada presented herself. "You look different, Jada. Taller or something."

Jada placed the few things she'd found in the trunk into her pillowcase. In the pale light it seemed like Suzanne looked different too. Smaller, yet more assured. "I didn't think you'd be here. Usually you aren't home for hours yet."

"It was an interesting night." Suzanne shut the door behind her. "I am glad you are here. I need to talk to you."

Jada steadied herself. Here it was. She wasn't sure she wanted to have this conversation yet.

"I realized tonight that you have been right all this time. All the letters, all the weird accidents, especially dear Ruby . . . they are more than simple coincidences. I think someone is trying to sabotage the Follies." Suzanne perched on the edge of the bed, a very serious expression on her face. "I am sorry I didn't understand before."

This is what Suzanne wanted to talk about? This and not their friendship? Her chin began to quiver as if deeply cold, and she couldn't stop the vibrations.

"You chose tonight to talk about this? After all that happened between us today, *this* is what you need to discuss with me? Not that you willfully held me back from working with Bert, nor that you belittled me in front of Julian and probably Mr. Ziegfeld himself. And let's not mention that you took Lillian's side over my own. No, you need to discuss what is happening to you." Jada resumed packing her bag. "I don't know why I'm even surprised."

There was a long pause. Jada shoved her nightgown into the pillowcase and moved over to the wardrobe, where her few gowns were hung.

"Jada," Suzanne said softly. "Jada, please stop."

"No." Jada shook as she spoke. "I've swallowed my own needs for too long. I refuse to do that for one more day. Just because you ran away with me doesn't mean you own me. I can't owe you the rest of my life."

Suzanne took a step back from Jada, her eyes wide. "I never asked you to ignore your needs. Never once. Every decision we made, it was together."

"Perhaps that was how it was once, but then you joined the Follies." Jada folded another gown and stuck it in the pillowcase.

"You wanted me to join. You were just as excited as I was, or was all that an act?"

"I was excited." Jada softened her tone. "Until impressing those girls became more important than me."

Suzanne threw her arms up. "And why shouldn't they be? The connections I am making now could send my career soaring. I won't be made to feel bad for this, Jada. I won't allow it."

"Allow it?" Jada practically shouted. She dropped her bag and pointed a finger at Suzanne's chest. "You don't own me and you can't dictate what I say or do. You are more like your father than I thought."

"Then you must be like your mother. Complacent to the point of insignificance. I wonder what Daddy ever saw in Cicely."

"Mother was a good worker."

"Who knew she did so much work on her back." Suzanne glared at Jada, her breath coming in short bursts.

Jada could almost feel the room shift around her. "On her back?" she repeated very softly. Jada took a step back from Suzanne. "How could you repeat such a horrible rumor? How could you throw that in my face?"

"It wasn't just a rumor. I heard Daddy begging for Mother's forgiveness the evening we left." The anger melted from Suzanne's body. "Jada, I'm sorry. I didn't mean to ever tell you." Suzanne grasped at Jada's arm, but Jada refused to be caught, pulling away at every turn.

"Never tell me?" Jada closed her eyes. "How long have you known?"

Suzanne stopped trying to grab for Jada's arms. Instead, she sat on the bed.

"How long?" Jada demanded again.

Suzanne exhaled. "Since the night of that big storm. The night your folks died." When Jada didn't say anything, Suzanne explained. "I walked in on Mother and Daddy fighting about Daddy's indiscretions. That's when I found out."

"The night they died?" Jada repeated. "And you never told me." Her voice was hardly above a whisper, but in the stillness of the room it felt like an exclamation.

Suzanne went to her friend's side. "Would you have wanted to know? They were murdered and we had to run. That certainly wasn't the time, and then more and more time passed and it became too hard to tell you."

"Why?" Jada's voice felt thick. She swallowed, trying to clear the emotion from her voice.

"I didn't want to tell you. I didn't want to be responsible for changing how you saw your ma."

Jada glared at her. "Perhaps you didn't want to look too close at dear Daddy either." Suzanne winced and looked at the floral wallpaper. Jada'd only said it to hurt Suzanne, which made the guilt bite harder.

"I didn't—" Suzanne cut herself off. "I suppose I didn't."

Jada could almost feel the air in the room stand still between them. Her face felt hot and her hands still shook. She clasped her hands in front of her and tried to cool herself down. She wanted to deny what Suzanne admitted, and yet, she knew it was true. Mr. Haskins often called Ma to his office for no reason or gave her special assignments in the house when Mrs. Haskins was traveling. Jada had been proud of her ma for being such an asset to the family. Now, with distance, she could see that something was amiss with his requests.

More than ever, she wished Ma was there with her. She and Pa had been so in love. Had she loved Mr. Haskins too? Had he forced himself on her? Jada would never know the truth. She bit her lip in frustration.

"Jada, this isn't what I intended." Suzanne's tone was low, as if approaching a wild dog. "How do I fix this? I don't know how to do this. What do I say?"

Jada picked her pillowcase back up and went back to the wardrobe. Was there anything Suzanne could say that would change how she felt? "Sorry would be a start."

Suzanne's face flushed and she sucked in her cheeks. "Sorry for what?" She was angry. What right did she have to be angry?

Jada shut the wardrobe door with more force than she intended. "For all of this. For not telling me what you heard that day, for not including me this last month, and for not realizing I have dreams like you."

"I can't say that," Suzanne said. "I'm not sorry. I can't do this without you. You make sense of the moves for me and help me smooth out the notes in the songs. Without you, I would fail. So I can't be sorry for what I did, but I am sorry that I hurt you."

The flame of Jada's anger was drowned by pity at Suzanne. Of course, she knew how much Suzanne depended on her, but she never thought

Suzanne would admit it. Despite wanting to be angry, Jada could only exhale and drop her bag on the floor.

"I'm still angry." She couldn't let Suzanne get away with what happened. "Do you think I'd abandon you? After all we've been through? After all you did for me?"

Suzanne opened her mouth to say something and then stopped. "I don't think I thought of it. I just, I can't fail. I left behind so much—Mother needs to see me a star."

"I know all you left behind; it has followed me. You may have saved my life, but it has been a bittersweet life. I can't watch you fulfilling my dream anymore. I won't do it, but that doesn't mean I don't want to be in your life still."

"Your dream? What do you mean, *your* dream?"

Did she really not know? "What do you think I was doing all those years I sat in on your voice and piano lessons? I had plenty of chores to do and could have advanced in the house staff much more had I not spent hours at your side."

"Oh." Suzanne looked out the window. "Daddy said he had assigned you to work with me."

Jada snorted. That sounded like Suzanne's father. He treated all the servants as if he owned them. Descendants of slaves did not make them slaves.

"How do we make this right?" Suzanne asked.

"You have instincts that I need both onstage and off. It was you who first thought the notes were something more, you who I didn't listen to. No one else should be injured like Ruby and, well, I don't want to lose your friendship."

Jada glanced at the wardrobe. One of her three dresses was still hanging, and her pillowcase bag now looked pathetic on the floor.

"I was offered a job tonight," Jada blurted out.

"What?" Suzanne's voice was barely above a whisper.

"At Roger's pub in Harlem. He wants me to sing there at night. I told him I'd do it." Jada picked up the pillowcase and waited for Suzanne's reply.

"I-I am happy for you." The words were laced with misunderstanding, but Jada didn't care. She would take any enthusiasm Suzanne showed her.

"But I can still help you with the dances."

Suzanne bounded off the bed and hugged Jada. "Thank you!" she whispered.

Jada pulled back. "I have one condition."

Suzanne bit her lip and nodded.

"No more lying. I am not Spanish. Ruby did receive threatening notes and that accident was not normal."

"It wasn't an accident. I think, I mean, it's possible that one of us girls is behind it." Suzanne looked at Jada.

"Well, of course. Those notes, they all spoke of talent and leaving the show. Someone wants to minimize the girls onstage. We just have to figure out who they are and what they want." The pillowcase was now empty and Jada turned to put the pillow back in it.

"I think I might know." Suzanne looked so unsure that Jada felt sympathy for her.

"Oh?" she asked to urge her friend on.

"Lillian?"

Jada blinked in surprise. "That is interesting. She did replace Ruby in both of the numbers. But Lillian? Really?"

Suzanne shrugged. "If not her, who?"

"I don't know."

A silence came between the women.

Clearing her throat, Suzanne asked, "Will you come to the theater with me tomorrow?" Before Jada could say no, she went on. "Someone needs to go through Lillian's belongings. While I am in rehearsal with her, you could search."

Jada bit the inside of her cheek. "I can't tomorrow. I am going to meet Roger to go over the contract; then I need to have a dress made for work."

"Oh," Suzanne was obviously surprised. Jada couldn't remember the last time she said no to Suzanne, but she had to draw the line somewhere. If she went to the theater, Suzanne wouldn't take her evening job seriously. She would lose ground. That wasn't an option, not anymore.

"Are you sure?" Suzanne pressed. "We leave

for Boston in a few days. I don't know if we'll still be roommates. What if something happens . . . something worse than Ruby?"

Jada turned away from Suzanne's pleading eyes and looked for some task to give her a moment to regain her resolve. After a moment of adjusting the pile of books on the bed stand, she shook her head.

"I promised Roger, and missing that appointment would be detrimental to my career. You have to see that." Jada crossed her arms.

It was Suzanne's time to pause. She sat on the bed and crossed her legs. "Well, perhaps I could do it myself tomorrow and if I need help, you can come in Tuesday."

Jada never thought Suzanne would bend so far.

"I will be there Tuesday," she said.

"Perhaps this will show you that I respect your new job." Suzanne's voice was thick. "If I'd known you wanted more . . ."

Jada held up her hand. "We can only start from where we are, not change what has already happened."

CHAPTER 23

Suzanne woke up earlier than she ever had before. Jada was already gone when she pulled on her dress and buttoned it up the front. She grabbed an apple from the kitchen and dashed out the door. Once on the front stoop she halted. A shiny Model T was parked directly in front of the boardinghouse. Jonathon was leaning against the side reading a newspaper.

"What are you doing here?" Suzanne tried to hide the smile on her face.

Jonathon looked up at her. "I wanted to give you a ride to rehearsal. I had hoped to have time to read the paper since it had come to my attention that you were not an early riser."

That comment stung, but Suzanne refused to let it show. "Perhaps not, but I am always on time to rehearsal."

Before he could answer, she walked to the car and waited as he opened the door. She slid inside and waited for him to walk around and sit beside her. She knew he hadn't meant his comment to offend her, but she still felt the sting of it.

"What got you up so early?" The car putted down the road. "I assume it isn't for rehearsal since you tend to rehearse in the evenings."

"How did you know that?" Despite herself, Suzanne's heart skipped a beat.

It was Jonathon's turn to be embarrassed. He turned away from her and looked out the window for a moment before saying, "How could I not know? You are hard not to notice."

"Oh, thank you." Suzanne rolled her shoulders back. "I wanted to get in first so that I might look through the dressing room. Alone."

"An excellent notion."

Jonathon settled into the bench and looked out the window as the buildings passed. He rested his hand on the bench beside Suzanne's. She looked down and her pulse quickened at how close he was to her. On purpose, she looked away and waited for them to arrive at the New Amsterdam. Once the car pulled up to the theater the pair stepped out. Jonathon instructed the driver to return at ten to take Mr. Ziegfeld to an appointment. By the time he was done giving his instructions, Suzanne was through the door and walking down the hallway. Jonathon caught up quickly.

"Lillian is notoriously late on Mondays and Thursdays. Flo and Julian have commented on it. If we are quick, we can check her dressing room things now." Suzanne was nearly out of breath.

"If you are sure." Jonathon held the door to the dressing room open as Suzanne entered. Ruby's vanity had been cleared off. Suzanne swept her hand over the white surface.

"What happened?" Suzanne asked.

"I don't know." Jonathon tapped the vanity top. "Her mother came in yesterday and collected all her things. She didn't say much, but I think she discovered the notes you mentioned."

Suzanne pulled her gloves off and laid them on the vanity. "Threatening notes and a sprained ankle. I can see where that worried her. Still, I'll miss her."

"We'll be sure to invite her back next year."

"Really?" Suzanne hung her bag on the hat rack. "That is rather generous for Flo."

"That's how he is. Once you are in the family, you are always welcome."

"Oh . . . Lillian's section is this one. She has the most horrible-smelling perfume, don't you think?" Suzanne lifted the bottle and sprayed some into the air.

Jonathon wrinkled his nose. "I prefer lavender."

Suzanne couldn't stop the grin that appeared on her face. He liked how she smelled. She stepped closer to him and opened the drawer on the vanity. Inside there was a line of various dimple pens and some lip rouge, but not even so much as a scrap of paper that implicated her in any of the happenings at the theater.

"Damn it!" Jonathon kicked the leg of the vanity.

"Calm down. This doesn't mean anything. Lillian may not be a smart woman, but that doesn't mean she wouldn't hide something she knew was incriminating."

"Or maybe she just didn't do it," Jonathon offered.

Suzanne opened the wardrobe and shuffled through the dresses. Lillian didn't keep much at the theater, preferring to bring what she needed from her home. So the few gowns and petticoats in there were things she wore for rehearsal and had a rather unpleasant stench to them. As she pulled two hangers apart, a box on the bottom of the wardrobe caught her eye. She knelt down and pulled the box out. It was made of oak and had Lillian's initials carved into the top. She opened the lid and gasped.

"What?" Jonathon asked, turning away from the photos Lillian kept on the vanity.

"Look!" Suzanne held up a small piece of paper. *"Lillian, one wrong step could be your last. Don't ignore me like your friend,"* Jonathon read aloud. "She's also receiving the notes?"

"That's how it appears." Suzanne agreed. "Clearly, I was mistaken about Lillian."

Jonathon handed the paper back to Suzanne. She shuffled some more through the box, but all she found were cards from genuine admirers and sentimental things. Why had she saved the threatening note along with all of these lovely things? She closed the box and put it back in the bottom of the wardrobe.

"You don't think," Suzanne began, then stopped for fear it was a ridiculous idea.

"What?" Jonathon prodded her.

"Well, you don't think she wrote herself a threat just in case someone was suspicious of her?" There was a brief pause; then Suzanne closed the wardrobe door. "Never mind. That was silly."

"Not silly," Jonathon said. "But if she wanted to prove she wasn't the culprit, why wouldn't she place it so that it is easily found? Why hide it so completely?"

"Yes, of course. I just had to say it out loud."

The grandfather clock in the hallway chimed 7:30.

"I had better leave. We don't need the girls gossiping any more about our relationship." Jonathon laughed nervously.

Suzanne met his gaze and smiled. "Craig Masterson walked in on you kissing me. Craig is many things, but proud is highest on the list. I assure you, he has told every one of my scandalous ways and why he is no longer pursuing me." She snorted. "Never mind, I'd been trying to shake him for the last few days."

Jonathon blinked. "I thought you were smitten with him."

"Craig?" Suzanne asked. "No, not really. He was someone fun. A gentleman to test my new-found fame on. He was never someone I'd consider actually letting into my life. He is too

305

full of himself for that. If I ever marry, I want someone who loves me more than his image."

"Ah, yes. That is something I understand. I would want the same thing . . . to be first to someone."

Jonathon looked down at Suzanne and smiled, and suddenly her feet trembled ever so slightly. She returned his gaze for a moment before breaking away and turning to her bag.

"I need to get ready." She paused for a moment before asking, "What's next?"

"Can I take you for dinner after rehearsal tonight?" Jonathon asked. "We should plan our next move."

Suzanne nodded. "Can you pick me up at Miss Mitzi's at seven?"

"Yes." Jonathon's face lit up as he agreed. He stepped backward and bumped against the table as he tried to leave. Feeling blindly behind him, he grabbed the doorknob and opened the door. "I'll see you then."

Suzanne grinned back. It didn't really matter what they were going to talk about together, only that someone wanted to spend time with her because she brought value to the conversation. Jonathon wasn't interested in her because of whom she danced for or because she was friends with some of the most beautiful women in New York City. He wanted to hear her opinions and thought she added virtue to the conversation. He saw her, and whether they were simply working out what was happening at the New Amsterdam or something more, she was glad to feel valued.

She leaned against the doorframe and watched Jonathon walk away from her, his coat slung over his shoulder. Once he had turned the corner and was no longer visible, she took a step back into her room; then the door across from hers swung open.

"Suzanne!" Laura's face shown with both surprise and awe. "Craig mentioned he saw you two together, but in your dressing room?"

Suzanne's face burned. "Nothing like that. Jonathon is a friend, an innocent friend."

"Sure he is." Laura winked. "What is he like? He always seemed kind of boring to me, but if you prefer him to Craig Masterson. Well, he must have something going for him." She walked past Suzanne to her dressing room door.

Suzanne stepped into the hallway and leaned against the wall. "Craig is an overreaching prig who won't take no for an answer. You spent time with him last night, didn't you get bored of hearing all of his stories about himself."

Laura shrugged. "The wine kept pouring and the music kept playing. Beyond that, I didn't really care. I mean, there are only so many millionaires in New York. Ann keeps half of them entertained. If I want one, I can't be too choosy, can I?" She entered her dressing room, followed by Suzanne. She sat at her vanity table and pulled out her bottle of lotion. She rolled up her sleeves and began applying the soothing ointment to her skin.

"Just be sure you like the person you choose. Millions are one thing, but a gentleman is worth far more."

Laura's eyes tightened. "I wouldn't expect you to understand. You ran away from your millionaire."

For a moment Suzanne's stomach clenched. Did Laura know about Elton and her? She took a moment and found a comment that fit for anything.

"Perhaps I did, but it wasn't for lack of trying." Suzanne offered Laura her bottle. "Some days I just don't think I'm cut out for the other part of this job."

"Other part?"

"You know." Suzanne waved at the dress hanging in the wardrobe. "The evening dances and celebrations every week. Don't you ever just want to go to bed and get some rest?"

"If you don't like the celebrations, why are you in the Follies? Isn't that half the allure? Being written up in the papers and having people follow your fashions. That is the dream." Laura had a hungry look in her eye. "And even with the Ziegfeld girl name, only a few of us really accomplish all that was promised us. Only a few of us become household names."

Suzanne nodded. "Ann and Fanny are very talented."

"You mean *Fanny* is very talented. Ann is simply beautiful. And when the room is as grand as ours, that's saying something."

Other girls started to come down the hall.

"I thought you liked Ann," Suzanne said quietly.

Laura waved her hand as if to dismiss Suzanne's question. "I can like her and still have an honest opinion of her. That doesn't negate my friendship. I like a lot of these girls, but that doesn't mean I think they all should be stars."

The honesty in Laura's voice made Suzanne pause. Before she could reply, Lillian came bounding into the room.

"Oh! You are here early this morning, Suzanne." She plopped her bag down on a chair. "You too, Laura. Did I hear right, Suzanne? Is that girl Jada singing in Harlem?"

"Where did you hear that?" Suzanne's tone was nastier than she intended, but she didn't soften it by saying more.

Lillian paused to think. "Someone told Ruby that and she mentioned it when I saw her yesterday. Is it true?"

"Yes."

Lillian and Laura both inhaled as if it were a huge scandal.

"After all you've done for her, she just left

you to pursue her own singing?" Lillian asked.

Laura stood up and paced the small room.

"I'm not sure I'd put it like that," Suzanne said. "I didn't have much use for her anymore and she was offered the opportunity."

"Didn't Bert also want her?" Laura's question had an edge of worry to it.

"Isn't one Negro enough for this show?" Lillian said dismissively.

Laura laughed. "Perhaps more than enough."

"We should get dressed," Suzanne said. Bert had never been a favorite, but pushing him out of the show wasn't an option Suzanne wanted to see happen.

Now that Jada had found a place somewhere other than on stage with Bert, Suzanne allowed herself a secret amount of pleasure for her friend.

CHAPTER 24

The crowd was loud with gay laughter and clinking bottles. Jada held the final note as long as she could before nodding to Danny and ending the song. The pairs of dancers stopped dancing and roared in applause. Danny applauded as well. Jada's grin felt as if it might tear her cheeks apart. Any concern that the thrill would wear off knowing she could return night after night was gone. This was what her life had been missing. This was what she needed.

"They love you!" Danny shouted.

Jada beamed. "I can't believe it!"

Requests were shouted from the couples on the floor. They came so fast that soon they were just noise in Jada's ears. Behind her the piano bench scooted back.

"We are going to take a five-minute break. The bar is open."

To Jada, Danny gestured to a door in the back of the bar. He opened it and followed her inside the much more quiet room. Though not part of the bar, the room had a small cart in the corner filled with bottles and glasses. Danny filled a glass with ice and poured brandy over it. He held it out to Jada.

"No, thanks," she said. "I don't like brandy."

"What do you like?" Danny grinned. "Last night you turned down beer, the night before gin. So, what's your poison?"

"This—" She pressed her hand to the entrance to the bar. "I like the feel of those people listening to me. I like the vibration of their applause. I don't like anything that takes away from that."

Danny took a sip of his drink. "Those are words I understand." He stretched his long brown fingers in the air. "I've never seen an audience take to someone like they have to you. It is exciting to watch."

"Thank you," Jada said. "I have wanted this for a long time."

The glass placed on the table, Danny bent over and touched his toes. "Don't mind me," he said. "I have a little routine I like to do between sets." He lunged to his side and raised an arm over his head.

Jada sat in one of the well-loved chairs and watched him stretch for a moment.

"Everyone has their rituals," Jada agreed. She didn't yet, but once she'd worked for a while she was sure she'd develop some.

The door opened again and Bert entered. Jada turned away and drank more of her water. She waited for her nerves to hit her, but her pulse kept steady.

"You are hot tonight!" Bert said warmly.

"Bert, you old chum! So glad you made it!"

Danny crossed the room and shook hands with the entertainer.

"Jada." Bert rocked back on his heels and smirked. "Well, we just keep running into each other."

Her breath didn't stop and her stomach didn't lurch. Instead, she tilted her head and smirked back. For the first time, Jada met Bert's gaze and she felt like an equal, not like some little schoolgirl.

"Perhaps if you didn't keep following me, we'd stop having these run-ins."

Danny stepped back and picked up his drink. "This is why you are lighting up the room. You have a spark, girl."

Bert took a glass and poured water into it.

"Roger has an eye for talent." He downed the glass. "Leon and I are trying to work out the end of a new number and the music isn't working."

"Bring it by at closing and I'll take a look," Danny offered.

"Thanks." Bert returned to Jada. "Maybe we can talk more then."

"Perhaps," Jada replied. "We should return to the stage, Danny."

And with that she opened the door and returned to the energy that was more potent than any drug or drink could ever be.

It felt like minutes instead of hours when Danny announced it was the final song of the night.

True, the bar was a bit less full and the couples a bit more unsteady on their feet, but Jada could've gone all night.

Roger turned up the light once Danny was done with the music. The brighter light ruined the mood and, looking around, the couples quickly filed out. Blondes with tall men, short dark men with their slender companions filed out of the bar. One of the blondes glanced over her shoulder and waved at Jada. On impulse, Jada waved back; then she realized who the girl was: Suzanne's friend Laura and that tall gentleman, Mr. Masterson. They walked out into the cool night air and Laura clung to her escort's arm. What were they doing here together?

"Jada?" Danny asked, pulling her away from her curiosity.

"Yes?" she asked.

"Can you wait here for Bert? I have to run upstairs and grab a new shirt." He gestured to himself. "It is too hot in here tonight. Thanks."

Jada laughed. "Anytime." Despite herself, she glanced at him as he walked by. His arms were muscled from his day job at the lumber mill and his shoulders were broad. She admired his assets until he turned the corner of the stairs and disappeared.

"Focus," Jada muttered to herself.

Danny jogged toward the back staircase and Jada sat at the piano. Her glass of water was still perched on the edge and she gladly took a drink. Glasses clinked from the bar as Roger collected the remaining dirty dishes from around the room. Jada prepared to help him when she noticed a song peeping out from behind the stack of papers in his pile.

She pulled out the music and started to play the first few notes of the tune. She put her glass down on the side table and added the left hand to the mix and started humming a melody along with it. It was a fun up-tempo beat that she hadn't heard before. All too quickly, she came to the bottom of the first page. She flipped the page over to find no more notes. It was unfinished. She turned the page back over and played the piece again. This time when the music stopped, she went back to the beginning and started again. The tune bounced in the air around them, filling the space with a joyful sound.

Behind her the last of the couples slipped out, leaving Roger drying the dishes alone behind the bar. As she continued to play, Roger hummed along, his voice matching the strength of the song.

"Wow," Danny said as he walked over. "You breathed some life into that piece. I've been working on it for the last week."

Jada took her fingers off the keys. "I'm sorry. It was just so fun to play."

The compliment brought a new smile to Danny's

face. "That is the kindest thing anyone has ever said to me."

"Hey, you two. Come have a drink on the house!" Roger called out.

Danny winked at Jada. "Two waters," he said.

It was a tiny gesture, insignificant really, but Jada blushed all the same. If Roger thought it odd at all, he didn't mention and brought three glasses up to the bar as the door opened. Leon Errol and Bert walked in.

"Evening," Roger called out.

"Mind if we keep you open a bit longer?" Leon asked.

"We wouldn't have it any other way." Roger pulled out two bottles and put them down in front of them.

Leon took a swig and looked at Jada for the first time. "Ah, hello again. You sing here?"

"I just started." Jada felt heat rush to her face.

"She is wonderful," Roger said. "I can't believe my luck."

Leon laughed. "Good for you. I know you've been looking for some time." He met Jada's eye. "Sometimes you just land in the right place at the right time."

"Thank you," Jada said. The tightness in her chest eased and her face cooled. Leon wouldn't press for reasons why she ran the other day.

"Well, our loss is Roger's gain. Congratulations." Leon lifted his glass to Jada and then took a drink.

Jada was about to reply when the door entrance chimed, announcing new guests.

"We're closed," Roger said. He rubbed the rim of a glass with a towel.

"Oh, yes, of course." Craig Masterson shuffled his feet on the welcome mat. "My friend Laura here believes she left a shawl behind. It is rather important. I assume you'll assist her."

"My mother is going to kill me," Laura whispered as she fidgeted next to Craig.

Roger put the glass on the counter and nodded. "Of course," he said. "I haven't had a chance to clean up yet, but Jada here will help you look for the lady's shawl."

Laura practically leapt from Craig's side. She pushed chairs aside as she looked around them. A few bottles fell over as she bumped against a table.

Roger watched her for a moment before looking to Danny and Jada. "Will you—"

"Of course." Jada took a rag and started wiping tables down. Most of the glasses and bottles had been picked up, so it was pretty quick work. Danny walked behind her, lifting the chairs onto the tables.

"What on earth are you doing?" Laura demanded as she bumped another table, sending liquid to the floor. "Why are you not helping me?"

Jada's hair stood on end. This woman had some

nerve speaking to her like this. Laura squatted next to a table, searching the floor for the missing shawl. She glanced at Jada and gestured to the table beside her. After a moment's pause, Jada gave in. If nothing else, finding the shawl would get her and Craig out of the bar.

"Where were you sitting?" Jada asked.

Laura jumped at the sound of Jada's words. "Why?"

"Because if you left the shawl here, that's probably where it is." Danny lifted another chair onto the table and smiled, alleviating tension Jada wasn't even aware had developed.

"Oh, yes, of course."

Laura stood up and sashayed to the back corner of the room. The far booth was not lit well, but Jada suspected that had been the point. Laura ran her hand over the booth's leather and then slapped the table in frustration.

"It's not there!" A hint of desperation colored her tone.

Jada hesitated. This woman wouldn't even look at her. She highly suspected the only reason she followed her advice was because of Danny's bright smile. But even as she debated that, she noticed a flutter of red on the gray floor beneath the booth.

"Is that it?" she asked, gesturing to the floor.

Laura stepped back and looked under the table. "Blast!" she swore.

Laura pinched a corner of the fabric and lifted it

off the floor. The scarf was matted to the ground in a puddle of dark liquid. As she lifted it, Danny shook his head at the sight of the dark splotches that dotted the red fabric.

"It's ruined!" Laura said.

"Give it to me," Jada said.

Once she plucked the fabric from Laura's grip she walked back to the bar. Laura followed after her, muttering more about her mother.

"Can I have some soda water?" Jada asked Roger as she slid behind the counter and grabbed the salt container.

"What are you doing?" Laura asked.

"I am trying to save your shawl," Jada replied as she first wet the stains with soda water and then covered them with a thick layer of salt.

Danny returned to putting up the chairs. The rhythmic thumping was oddly soothing. It somehow proved that there was action around her, a purpose. On her other side, Craig slung back a shot of some dark liquid while Roger hung the now-dry glasses.

"I hope this works." Laura was fidgeting again. "I borrowed it from my mom's shop. It is being picked up tomorrow."

Jada glanced at Laura. "I will do my best," she promised. "I didn't know you were from New York."

"I don't tell many people." She swayed a little on the stool. "Flo doesn't need another poor girl from the Bronx trying to make it big in his show. He wants a new story to captivate audiences. Mother's shop is so close to the theater I can walk. Not exactly exotic." She picked a bit of dirt out of her nail.

"I didn't think Mr. Ziegfeld cared where you grew up, as long as you were talented."

"Well, you'll never be a Ziegfeld girl, so it doesn't matter to you."

Jada swallowed any retort. This girl wouldn't hear any of them anyway. Instead, she asked, "Does she only make shawls?"

"Heavens no. She is a full-fledged tailor. She even rents out her front window to a friend who makes hats." She giggled. "You wouldn't believe the hats some people buy."

Jada smiled, thinking of the woman who sold Suzanne that horrible bird hat.

"You said the shop is close to the theater?" Jada asked.

Laura nodded. "It is right off Forty-fourth Street."

Jada smirked to herself. Laura's mom was that horrible woman who pushed that horrible hat on Suzanne. What a small world. She was about to say as much, but Laura leaned forward and touched the shawl's edge.

"She's been working on it for a month. All that fine embroidery takes time."

Jada poured more salt on the darker stain before

320

walking over to Laura. She took a clean glass and poured some water for her.

Laura stared at the shawl as if the stain might stand up and walk away if intimidated enough.

"Can I ask, why did you take it? You are in the Follies. Go into any dress shop or department store and people will fall all over you to help you find accessories." Jada leaned back and waited while Laura took a drink.

"I don't know." Laura laughed at herself.

There wasn't much to say in response to that, so Jada smiled and nodded.

"How did you know I was in the Follies?" Laura asked. She leaned forward, looking at Jada. "Oh! You're Suzanne's girl." Once she said Suzanne's name, Laura glanced at Craig, but he was too interested in his drink to notice much else. "Lillian said you were singing in Harlem?"

"She has the best voice I've heard in a while," Danny said as he slid behind the bar with Jada.

"We are lucky to have her," Roger agreed.

Laura glanced at the two men and giggled. "Well, that explains it."

"Explains what?" Jada asked.

Laura leaned close and whispered, "Why Suzanne is floundering."

Jada's hands went cold for a moment. Floundering? That couldn't be. They'd gone over every step together. Had there been a shift in the performance that Suzanne hadn't told her?

"Oh?" she asked, hoping her concern didn't show.

"I don't know if everyone has noticed yet, but she is struggling. Rehearsing all hours of the day, not attending as many parties as most, and she has turned away suitors." Laura nodded toward Craig. "Not that I am complaining. Leaves more for the rest of us to play with, but it isn't like her. I miss going out with her."

The last complaint had an edge of truth to it that made Jada sad. She missed Suzanne too, but the person she missed sounded more like the girl Laura was complaining about. Hardworking, serious, and focused. That was the friend who had run away with Jada. That was the friend Jada valued above all else.

"As long as she is happy." Jada tried to sound nonchalant, but it sounded wrong. "Let's see if this stain will wash out, shall we?"

She took the other cup of soda water and poured it over the piles of salt. Laura watched as the fabric appeared to be good as new.

"Oh my goodness! You did it!" she exclaimed. "Craig, look!"

"Top drawer," Craig said. "Shall we depart? The night is still young."

Without waiting for a reply, he slung an arm around Laura's waist and escorted her out the door.

Roger snorted. "He didn't pay. Figures."

"Go after him." Danny lunged toward the door.

"No," Roger said. "It isn't worth it. Not for his kind."

Jada silently pulled out the broom and swept up the salt from the floor.

CHAPTER 25

Buildings whooshed past one after another as the train made its way from New York to Boston. Suzanne leaned her head against the cool window glass and tried to get the movement of the train to settle her nerves. She, Ann, and Laura sat at a table in the club car, a plate of sandwiches untouched between them. Ann shifted so Lillian didn't bump her and she walked through the car's aisle.

"Of course you know the cast isn't set in stone yet," Lillian explained to Kay.

"Oh?" the tiny girl replied.

"They call it previews for a reason. If something or someone doesn't work, Flo will adjust the show." Lillian waved her hand in the air dismissively. They opened the train car door and left the club car.

Laura shifted in her seat. "That girl is impossible. She got the parts she wanted and is still bitter."

Suzanne lifted her head from the cool window and turned to look where they had disappeared. "She may be in our number, but Kay isn't. Perhaps she is trying to be nice to the girl?"

Ann snorted. "Lillian nice? Those words don't belong in the same sentence." She reached forward and took one of the tuna salad sandwiches.

"Kay is beautiful, but her parts speak to her talents, a lovely background statue." Laura smirked. "What exactly did Flo see in her?"

"Stop it," Suzanne demanded. "This isn't fitting."

"You heard Lillian. If she is wishing us ill, why should we be kind in reply?"

"Because it is what is done." Suzanne rested her head against the window again. Arguing with Laura was like arguing with a child. She suspected that she sounded much like her mother, but at that moment she didn't care. The movement of the train along with the nerves for the previews were not working together. Her head pounded like her heart was in her temples.

"Are you ill?" Ann asked. She glanced at her sandwich and then put it down, as if eating in front of Suzanne was distasteful.

She closed her eyes. "I'll be fine."

"Eat something," Laura said, pushing the plate closer to her. "It won't do to be hungry once we get to the hotel and start toasting the company and each other over and over."

"Ugh," Suzanne moaned. She'd drunk enough champagne these last few months to last her a lifetime. And she didn't like the stuff, not really.

Ann laughed. "It won't be that bad. Small sips will save your stomach."

"Or no sips," Suzanne said. "Flo can't watch all of us."

Laura stood up. "I'll go get you some crackers." Ann nodded to her and watched as she walked down the club car to the cart. A few gentlemen watched her as she moved. Suzanne wondered how serious she and Craig were, or if she'd allow gentlemen in Boston to call upon her as well.

Ann cleared her throat. "It is just us now. Are you ill?"

Suzanne rubbed her temples. "Not ill. It is just a headache. I am well. Will we rehearse tonight?"

"Well, that is up to Flo and Julian, but probably not. I suspect we will all be instructed to bed for rest, but many will go out dancing. Just be sure not to get caught." She took another bite of the sandwich.

Suzanne nodded. "Bed sounds perfect."

Ann looked up at her tone. "The parties are not mandatory. Flo likes for us to be seen in society, of course, but that doesn't mean that we have to go out every night. If you are tired, stay home. He will not think less of you. He'll probably commend you for taking care of yourself."

"Really?" The pounding in her head subsided a bit.

"Of course." Ann reached across the table and squeezed her friend's hand. "We are performers above all else."

Suzanne laughed despite herself. "Performers who bathe in milk and lavender."

"Well, we are special women," Ann said in return.

Laura returned with a small pile of crackers on a plate. "Here you are." She smiled.

Suzanne took a cracker and nibbled on it. The rocking of the train felt less intense. Across from her, Ann took another sandwich and leaned back in the seat. Laura stood, swaying back and forth with the rhythm of the train.

"Is the cracker helping?" Laura asked after a time. "I can get tea if that would be better."

Suzanne was about to reply, but a side glance at Ann silenced her. Ann's face was turning pale, almost green. With a moan she gripped her stomach and lurched over. Her chair jutted out behind her and bumped another passenger.

"Ann?" Suzanne asked, dropping her cracker.

Laura jumped back from the table as Ann leaned over and retched onto the floor, spewing partially eaten tuna onto Laura's shoes.

"Ann!" Laura jumped back.

Suzanne pushed back from the table and stood up. "Don't just stand there, Laura. Help her!"

Laura's lip curled in distaste. "What?"

Suzanne grasped Ann's arms and pulled her to her feet. "Let's at least get her out of the club car."

She put one arm around her shoulder and instructed Laura to do the same.

"I don't feel good," Ann muttered.

"I gathered," Laura muttered back.

327

The two dragged her down the aisle. The other passengers leaned away from them as Ann tried to conceal another heave.

Laura opened the door to their private room and the two helped Ann take a seat. Suzanne sat on the bench facing her and worked on opening the window. The latches were harder than she expected, but after a moment the top leaned out and a gust of fresh air flew into the room. Laura stood in the doorframe, a look of distaste and fear on her face.

"Sit here and breathe in the fresh air," Suzanne instructed Ann. To Laura she demanded, "If you aren't going to come in, perhaps you could get a towel or bucket from the kitchen in case she gets sick again?"

Laura nodded. "Yes, of course, thank you." She was gone before Suzanne could say anything else.

Ann leaned against the train's window and took a deep breath.

"What is wrong?" Suzanne asked.

"I don't know," Ann said, wincing as she spoke. "I just—"

She glanced around with a panicked look on her face. Suzanne jumped up onto the bench, grabbed a hatbox off the shelf, and tossed the container to Ann, who promptly tore off the top and threw up in the box."

"Oh no," she said. "Your hat."

Just over the rim, Suzanne could see the little

bird bopping up and down. She stifled a grin. "Don't worry, Ann. I never really liked that hat."

"Do you think there were onions in that sandwich?" she asked.

"I doubt it. Wouldn't you have tasted them?"

"I guess." She burped and re-covered the hatbox.

The train jolted and both Ann and Suzanne lunged to one side. Ann moaned and rolled over to lie down. A queer sensation came over her as she sat, watching the trees go by.

"Ann," she said loud enough that her friend opened her eyes. "Have you received any threats?"

Her eyes opened wider and she pushed herself back up to a sitting position.

"Threats?" Her voice sounded thick.

Suzanne nodded. "Has anyone threatened you? Perhaps by note or something?" Her pulse pounded in her ears as she asked the question, but she had to know.

Ann's face went grayer than it already was. "No, no threats. Have you?"

"Some of the girls have." Suzanne deflected the question.

"What?" Ann sat up, fully alert now.

The train swayed again as Suzanne checked the hallway for Laura or other girls. For some reason, she knew this news shouldn't spread far.

"Before Ruby was injured she received some threatening notes. And the day she fell there was a grease mark onstage. Now, I don't know if that was there on purpose or accident, but it feels connected."

"Have you received any?" Ann asked.

Suzanne looked away. "Not like Ruby's, but I have gotten strange notes. I just wanted to be sure this illness isn't contrived."

"Contrived!" Ann asked, insulted. Then she retched again and held up a hand. "I am not that good an actress."

"No," Suzanne laughed. "I meant that it isn't someone else's doing."

Ann reached her hand out for the hatbox. All thought of being sick seemed to disappear from her face. "You mean poison?"

"I'm afraid so."

"But . . ." She grabbed the hatbox just in time. After she regained herself, she asked, "Who? If you believe me poisoned, then you believe it to be someone within the company."

The door to their small cabin opened and Laura returned. She made a face and propped their door open. Suzanne hadn't realized how bad it smelled in their room until fresh air spilled in. She took a deep breath to clear the stench from her nose.

Laura held out a metal pail. "Here, Ann. It is the best I could find." She pulled the hatbox from Ann's grasp and covered it up. "They promised a boy would be around any moment to help tidy our cabin. He can dispose of that."

Ann nodded and lay down on the bench again.

After a moment she reached for the pail and retched again. Suzanne turned away.

"If you don't mind, I think I'll visit some of the other girls." Laura's nose wrinkled as she looked around their cabin.

"Of course," Suzanne said. "I'll stay with Ann. Go have fun. Let me know if any plans are made for tonight."

"Thanks, Laura," Ann said. Laura waved to Suzanne before ducking out and leaving the two alone with the open door.

This time her eyes closed, and Suzanne knew she wouldn't get much more discussion from her. But one thing stuck in Suzanne's mind: Did she think someone in their small company capable of such acts? She had thought Lillian capable of threats, but poison? Suzanne returned her gaze out the window.

A few hours later the entire company was standing on the stage of their Boston theater. Ann had been dismissed to the hotel when Julian saw that she was genuinely ill. Suzanne didn't dare voice her concerns aloud to the director, as she hardly knew what to make of the events herself. Instead, she stood with Laura at the far right of the company, waiting for dressing room assignments and her call sheet.

"Previews start in one week, ladies and gentlemen. I would hate to see anyone's hard work ruined by too many late nights. If it were

331

up to me, I'd enforce a curfew on all of you, but I was overruled. So, let me say this. If any of you are late to rehearsals or final fittings, there will be severe consequences."

Laura leaned over to Suzanne and whispered, "Last year Ruby was three minutes late to the final rehearsal due to a final fitting and Julian sentenced her to running up and down every row in the theater. It would have been comical if we weren't all so angry with him for it."

Suzanne looked out over the vast audience. Rows upon rows reached far back into the shadows and then started again in the balcony. Mentally, she promised herself she'd be in bed by nine each evening.

"Julian?" Laura asked with her hand in the air.

"Yes, Laura?"

"When is our full dress rehearsal?"

Julian rubbed his temples and closed his eyes before explaining. "We will do a complete run-through with the cast this Friday. That gives us three days to adapt to this stage and put those final touches in that make us special. It will be a hard week, but worthwhile."

"Thank you." Laura stretched her legs out far in front of her and pointed her toes.

Jonathon walked onto the stage and whispered in Julian's ear.

"Suzanne Haskins?" Julian called out abruptly.

Suzanne jumped to her feet. "Yes?" she asked.

"You are wanted in the main office. Jonathon will show you the way." He held out an envelope. "Your call sheet and dressing room assignment. Your belongings will be delivered in time for rehearsal tomorrow, and your hotel key is in the envelope as well. I assume you can find the hotel without direction?"

Jonathon stepped forward. "I'll be sure she arrives to the hotel after her meeting."

Julian nodded. "Very good of you. Plenty of rest, Suzanne." He tapped his nose and then turned back to the rest of the theater.

Suzanne fell in step beside Jonathon as he led her through the wings and down the side hallway of backstage. His pace was swift and her shorter legs had to work double to keep up with him.

"Where is this office?" she asked when he opened a door and they found themselves in the theater lobby.

Jonathon blushed. "We aren't actually going to the office."

"What?" Suzanne stopped walking. "But you pulled me offstage. If Julian finds out—"

Jonathon took her hand. "Leave Julian to me. Flo knows where we are going, and nothing else matters."

His hand was soft and his grip gentle, but Suzanne refused to be wooed so easily.

"I deserve to know where you are taking me," she said.

Jonathon blinked. "I would have thought it obvious. We are going to see Ann. As luck has it her room is directly across from yours, so if anyone sees us there it will just appear that your meeting was short and I escorted you back to the hotel as promised."

"Has Ann worsened?" Suzanne asked as she started toward the door.

Jonathon held it open for her, and the autumn air felt fresh and bright on her skin.

"Flo sent a doctor to see her, but they suspect food poisoning. While she is sleeping, he wants us to investigate her room."

"Us?" Suzanne asked. "He thinks me credible to investigate this mystery?"

"Well, not exactly. He asked me to look, but I told him I needed your help. You are the one who found the cards and tied them to the other girls. Without your keen eyes I'd likely miss something."

Suzanne's steps slowed. "The credit really lies with Jada, not me," she admitted. He was still holding her hand. She squeezed it. "But thank you for your confidence, Jonathon."

A breeze shifted the part in his hair so he looked younger than he already appeared. She smiled as she looked up at him. Jonathon didn't reply. Instead he took her hand and tucked it through his arm so they were walking closer than before. Suzanne felt her skirt move back and forth against his legs as they walked, and it left goose bumps all over her. Craig had been closer to her when his slithering hands tried to hold her close, but the thrill of being so naughty was nothing compared to the thrill of being close to someone who actually cared for her. She looked up at his smooth face and let the warm glow of happiness spread over her. This was good.

"Here we are," Jonathon said, gesturing ahead to the Lenox Hotel. The tall, square building sat on the corner of the block, making an impressive figure. A line of carriages and automobiles sat in front of it, waiting for passengers. Jonathon gestured toward the line. "Flo or Julian will be tipping those drivers to let them know which girls are out late."

Suzanne nodded. "I am not surprised. Julian was very clear about the expectations this week."

The doorman opened the door and tipped his hat to Jonathon.

The hotel lobby was spectacular. Red velvet circular couches dotted the grand room while gentlemen sat at a pillared bar sipping from wide glasses. The gold-leafed ceiling gave the room a shine of luxury. The check-in desk was made of marble and extended the length of the lobby. It presented the world with an air of both confidence in business and beauty in design.

"Flo has exquisite taste in hotels," she said.

Jonathon grinned. "Ann and you are on the third floor."

They took the elevator up in silence; then Jonathon guided her to the correct room.

"Ann?" he asked as he keyed into her room.

Neither expected the jubilant "Jonathon?" that Ann declared as the door opened.

She lay on a rose-colored sofa, her dressing gown draped loosely about her waist. Her brown curls rested on her back and shoulders. A cup of tea was nestled in her hands.

"Ann?" Suzanne said. "You seem much better."

The pair walked into the small sitting room. Jonathon shut the door behind them and ran his hand over the entryway table.

"I feel much better. Flo had someone drive me here and they nearly carried me up to the room. But once all that train food was out of my system it was as if a cloud lifted off of me and I could see again. I hope I didn't miss much at rehearsal."

Jonathon snorted. "You know the drill. Julian is scaring everyone into early bed this week and handing out room assignments and call sheets."

Ann glanced at Suzanne. "Don't push Julian. He makes good on his threats."

"Laura told me about Ruby."

Ann smiled. "That was horrible to watch. But what a good story."

"Not one I would like repeated about me, however," Suzanne admitted.

Ann smiled. "I doubt anyone could find a bad story about you."

If Ann only knew the skeletons Suzanne buried in her closet. She instantly redirected the conversation. "Do you remember what we talked about on the train?" Suzanne said.

The smile fell off Ann's face. "How could I forget?"

Jonathon moved to the bouquet of flowers on the center table. He reached in and pulled out a card.

"May I open this?" he asked Ann.

Ann and Suzanne turned their attention to Jonathon. Ann walked over and took the card from Jonathon. She tore the envelope open and pulled the card out.

"Darling, Suzanne," she began.

"Me?" Suzanne asked.

Ann continued reading: *"Darling, Suzanne, perform with that Nigger and it will be the last performance you dance. Do not ignore me again. That blue gown is too pretty to waste for a funeral."*

Suzanne took a step back, as if being too close to the flowers would bring ruin as well as the card. Blue gown? Was she referring to the blue gown they were wearing for the Williams-Errol number?

"Ann. The dress." She stared at her friend.

"The dress?" Ann repeated. "How did they know?"

337

"Know what?" Jonathon asked.

"Before we got on the train this morning Julian told us we'd have to meet with the costume staff first thing tomorrow because they changed our dresses for the Williams-Errol number. We were to wear these pink French things, but after seeing it onstage, they want to prevent us from blending in and are changing them to these bright blue gowns. They are working around the clock on them and we have a fitting first thing tomorrow. He only told Suzanne and myself. I don't think Lillian even knows."

"So, whoever is sending these notes is in the costume department?" Jonathon asked.

Suzanne sat on the edge of one of the satin chairs. "It *is* someone in the company. Someone in our family is trying to push girls out."

CHAPTER 26

Jada perched on the large bed, a book on her lap, but her mind was elsewhere. A gentleman had come the previous day to collect Suzanne's trunk. The room was empty without it. Angry or not, Suzanne's presence changed a room. She made the room shine with her excitement and frivolousness. Without her, the room was quiet, but not peaceful. No matter how much Jada had longed for this silence, she missed Suzanne's energy.

She tried to read more of the essays, but the room was simply too quiet. And that is how it would remain until Suzanne returned from Boston. She placed the book back on the nightstand and stood up. She was in charge of the room until Suzanne returned, perhaps she should make it feel more like her home.

Sally knocked on the door. "What are you doing in here?"

"Oh!" Jada jumped. "I was straightening things." She wasn't sure if she should admit that she missed Suzanne. Not to Sally.

"You don't have to do that. You don't work for her no more." Sally cocked her hip out.

"She shouldn't come back to such a mess." Jada replaced the book on the nightstand. "Perhaps I

339

don't work for her, but she is still family. Besides, much of this is mine too."

"I suppose." Sally glanced over her shoulder. "I was sent to fetch you actually. You have a visitor."

"A visitor?" Jada asked. Instinctively she glanced in the mirror. Luckily she wasn't a mess. Sitting on the bed reading for so long had wrinkled her skirt a bit, but her hair was pinned up with small ringlets framing her face.

"Danny is here." Sally couldn't keep the grin from her face. "Are you two . . . ?"

Jada scowled. "I don't think so. Not at all."

Sally stepped into the room defensively. "But you're interested?"

An image of Danny's strong arms came to mind, but Jada shook it away. "No. Don't misunderstand, I enjoy Danny. He is a good guy. I just don't have time for a good guy right now. It isn't the right time." Jada pinched her cheek to give herself a bit more color.

"Well, he asked to speak with you." She picked a nut out of the bowl and popped it into her mouth.

"Very well." Jada looked around the room one last time. She'd figure out what to do with it later.

Sally nearly pulled her out of the room and then pushed her down the hall. "You be nice to him. He doesn't make visits often."

"How else would I treat him?" Jada shook her head, amused before she walked away and down the stairs to meet the piano man.

"Danny?" Jada asked once she was in the doorway to the parlor.

"Jada!" He spun from the window and smiled at her. "I was hoping you would be here."

The room buzzed with excitement. Danny held his hat in his hands, turning it round and round nervously. The white around his eyes was more pronounced than usual. Jada gestured for him to sit.

Once he settled into the sofa and she perched on the green chair, she asked, "What can I do for you?"

Alone in the room together, Jada realized she didn't know much about Danny. Sure he played a great tune and had always been kind to her. But that didn't help her know what to say when sitting in a room with him alone looking for a way to break the ice.

"Oh my," Danny said. "I didn't realize how inappropriate this visit would feel." His cheeks flushed as he cleared his throat and shifted in his seat. "Roger gave me the address once we received the news and I had to rush over."

His formal tone wasn't what Jada expected. She leaned forward. "Danny, I'm not upset. I'm surprised to see you here. You are welcome to visit anytime. If we are going to work together, there should be as few walls as possible between us."

A long exhale slid from Danny. "I'm glad you

feel the same way I do. I have come with news . . . exciting news." He grinned.

"Oh?"

"You know Bert comes to the bar frequently."

She laughed despite herself. "I've seen him there more times than I ever expected."

"Well, before he left for Boston with the Follies, he left a message for me. For us, really." Danny nearly bounced with excitement. "When they return, Mr. Ziegfeld is going to visit us. He is interested in us for his new revue, Darktown Follies."

"The what?"

"At the Bijou Theatre on Broadway. He is starting a revue with Negro acts and is thinking about signing us. What do you think?"

For a moment Jada couldn't move. Her hands felt like two dead weights in her lap and her ears buzzed. Then, suddenly, her heart pounded in her ears and she gushed, "Really? He wants to put us on Broadway?"

Danny nodded. He stood up and came over to her. "I'd be a fool not to see that this audition is directly related to you. I don't know how to thank you."

"I doubt that very much. You are incredibly talented, Danny."

"And yet, Bert only got the audition for me once I paired with you. We make a good team."

"We do." She smiled.

Performing at the Bijou Theatre was something she never considered. Oddly it seemed less obtainable than the Follies. Only the very best Negro performers played there, and she had only yet performed in a nightclub. But if Mr. Ziegfeld was starting a Negro revue, suddenly it seemed possible.

"I never imagined Flo would seek me out." Jada stumbled over her words. "I don't know what to say. This is amazing."

"You sound like I feel." Danny laughed. "In a matter of weeks we will be sitting in the same room as Florenz Ziegfeld."

Jada swallowed her rambling. "We should practice a defined act, shouldn't we? Really choose songs that highlight your skills and my voice."

Danny nodded. "Roger has offered his bar for us during the day if we need a space to rehearse."

Jada stood up. "Do you have time now?"

"You aren't busy here?" Danny looked around. "I thought you worked for that girl?"

"No, this opportunity comes first. Regardless, I do not work for Suzanne anymore, not in an official capacity."

Danny blinked but did not ask questions. "Let's get started then."

"Is this all the music you have?" Jada asked.

She and Danny were sitting side by side with

their backs against the piano legs. Sheet music was strewn all across the small stage. Between them sat a pile of three sheets, which they saved as possible songs to perform. But three, out of nearly a hundred? Surely there was more than this.

Danny rubbed his face and looked around them. "Perhaps we are being too picky. Where is that one about the blue-eyed man? That one might have potential if we spruced it up."

Jada snapped her fingers. "That is what these songs are missing!"

"What?"

"Where is that song I found on the piano a few weeks ago?" Jada got to her feet and shifted through the sheets on the ground.

"The night we helped that girl find her scarf?" Danny asked.

"Yes."

"You won't find that number among these sheets." Danny tried to pull the mess into one big pile. "That song was mine, I wrote it. And last week, I gave it to Bert to look at."

Jada pouted. "Darn. We could have done something with that." She sighed. "Oh well, let's keep looking."

Danny put his messy pile on the back of the piano. "Well, we could see if he left it in the back room."

"Back room?" Jada put a pile on top of Danny's. "Why would it be there?"

344

"I don't know. Roger lets me keep music in one of the back storage rooms, and sometimes Bert works in there. Something about the muted noise of the nightclub inspiring him. I think he worked in there the night I gave him the music." Danny shrugged. "It's worth a look."

Jada hesitated. "Will he mind us looking through his private things?"

"They aren't his. That is a public room. He understands that. If he leaves things behind, he knows they might get moved." Danny took her hand and nudged her toward the hallway.

"Very well." Jada grinned as she pulled her hand free from his grasp.

They crept up the narrow staircase and into the dark hall. There were three doors, all shut. The light from downstairs gave them just enough light to see their way, but not much else.

"That one there is my room." Danny gestured toward the door at the far end of the hallway. "And this here is Roger's."

"You live here?" Jada asked.

Danny shrugged. "It is better than some cramped apartment far from work. I help with the cleanup after work and Roger cuts me a deal on the rent."

"Roger is a good man," Jada said. Sally was lucky to have found such a good gentleman.

"One of the best." Danny took a step toward the last door and jiggled the latch. It was locked. He reached up and tapped the top of the door until he found the spare key. Then he unlocked the door.

The room smelled of leather and wood. A tall bookcase covered one wall, and a fine dark leather chair sat in front of it with a gaslight hung overhead. The whole room was soothing and quiet. Jada could see why he wanted such a room. From the little she knew of the man, this felt like him. She could see him sitting in the chair reading or meditating on life.

Danny walked over to the bookshelves and started fingering through the top shelf's contents. Jada blinked as she realized that the shelves were not all filled with books. Some of them, like the one Danny was working through, were filled with sheet music.

"Gosh," Jada said, looking around in amazement. "I can't imagine having so much music."

"Isn't it glorious?" he exclaimed. "This top shelf is yet to be published, but you can look through the pile on the table if you want."

"That whole shelf is unpublished?" The very idea made her feel small in comparison. So many artists were trying to break into the performance world and she and Suzanne had done it. Or at least Suzanne had. A tickle of pride poked her into smiling. Whatever else happened, she and Suzanne had accomplished something big together.

The pile on the table was tiny compared to the shelf, but Jada looked through it carefully. Not one of the sheets had Danny's name on it. She put them back on the table and plopped on the chair, disappointed. Danny was only a quarter of the way through his shelf. She looked around the room, hoping for another place to look. The trunk.

The latch was open on the trunk, so it opened easily for Jada, but instead of sheet music, she found it to be mostly empty except for a box of spiced nuts, an envelope of square paper, and a shawl. The shawl was red and covered with delicate embroidery. Jada pulled it out and held it up to the window to see it better.

"Why is this here?" Jada asked.

Danny looked over his shoulder. "Oh, I don't know. Bert did say he was storing some things in the trunk for an upcoming anniversary with Lottie. She likes red, perhaps he bought it for her."

"It is the shawl Laura came back for, isn't it?" Jada smoothed the ends of the garment, looking for any signs of the stains, but she didn't see any.

Danny shrugged. "I don't know. Maybe."

Jada frowned. She folded the shawl carefully and put it back in the trunk. Then she pulled out the envelope of paper. She flipped through them.

"These are all notes written to him. Horrible notes."

She handed the envelope to Danny. He took it and flipped through the pieces of paper. He handed it back and returned to looking for his music.

"Bert gets a lot of disagreeable mail. It is part of the job."

"No, this is more than just hate mail. Others have been getting notes just like this." She unfolded another. "This is not normal."

"Everyone knows Bert gets hate mail. He is a black man onstage with some of the most beautiful women on the planet. People are going to complain. Don't go reading into it. It makes people feel important to try to tear another down." Danny glanced over his shoulder and his eyes perked up. "Are those nuts?"

"That is what it says on the canister," Jada said as she continued to read through the notes.

Danny put a marker in his spot on the shelf and sat on the floor next to Jada. The canister of nuts was easy enough to open, but neither moved once the spices permeated the room.

"What is that?" Jada asked.

She put the envelope down and took the nuts from Danny. The open canister smelled wrong. She put the lid back on them and shuddered.

"What is that smell?" she asked again.

Danny took the jar back from her and sniffed. "Ipecac. I'd know that smell anywhere." He pulled out a nut and pressed it to the tip of his tongue. He instantly shuddered from the taste. "Yes, ipecac."

"Why would nuts have ipecac on them . . . ? Oh no!"

"Someone poisoned them," Danny said, reaching the same conclusion as Jada.

"Well, of course they were poisoned," she replied. "But the point is that they were sent to Bert. The notes, the nuts, the grease—it all has to do with Bert."

She dropped the box and jumped to her feet. She had to go to Suzanne.

"I have to go," Jada said. "To Boston. I have to go now. I'm so sorry. I think my friend is in danger."

Suzanne was never one to turn down free food. Half the chocolates she received as gifts were gone before they reached home.

"Can I take you?" Danny asked.

Jada shook her head. "No, tell Sally where I've gone so she won't worry, and explain to Roger I will be back as soon as I can. I'm sorry. Bye."

She squeezed his hand in thanks before she fled from the room. She didn't stop to pack a bag, but rushed to the train station. The quicker she got to Boston, the quicker she could return.

CHAPTER 27

A tray of half-eaten scones sat between Ann and Suzanne. The girls were lounging on the two sofas in Ann's sitting room, their rehearsal attire strewn about the room and robes tied loosely around their waists. Suzanne's feet were curled up under her and she sipped her tea.

"I thought Julian's head would explode at that last rehearsal." She laughed.

Ann coughed on a bite of scone. "If Josephine isn't rehearsing that turn all night, she is a fool. Did you see the vein in Julian's forehead?"

"It was purple!" Suzanne took another sip of tea. "Bert was in rare form."

"He gets that way during rehearsals. Focused." She put down her sandwich. "Did you hear Lillian during lunch?"

Suzanne shook her head. "You would have thought he tried to kiss her or something. The way she talks about him . . . I'm amazed she got Ruby's part in our number."

Ann's whole body tensed as she shook her head in frustration. "It is not right. He is one of the best men in this production. He doesn't sleep around and is happily married. Why Lillian continues to hammer on about his inappropriate stares is barbaric. I don't think we will ever see eye to eye." She harrumphed and grabbed another sweet off the tray.

Suzanne shifted uncomfortably. "I think I've eaten too much."

Ann looked at the sandwich square in her hand. "I am still hungry."

The two laughed. It felt good to enjoy some time one-on-one after such a long day of rehearsal. Julian ran them through the first act three times. Not only did Suzanne open the show with the Rose quartet, but she closed act one with her tango number. Luckily she wasn't in too many of the chorus numbers, so she had plenty of time to change backstage.

A knock came from the door.

"Come in," Ann called.

A maid entered, pulling a cart laden with silver pitchers. "Shall I draw your bath, ma'am?" she asked.

"Yes, please, Hilde. Thank you." Ann took one last bite before placing it on the tray.

"Yes, ma'am." Hilde walked into the bathroom.

Suzanne stood up and leaned over to stretch her back. From her angle she looked into the pitchers and laughed.

"Oh my! The rumors are true?"

Ann blinked. "What rumors?"

Suzanne peered again into the pitchers to confirm what they contained. "You bathe in milk? Does it really keep your skin soft?"

Ann laughed. "Well, not every bath, but often enough to keep up the glamour."

Hilde walked back into the room and pushed the cart into the bathroom.

"If you want to capture the imagination of audiences, you'll have to find something to take their imaginations by storm." Ann eyed Suzanne up and down. "Ha, I've got it."

"Got what?" A note of panic fluttered in Suzanne's chest.

"Hilde!" Ann called.

She lifted her finger to her lips and winked at Suzanne. A feeling of dread settled in Suzanne's stomach at the same moment butterflies of excitement bloomed. She set her tea down and steadied herself before she got ill.

"Yes, ma'am?" Hilde rushed out to them.

"Has anyone brought Suzanne her tea?"

"Tea?" Hilde repeated. The tray of tea and sandwiches seemed to glow between them.

Suzanne's head spun. What did Ann have planned?

"Yes, for her hair." Ann sounded exasperated. "Surely someone told you."

Hilde glanced at Suzanne, pausing at her hair. "Tea for hair?"

Ann sighed dramatically. "How else does her hair retain this luminescent brown shine?"

Hilde paused, then said, "Oh my! Of course. That beautiful color must be protected. Tea does that?"

Both women looked to Suzanne. This was it. This was the moment Suzanne had waited for since joining the Follies. This was her chance to make her mark. She ran her fingers through her hair.

"The tea is a family secret. I rinse my hair with tea every night to keep it healthy." She thanked her lucky stars that her hair looked so good today. The curl sat on her shoulder just right, and her pins were in place without any frizz.

Hilde fingered her own graying bun and nodded. "I will be sure you have pitchers of tea in your room every night."

"Thank you, Hilde," Ann said. "I knew we could count on you."

The maid stood a bit taller as she smiled back. "Yes, ma'am," she said. "Would you like your bath now?"

Ann glanced apologetically at Suzanne. "If you don't mind?"

"Of course." Suzanne stood up and dusted any remaining crumbs from her gown. "I'll see you tomorrow."

Ann retired to the bathroom as Suzanne left the room and went across the hall to her own suite. She went to turn the key, but the door was already ajar. Her heart beat a bit faster as she pressed her hands to the door and pushed it open.

"Hello?" she called out. The maid must be delivering something or was still cleaning the room. "Who is in here?"

A clatter came from the back bedroom. Instead of fear, Suzanne felt instant frustration. Who was causing chaos in a place that was to be her home for the next few weeks? This was intolerable! She stormed into the back bedroom, but stopped in the doorway.

"Wh-What is this?" she demanded.

Jada was seated in front of Suzanne's pile of treats, tossing everything into a canvas bag. From the looks of it, everything that was sent to Suzanne was being thrown away. She glanced up at Suzanne with a defiant look on her face.

"Bert was sent poisoned nuts."

"And?" Suzanne replied. "He gets such mail often. Why are you tossing my gifts out?"

"You get mail too," Jada said, cutting her off.

"I know I do. Same old, 'Don't dance with Bert or else' nonsense." Suzanne forced her tone to be light.

Jada looked up at her. "You got some at the house too. One referring to a dark secret."

"A dark secret?" Suzanne wasn't sure how she felt. "That could mean anything."

"Or it could mean more. It was a threat no matter what else." Jada shoved another box of chocolates into the bag.

"Why didn't you tell me?" Suzanne crossed her arms.

"At first I didn't think they were anything; then there never seemed to be time between all the parties and dress fittings. And then, well, other things clouded my mind and my judgment." She stopped her cleaning and looked up at Suzanne. "I am sorry. I should have told you."

Suzanne sat on the soft white bed. "Had you told me, I wouldn't be here. I don't think I'm that brave."

"You are braver than you think."

An awkward silence passed between the two girls. Suzanne scratched her arm as she tried to think of something to say to her friend that would make things less awkward, less thick between them, but nothing came to her. She pulled a box of sweet cakes from her vanity drawer and handed them to Jada.

"Better safe than sorry. How did you find out about the poison?"

"Danny and I found in the back room a box of nuts someone sent Bert. They reeked of ipecac."

"Ipecac?" Suzanne glanced over her shoulder toward Ann's room. "Ann had a bout of food poisoning on the train ride here. She couldn't keep anything down."

"And now you wonder if it was poison?" Jada asked, finishing Suzanne's thought.

"She kept asking me if the sandwich had onions in it since it tasted funny." Suzanne bit her lip.

"If Ann was poisoned on the train, then Bert is surely in trouble." Jada shoved her bag of food in the corner. "We need to find him. Do you know where he is staying?"

Suzanne thought for a moment. "I don't, but I don't think it is here. Ann will know."

Jada followed Suzanne out of the room and across the hall. "Has Ann had any problems?"

"I asked her about the notes and she didn't know anything about them. I suspect she isn't a target."

"Interesting."

Her thought was interrupted when Hilde answered the door.

"Yes?" she said.

"Hi, Hilde, I know Ann is probably in the bath, but I must speak with her." Suzanne nearly pushed Hilde out of the way as she entered the room. "Ann?"

"Suzanne?" Ann's voice was just audible through the closed door.

"Where is Bert staying?" Suzanne asked. She cracked the door open slightly. She couldn't see Ann in the bath, but it still felt invasive. She'd explain her behavior after.

Water sloshed in the tub. "I'm not sure. I think it is somewhere downtown. Do you need him? I think he and Leon were staying late at the theater to practice tonight."

Thank goodness, Suzanne thought. "Thanks, Ann. Enjoy your bath."

"Milk soak, dear, and thanks," she called back.

Suzanne tried to hide her grin from Hilde.

Hilde held the door open for them. Jada was out the door when she turned and met Suzanne's eye. The look of concern said it all.

"Hilde?" Suzanne said. "Miss Pennington has a weak stomach. Could you get rid of all the goodies that were sent to her room so she avoids becoming ill?"

The maid looked around at the table of gifts and said, "Very well. I will dispose of them."

Jada made a face and then stepped toward Hilde. She leaned over and whispered, "Be sure no other hands touch them. Mr. Ziegfeld dislikes when treats are passed around. A box of chocolates is not worth a job."

Hilde's eyes widened and she nodded. "Thank you. They will go straight to the trash."

The theater was a few blocks from the hotel. The evening air was warm, but Suzanne still hugged her shawl around her shoulders. It felt like a layer of protection from whatever was happening around them.

"How many letters did I get?" The question left a bitter taste in her mouth.

Their pace was brisk, but Jada didn't miss a beat. Suzanne wondered if she'd even heard the question. "Six maybe? Not as many as Ruby, but they were a bit more graphic. They definitely came quicker once you were working with Ann

357

in Bert's number." Jada tripped over a crack in the sidewalk.

"I visited Ruby before we left New York. She hasn't gotten any letters since her accident." Suzanne shrugged.

"So the accident achieved what the sender wanted?" Jada thought out loud. "But that can't be right, or Bert wouldn't have gotten those nuts and I wouldn't be here."

"So Ruby left the production and Lillian stepped into her role for the time being, although it looks like she'll be in the number for the duration of the show."

"What is this person after?" Jada asked out loud.

They turned a corner and the large marquee stared down at them. Suzanne gestured at the entrance and said, "This is the theater."

CHAPTER 28

Jada opened the stage door for Suzanne and was nearly toppled when it swung open from the other side.

"Whoa!" Jada exclaimed.

"Suzanne?" Jonathon stopped dead in his tracks. He turned and his eyes widened. "Jada? What are you doing here?"

Suzanne didn't allow Jada to answer. She quickly recounted why they were there. Jada noticed how she stepped closer to Jonathon.

"Poison? In Bert's trunk?" Jonathon repeated. He paused. "Did either of you eat anything toxic?"

"Suzanne is tougher than she looks," Jada said, smiling at Suzanne. "And, no, neither of us has eaten anything."

Suzanne smiled back. "Jada threw out everything that was sent to me from admirers."

"Thank you, Jada." Jonathon ran his hand through his hair. "We had better find Bert."

"Ann said he was rehearsing with Leon," Suzanne said as she walked through the door.

Jonathon shook his head. "I don't think so. Leon is meeting with Flo right now, making sure we have all the staff we need to open."

Jada fell in step beside them. "If he is here this late, I'm sure he is onstage. This will be his return to the Follies, and many people want to see him fail. He will be perfecting every detail."

Without another word the trio rushed through the theater and to the stage. Jada tried to stop the uneasy feeling that was welling up inside of her.

They opened the door and blinked. The house and stage lights were off. Jada pursed her lips. This was not right. Bert was a workhorse. He should be there.

"Shall we look in his dressing room then?" Suzanne asked.

"No," Jada said. "This feels wrong. There are what, two days before you open and the stage is empty?"

Jonathon went past Jada and started feeling on the wall for the light box. Suzanne left his side and stood close to Jada.

"I don't like this," Jada repeated.

"We will find him," Suzanne promised.

"There," Jonathon said, and the lights flickered on. The footlights were still off, but the light from the wings gave off enough light that they could see across the stage.

"Bert!" Jada exclaimed.

In the middle of the stage lay a dark pile of cloth. As the lights warmed up, a slight movement was just visible. Jada rushed forward and pulled back the black tarp. Bert was lying on his stomach, his hand pressed against the stage as if he were trying to get up. His already pale face looked almost chalky in the shadows.

"Jonathon, help me," Jada said.

She sat beside the man and tried to turn him to his side, but he moaned as if her efforts pained him and she stopped.

"Maybe we shouldn't move him," Suzanne said.

Jonathon leaned his ear and listened to Bert's breath. "What happened?" he asked Bert, but there was no reply.

Jada looked up at Suzanne. "Do you think he was injured?"

"It's possible." Suzanne glanced around them for a container of something, but the stage was remarkably clean. Even the first few rows where the girls sat as they waited for their number to go on showed no signs of garbage. "Did the cleaning crew already clean up?" she asked.

Jonathon shook his head. "I don't think they come until morning."

Jada looked around and quickly followed on Suzanne's thought. "Let's assume that Bert ate something laced with ipecac. What do we do?"

"Roll him over," Suzanne demanded.

Jonathon forced his arms under Bert's shoulders and rolled him over.

"Ugh," Suzanne declared at the puddle of bile that was matted to his chest and the floor.

"We need to get him to a doctor," Suzanne said.

Jonathon nodded. "I'll get the car."

Jada looked at the pool of bile and raised her hand. "Wait. Your dressing room has water, right?" Suzanne nodded. "We need to get him hydrated."

"But a doctor can control the poison," Suzanne said.

Bert's eyes flickered open and he turned his head to Jada. "Water," he croaked, then closed his eyes again.

"Water and then the hospital," Jada said firmly. "Carry him to the car, Jonathon. We'll meet you there."

Jonathon nodded. "If you see anyone—"

"We'll send them to help," Suzanne promised. Then she led Jada to the dressing room.

The lights from the hallways gave the staircase just enough light by which to see. Jada walked a few steps ahead of Suzanne and looked down the hallway. Jada's hearing peaked as echoes of falling jars clanked from one of the rooms. Looking carefully, one door about halfway down the hall was ajar, revealing the flickering light from a candle inside.

"Whose room is that?" Jada whispered to Suzanne, who was now standing beside her in the hallway.

Suzanne counted the doors twice before she glanced nervously at Jada. "Mine."

"Do you still share with Lillian?"

"Yes," Suzanne whispered.

Jada's eyes widened. It was time to confront Lillian with these crimes. She motioned to Suzanne to stay quiet as they moved closer to the door. The flickering light from inside sent moving shadows over the wall. Jada worked hard to focus on the task at hand.

Suzanne walked behind Jada, her breath coming out in jagged spurts. Jada turned to her and pressed a finger to her lips. Whoever was in the room must know they were coming with Suzanne's loud mouth. They stopped just outside the room and glanced at each other. Jada closed her eyes and readied herself to enter.

"Blast!" a woman exclaimed as something toppled to the floor.

Jada took her chance and swung the door fully open. It banged against the wall, and the blond woman dropped the bottle in her hand and knocked over the piles of towels behind her. The clear liquid quickly seeped into the carpet.

"Laura?" Suzanne demanded. "What on earth are you doing in my room?"

Laura sat in the middle of the room, surrounded by small bottles and a black medical bag. Her normally perfect hair was disheveled, and the sleeves of her blouse were rolled up. A toppled pile of towels was strewn across the floor behind her. She grabbed one of the towels and pressed it into the carpet, coughing at the strong stench of rubbing alcohol that was now filling the room. She glanced up as they entered, but went back to measuring a dark syrup from one bottle to another.

"I had to get my bottles." Her words came out quickly and unfocused. She shifted so that Jada couldn't see exactly what she was doing with the liquids. "It wasn't supposed to be so strong."

Jada and Suzanne exchanged a glance. Jada inhaled and made a face. The room smelled faintly of ipecac.

"What wasn't?" Jada asked.

Laura kept measuring the liquid in the bottles and didn't reply. Jada stepped to the right slightly so she could see what Laura was doing. With a measuring spoon, she measured some of the syrup out of one container and moved it to the other. She was doing inventory.

"What was too strong?" she asked again. Laura didn't even flinch at the words.

Jada leaned closer to Suzanne and whispered, "You need to talk to her. You know her better. She'll confide in you more than me."

Suzanne nodded. Slowly she lowered herself to the floor and moved toward Laura. When she was close enough she settled onto the floor beside her friend.

While Suzanne tried to get close to Laura, Jada looked around the room. Had Laura left Suzanne a present here? The vanity was clean except for a container of powder and a brush. The wardrobe was shut. Even the floor looked swept. There was nothing amiss. Then her eyes fell on the water pitcher. Suzanne had promised there was water in the room and glasses, but the glasses were in the trash and the pitcher was empty.

"What are you doing, Laura?" Suzanne asked.

"He shouldn't have gotten so sick," Laura said softly. "I must have given him too much."

"Gave who too much?" Suzanne pressed.

Laura didn't reply.

"Suzanne?" Jada said, drawing her friend's attention. "Didn't you say there was water here?"

Suzanne nodded and then glanced at the pitcher. "Where are the glasses?" she asked.

"All the same. Nosy niggers. Can't leave well enough alone without horning in on our lives and taking what should be ours." Laura looked up at Jada and shook her head. "The glasses are in the garbage. I couldn't take the chance."

"Take a chance?" Suzanne repeated.

Jada glared at Laura. "She poisoned your water. Didn't you?"

"Yes." Laura's voice was flat. She looked up at Suzanne. "But not to kill. Never to kill. I never meant for anyone to die. You have to believe me on that."

Suzanne reached forward and took Laura's hands, which were shaking. "I believe you. But you must tell us, what happened to Bert?"

Laura looked back at her bottles. In one motion, Jada swiped them off the floor and into the small black medicine bag. Laura looked away and her shoulders collapsed.

"I knew he'd be rehearsing alone after we all left for the evening. So I rubbed some ipecac onto the rim of his glass. I just wanted him to get sick and have to miss opening night. If Flo could only see how good the show was without him, perhaps he wouldn't be so intent on keeping him on. It is dangerous."

"How is Bert dangerous?" Suzanne asked. "He's always been a gentleman."

Laura rolled her eyes. "That is what they want you to think. They act all nice at first, but when their animal urges take over it is too late." She leaned close to Suzanne and whispered, "They rape the women. It doesn't matter if they are pretty or ugly. They are like dogs in heat."

"Excuse me?" Jada spoke up. "Bert would never hurt anyone!"

Laura snorted. She turned her back on Jada and turned to Suzanne. "I was only trying to protect everyone. If Ziegfeld won't protect us, one of us had to step up and do something."

Suzanne put an arm around Laura and patted her head. Jada met her gaze, and from her glare knew that Suzanne was angry with Laura as well.

"What happened with Bert?" Suzanne asked calmly.

"I must have put too much on the glass." Laura frowned as she tried to put the pieces together in her mind. Then she looked up at Suzanne. "He's dead, isn't he?"

"No, but he is very ill." Jada stood up, leaned over, and took one of Laura's elbows. "We can't wait around here any longer. Bert needs to see a doctor and we need to make sure Jonathon leaves. We can deal with Laura after they have left."

Suzanne held on to Laura's other arm. "I'm not sure I'd trust any of the glasses here," Suzanne said. She glanced at the pile of broken glass at the bottom of her trash can.

Laura repeated, "I never meant for him to get so sick. There was vomit everywhere and then he just collapsed." She shuddered at the memory. "It wasn't supposed to be like that."

"Maybe think of that before you try to poison someone next time," Jada muttered. She looked around for something to confine Laura in so they could take her up to Jonathon and call the authorities. One of Suzanne's scarves was draped on the wardrobe handle. She took it and wrapped Laura's wrists quickly.

The trio walked awkwardly up the stairs with Suzanne leading Laura and Jada pushing her along. Laura didn't try to escape, but her stride was slow. Suzanne looked over Laura's head and met Jada's eye. "To Jonathon," Jada mouthed, and Suzanne nodded.

"Laura," Suzanne asked, "if you felt so threatened, why did you stay in the Follies? Why not voice your concerns and then leave?"

Laura's face tightened and her lips tensed. "You wouldn't understand. Your family gave you a life, an ability to make your own choices."

"Doesn't every family teach their children to make choices?" Suzanne pulled Laura out into the hallway. Both girls put a firmer grip on the culprit.

"I didn't think you'd understand," Laura muttered.

Suzanne glanced at Jada, confusion written all over her face. But Jada suddenly understood Laura. She cleared her throat.

"Laura's mother owns that dress shop near Miss Mitzi's," Jada began. Laura tried to pull away from her, but Jada's grip was too strong. "Perhaps her father died, or was never around, I don't know. But she doesn't feel like she had an interesting enough background to attract a man like Ziegfeld. But somehow she got into the Follies, and I don't think she was going to give up her big break. She'd rather ruin someone else's life than her own."

"Oh," was all Suzanne said.

Laura spun on Jada, her eyes nearly slits. "Don't you act so high-and-mighty. Isn't that what we all do—put ourselves first. I'm not doing anything unnatural. If you were me, you'd do the same."

"No," Suzanne said instantly. "I'd never take someone's career from them. I'd never attack them to keep a part." She looked at Jada. "Friendship is worth far more than any success."

"If you don't understand, your girl does," Laura insisted. "How do you think she got that gig at the nightclub? She betrayed all you did for her to advance herself."

They were approaching the back entrance and Laura started to pull on their grips. "I didn't mean to hurt him, really. Flo can't know I did this. He'll fire me."

Suzanne opened the door to the back alley and turned to Laura. "There are worse things than being fired, Laura."

The trio walked out the back door and toward Jonathon, whose mouth had dropped open in an O of surprise.

CHAPTER 29

A lot had changed since Suzanne had sat on the opposite side of a desk from Flo Ziegfeld. She, Jada, and Jonathon now sat on soft cream chairs while he finished reading the police report the officer had been kind enough to write up. Bert was resting comfortably in the hospital. They hoped that he would be well enough to attend the dress rehearsal the following day, perhaps even perform in it.

"This is very well-written," Flo said. He lifted the report to the light and with a single motion tore the document in two. "But it cannot be put into public record. I will not have it known that one of my girls would injure another."

Suzanne's mouth dropped open. "You cannot be serious," she said.

Jada patted her hand. "Mr. Ziegfeld is correct, Suzanne. If this got out it would injure the entire reputation of the empire he's built." She glanced at the man himself. "Although it does seem unfair."

Flo raised his hand. "Laura will be punished. Her crimes will not go unanswered. But it will not be fodder for gossip. Her name has already been stripped from the production documents."

"Yes, sir," Jonathon confirmed. "I put in a call

to Dr. Rearden at the women's clinic upstate. He is arranging a room for Laura as we speak."

Suzanne couldn't listen to this another moment. "Jada, you can't agree with this! That woman tried to poison us and Bert, and they are going to send her to a clinic? That is hardly punishment to fit the crime."

Jada smiled. "What punishment would fit? Luckily she didn't truly harm anyone. If Mr. Ziegfeld let this become page six gossip she could ruin the Follies and then she would have won. At least she is losing the very thing she hoped to retain through her actions."

"She won't be working in New York ever again." Mr. Ziegfeld scoffed. "She may not even leave Dr. Rearden's facility quickly." He dropped the torn paper in the trashcan.

"I still don't like this," Suzanne said. "And I can't see how you are all being so calm."

"Things aren't always fair," Jada said.

After all the things they had run from and hidden from each other, for Jada to say that made everything else worth it.

Suzanne smiled. "Perhaps they aren't," Suzanne agreed.

"Do you need anything else from us?" Jonathon asked. "It is getting late and I know Jada needs to get back to New York. There is an overnight train if we do not delay."

"Yes, of course. Jada is needed in Harlem." Mr.

Ziegfeld winked at Jada. "Send the police chief back in. I'll have a talk with him. I will see you and Suzanne at the theater tomorrow."

"Thank you, sir," Jada said as she stood up. "It was very nice meeting you."

The two shook hands.

"I will see you again soon," Flo promised. "Will you stay a moment, Suzanne?"

"Of course," Suzanne said. She could almost feel her back tighten.

As she turned to leave, Jada squeezed her hand and winked at her. She left with Jonathon, who shut the door behind them.

"I know you disagree with how I am handling this situation. But I must ask that you keep what happened secret from the other girls."

"You realize that I can't stop any rumors that come from this. I imagine there will be many," Suzanne said.

"Let me handle the rumors. I doubt any will come close to the truth. Laura worked hard to stay in my good graces. She didn't speak ill of Bert at rehearsal, and few knew of her New York connections. I myself thought she was from New Orleans until tonight."

"Very well. I'll not say anything."

"Even to Ann?"

He clearly did know her well. "Even Ann."

"Go see that Jada makes her train. If you are needed for anything else I will call for you." Flo returned his attention to another stack of papers on his desk.

"Thank you," Suzanne said, and she slipped out of the room while she still could.

The train station bustled with travelers moving in an endless circle. Suzanne stayed close to Jada as they purchased her ticket home. Jonathon insisted on footing the bill for the fare.

"Mr. Ziegfeld would have it no other way," he said.

The trio wound their way through the people until they found the correct platform. Jada turned and held out a hand to Jonathon. "It was lovely seeing you again, Mr. Franks."

He shook her hand. "And you."

She turned to Suzanne. "Break a leg!" she cried. "I'm sorry I'll miss the opening."

"You need to be in New York," Suzanne said. "I'll have tickets for the opening there."

Jada's face lit up. "I wouldn't miss it."

The conductor walked down the platform. "All aboard!" he called.

"I'll see you in a few weeks," Jada promised before turning to get on the train.

Suzanne stopped her by taking her hand. She pressed a few bills into Jada's hand. "Promise me you'll take a cab from the train to Miss Mitzi's. I don't want you alone on the streets."

"I promise," Jada replied. She boarded the train.

Jonathon and Suzanne stood on the platform and waited for the train to depart. In a matter of moments the crowds parted and people stood in groups of two and three across the platform. The train started to humph and chug as it slowly made its way into motion. Jonathon and Suzanne raised their hands to wave despite not being able to see Jada in any of the windows. They stepped back and the steam blew from the engine.

"Can I take you back to the hotel?" Jonathon asked.

"Please," Suzanne nodded.

They walked back to the car that was waiting for them, their arms bumping against each other. *What a long day,* Suzanne thought to herself.

Jonathon cleared his throat. "This may be the wrong time to say this," he began.

"Yes?" Suzanne replied. She adjusted her glove as they walked.

"Now that this thing with Laura is over, I was wondering if I could take you to dinner one night."

"We've had dinner a few times," Suzanne replied. "You are always welcome to dine with Ann and me."

Jonathon fell over his words. "What I mean to say is, would you allow me to escort you to dinner? I think you know that I am rather fond of you and, despite my brazen behavior at that party, I respect you."

Suzanne looked away and smiled. An image of Elton came to mind and how he first announced his intentions. It was time to let another man into her life. She eyed Jonathon out of the corner of her eye. Mother might even approve of him.

"If you are free, I do need an escort to the opening night party." She smiled. "If Flo can spare you."

Jonathon beamed. "I will be sure he can."

He held the door for her and she walked out into the warm spring night.

CHAPTER 30

Late July 1914

Jada had been through plenty of opening nights with Suzanne, but tonight felt different. The nerves and doubts that used to plague Suzanne were absent. Her dressing room was full of chorus girls, twittering about mistakes for the last week of dress rehearsals, but to Jada it was all a buzz of noise. In thirty minutes she would be a Broadway performer.

For the last time, she picked up the sheet music on her vanity and read through the songs that she and Danny would perform. There were only two in which they were featured, but that was more than she had expected. She was even in the finale number, "Ballin' the Jack." It was more of a dancing than a singing number, but she was thrilled to stretch her legs and perform that way as well. It was a new dance that she'd never seen before. Lots of hip swaying and leg kicking to a tune chockful of pep and vigor. Hopefully the audience would find it as fun as she did.

She rubbed on her lip rouge as she hummed the tune of her first number, "I Love a Piano." It was up-tempo and featured just her and Danny onstage. He accompanied her on the piano while she danced around him declaring her adoration for the instrument. Danny gleamed with pride during that number, and it highlighted her voice perfectly without being too challenging.

One last look at the mirror and she was ready to head up to the stage. Her black skirt and red top were perfect. She fixed one strand of hair so that it fell where she wanted it to and slipped out the door.

"Later, girls," she said as she left.

"Break a leg, Jada!" one of the dancers shouted back.

It was fifteen minutes until curtain. Danny would be waiting in the wings for her.

She opened the staircase door and stopped. Sitting on the stairs was Suzanne. She wasn't in her costume for the Follies, nor was she dressed up for an evening off. Jada's stomached lurched in preparation for bad news.

"Is something wrong?" Jada asked. "You should be across town dressing for tonight's Follies."

Suzanne stood up and kissed Jada's cheek. "Ava is filling in for me tonight. Her family is in town and she deserves to showcase her talent for them." She feared she'd misspoken. "That isn't important, though. I am here for you. I couldn't miss your opening night."

"Really? You came to see me?" In all her visions of her opening night, she never expected Suzanne to attend.

"You are such a ninny," Suzanne said. She pulled a small rosette from her clutch and handed it to Jada. "You have been there for me for as long as I can remember. I couldn't call myself your friend if I wasn't here."

The two walked up the stairs to the stage. It wasn't as glamorous as the New Amsterdam. The walls were not plated with gold and the stage had scuffs from years of use, but to Jada that just made it better. There was a history here where you could literally see the success and failures of productions past in the imperfections.

Danny sat at the piano onstage stretching his neck and wiggling his fingers over the keys. A dull murmur could be heard from the audience that was filling quickly. Despite every rule she knew, she peeked out through a seam in the curtain and smiled. It was nearly standing room only and there were still ten minutes to curtain.

Suzanne placed a hand on her shoulder and pulled her back. "I am so proud of you," she whispered.

Jada grinned back and said, "I'm proud of you too."

Suzanne walked back into the shadows of the wings and found a chair that was out of the way of the stage manager. Jada swayed back and forth and rotated her arms in a grand warm-up routine that she and Danny had created for her. From the corner of her eye she could see Suzanne sitting and she smiled at her friend.

Had she thanked her for coming? Jada couldn't remember.

She made a move to do so when the orchestra started the overture. Her stomach tightened with nerves. She finally felt what Suzanne went through. All lyrics and moves disappeared from her mind and she was left frozen onstage.

Danny scooted off the piano bench and took her hand. "It will be all right when you hear the music." He led her to her starting mark and patted her shoulder for good luck.

Jada closed her eyes and leaned her head back as she tried to physically shake the nerves out of her hands. The last few notes of the orchestra played; then there was silence.

The curtain rose and Jada began to sing.

Author's Note

This novel is a culmination of a lifelong passion for theater. Growing up, I watched every musical from the forties and fifties that I could get my hands on. One day I rented *Ziegfeld Follies* from Blockbuster and was entranced by the amazing costumes and eclectic range of performances. I had the Ziegfeld Follies paper dolls and loved making different productions out of the various costumes.

Jada and Suzanne came to me as a pair. What would the relationship be like between a white and black performer in pre–WWI New York? I wanted to look at that relationship and how the pressures of being in the Follies would affect each of them.

While the two main characters are fiction, many of the characters in this novel are based on real people. Ann Pennington, Bert Williams, Leon Errol, Julian Mitchell, Billie Burke, and, of course, Florenz Ziegfeld himself. Many of their subplots were based on fact as well. Flo did try to seduce Ann Pennington, and she did gift him with an "artistic" photograph of herself. Leon and Julian worked with the 1914 Follies, and Flo was dating Billie Burke, the future Glinda the Good Witch of the North in the 1939 *The Wizard of Oz* movie. They actually got married during the 1914 Follies.

Of all those people, Bert was the most interesting to me. Before I started researching this book, I had never heard of him before. And yet, he was the man who integrated the Ziegfeld Follies' stage. And more than that, when the Ziegfeld girls threatened to walk, Flo himself stood up for Bert and informed the girls, "You I can replace, he is unique." I kept that line in my novel as I felt it was such a strong vote of confidence from this man I have come to really respect.

I should say that the fact that women were allowed onstage with Bert may not be 100 percent accurate. Two different texts I consulted quoted two different years. Regardless of that, in either 1912 or 1914 Bert was at least allowed to speak to women onstage. I chose 1914 as the year to set this story because it was nestled between so many dramatic events.

Most women have had relationships that were both beneficial and detrimental. Jada and Suzanne are like sisters, and as such they are not willing to give up on each other. They give each other strength but also hold each other back. Their story is one of love and acceptance. I hope you enjoyed their story and are inspired to learn more about Broadway at the turn of the twentieth century.

Acknowledgments

This book, nor any of my work, could not be possible without the love and support of so many people. I appreciate the work my agent, Steven Chudney, and editor, Martin Biro, did to bring Suzanne and Jada to the page. Thanks to my writing group who endured many years of reading variations of this story. Jenny, Jenn, Jenifer, Natalie, Laura, Kym, Cherie, and Lisa, as well as many more—I am so grateful for your input. Especially Jenifer for reading the final draft when I was sure it was garbage. Huge thanks to my mom and dad for instilling in me a love for old movies and history, as well as watching my girls so I can write. A special thank-you to my husband, whose support and love make it possible for me to write. Last, but not least, to my girls—thank you for continuing to nap and play so Mommy could get in her daily word count!

Discussion Questions

1. Much of the conflict between Jada and Suzanne is centered on the ideas of entitlement and guilt. It never occurs to Suzanne to think of Jada's dreams, just as it never occurs to Jada that Suzanne might have benefited from leaving Richmond. Have you ever experienced such conflict with a friend of yours? Do you think, given the time period, these misunderstandings could have been avoided?

2. Per Mr. Haskins's orders, Jada was given many privileges. She attended Suzanne's tutoring sessions, as well as all her piano, voice, and dance lessons. Do you believe there was another reason that Mr. Haskins provided Jada with such a valuable education?

3. Suzanne chose to run away with Jada. Had she not chosen to do so, how do you think both of their lives would be different?

4. Do you think Jada had any option other than to run away once she found her parents lynched?

5. Suzanne and Jada's relationship is affected by their race. In what ways do you think their relationship would be different today? In what ways the same?

6. Laura struggles in her role as a Ziegfeld girl because of her middle-class status and because of her fear of black men. How do you think race and class impact your life and prejudices? What do you think about how far or little your community has come in race relations since 1914?

7. Jada stays involved in current affairs, while Suzanne is not politically minded. As WWI and the suffragette movement take hold, what do you think both girls' roles will be?

8. Every time Jada was offered a chance to work with Bert Williams, she ran away. Has there ever been something that you ran from, and how did you face that fear in the end?

Center Point Large Print
600 Brooks Road / PO Box 1
Thorndike, ME 04986-0001 USA

(207) 568-3717

US & Canada:
1 800 929-9108
www.centerpointlargeprint.com